TANTALUS

By the same author

THE ALCHEMIST
PZYCHE

TANTALUS

by

Amanda Hemingway

ARBOR HOUSE
NEW YORK

BGT M-22515 1-30-85 $14.95

Library of Congress Catalog Card Number: 84-70881

ISBN: 0-87795-595-6

Manufactured in the United States of America
10 9 8 7 6 5 4 3 2 1

This book is printed on acid-free paper. The paper in this book meets the
guidelines for permanence and durability of the Committee on Production Guidelines for Book Longevity of the Council on Library Resources.

'I also saw the awful agonies which Tantalus has to bear. The old man was standing in a pool of water which nearly reached his chin, and his thirst drove him to unceasing efforts; but he could never get a drop to drink. For whenever he stooped in his eagerness to lap the water, it disappeared. The pool was swallowed up, and all he saw at his feet was the dark earth, which some mysterious power had parched. Trees spread their foliage high over the pool and dangled fruits above his head – pear-trees and pomegranates, apple-trees with their glossy burden, sweet figs and luxuriant olives. But whenever the old man tried to grasp them in his hands, the wind would toss them up towards the shadowy clouds.'

HOMER: THE ODYSSEY
(translation by E. V. Rieu)

For Robert

Prologue

They met in a beachside bar on one of the Greek Islands. He was on one side of the bar, serving; she was on the other. Neither of them had any premonition that there was anything fatal or even important about their meeting: they exchanged a few words, as people do in bars; the next day, they exchanged a few more. He was not to know that in the future his one regret (he was not a person who regretted many things) would be that he had ever spoken to her at all. And she would have laughed at the suggestion that this casually encountered local, with his predictable dazzling smile and facile charm, could actually intrude on her rarefied existence and disrupt it forever. She was hot and wanted a drink; the bar looked sunless, dim and pleasant. She went in. Human lives are supposed to be influenced by decisions and dilemmas, by freedom of choice, but she could not know how much that one careless decision might mean. He spoke; she answered; the choice was made.

The bar was little frequented in the afternoons and, liking the quiet, she got into the habit of stopping there on her way back from the beach for a glass of lemonade and an occasional vodka. He paid her compliments, which she dismissed, but he was always polite and friendly, and after a few days she even allowed herself to fall into conversation with him, having little idea that his charm was more insidious than she knew. It was a fairly serious conversation, about attitudes and national differences; she felt the same kind of interest in him, or so she believed, that Captain Cook must have felt in the aborigines. To her, he was just another Greek, maybe a little taller and fairer than most, with a rather dated frizzle of khaki curls, white teeth in a wide smile, a greeny-bronze skin. He had the slightly curved nose and strong bone structure usually seen on the side of a vase. One day, she decided he was almost classically good-looking; the next, she found his features crude, somehow repellent, reminding her a little of the devil-masks she had seen being sold on the souvenir stalls. He told her his name was Ulysses, a fact which she accepted at the time although long after she wondered if it was an exotic touch for the benefit of the tourists. Probably it was a middle name, or a first name not intended for everyday use. The Stavrakis Bar was a family concern and his mother and sundry cousins came in now and then. They called him something which sounded like Nico, but she was too indifferent to inquire about it. For her, he always remained Ulysses. She did not think it was particularly appropriate.

Her name was Caroline Horvath. She was tall, slender and blonde, superficially indistinguishable from many of the other English girls proliferating in Greece that summer. Her skin was fair and unused to the sun. She drank less than most and talked without the usual northern or cockney accents, which made him think she must be upper-class. He decided she was reserved, in an old-fashioned British way, and therefore, behind the reserve, inhibited or unhappy or possibly both. There could be no other reasons for being reserved. He imagined her, as a small child, having to sit straight-backed through endless genteel tea-parties, taking very small bites out of very thin cucumber sandwiches. Occasionally, he tried to fantasise about making love to her, since he fantasised about making love to most of the better-looking girls who came into the bar. But althought the vestigial bikini showed all of her body save the usual brief triangles, he found it strangely difficult to picture himself actually caressing it, or arousing her to any kind of response.

'What are you running away from?' he asked her once, apparently unaware of triteness. Much of his English had been picked up in America, watching television.

'Work,' she said with a faint smile. 'Like everyone else who comes on holiday.'

He shook his head. She was sitting up at the bar and he leaned on the counter in front of her, studying her face so intently she could not be sure if he was serious or subtly mocking her. She was not quite convinced that he had a sense of humour. She noticed for the first time that his eyes were not dark as she might have expected but light, almost golden in colour. There were cats in the village, undersized, dusty-flanked cats who prowled the restaurants by night in search of scraps and fixed you with a hungry yellow stare. His eyes, she thought, were just like theirs, hypnotic unhuman eyes trying to fascinate you into doing or saying something you had never really intended.

She told herself she was letting him seduce her, mentally if not physically. The unaccustomed sun was affecting her mind, making her feel too relaxed, too warmed, too much at ease with the rest of the world. They were playing games with each other – light-hearted sex-games that would never reach beneath the surface of emotion or desire. What he wanted to know of her had so little to do with her more painful memories. She might as easily tell him she was a princess in disguise.

'Naturally, you are running away from something,' he was saying. 'Probably a love affair that went wrong. Everyone has a love affair that went wrong. Did you leave him or did he leave you?'

'Neither,' she retorted, truthfully enough.

'But there was someone, wasn't there?' His teasing held a cruel note which should have warned her of many things. 'Someone who hurt you.'

Afterwards, she never knew what made her answer as she did, what made her give away even so tiny a fragment of herself.

'My father,' she said.

PART 1

PHILIP

1

Until she was six years old, before the breakdown of her parents' marriage, they lived in a house in Kensington. It was what the estate agents call 'a slim, elegant house in the Regency style', meaning a narrow, terraced house in a row of other narrow, terraced houses, built by an architect with no imagination. The rooms were small and graceful, the furniture, inherited from a paternal grandparent, large and ungainly: mahogany sideboards, gilded mirrors, huge leather-covered armchairs with sunken cushions. Her father's first wife, Philip's mother, had a penchant for modern sculpture, odd examples of which sprouted incongruously from occasional tables. There was a tree of black metal spikes, a wooden nude with no head ('Parkinson's Venus'), a meaningful empty space encased in alabaster that subsequently got broken, and a bald marble bust which the children called Horace. Like Philip, Caroline thought when she was older, she must have been an unsuccessful aesthete, artistic without taste. Her own mother collected china figurines which might have looked right on the mantlepiece if it had not been for the juxtaposition of the modern sculpture. The ceilings were too low, the pictures too large. Her father's study, where he wrote his articles for the *Lancet* and letters to *The Times*, was only twice the size of his work desk. In Caroline's memory, it was always evening, and the lights were always turned down.

Her bedroom was on the second floor. There was a large wardrobe and a small bed. When she opened the wardrobe doors, yawning inset mirrors showed her reflection, pale and shrunken against a background of shadows. Her wallpaper was blue with a pattern of little white stars. Lying in bed at night, she would join up the stars to make pictures: angels and flowers and cats. 'I can't see any cats,' Philip would say.

'I can see a peacock, with its tail open. And a winged horse. . .' 'Where?' asked Caroline. He tried to explain, but she couldn't see the horse or the peacock, although she concentrated very hard. Philip's own wallpaper had pictures of old-fashioned motor cars, with yellow wheels and carriage-lamps, but he thought these very dull. Caroline's room was tidy; Philip's wasn't. There were paintboxes on the floor and books and crayons in the bed and Philip's drawings pinned on the walls. 'I wish,' he complained, 'Mummy wouldn't pin them up when they aren't finished.' He always called Caroline's mother 'Mummy' although she wasn't his real mother; his real mother was dead. A car accident. There was a photograph of her on top of the chest of drawers, a black-and-white studio portrait of a woman with smooth wavy hair and pale delicate features: 'Valerie Horvath'. Her writing was still in some of the books: 'Val' in big sprawling letters. But gradually the books vanished and even the photograph was put away. Caroline could not remember when she first real-ised Philip's mother must have committed suicide.

In her photograph, Valerie Horvath looked young and rather pretty. Mothers, Caroline thought, weren't supposed to be young and pretty: there was something unreliable about youth and prettiness, something alien and mutable. Her own mother had a round unremarkable face and a comfortable figure. She wore the sort of clothes that did not look very exciting but felt nice against your skin, lambswool and viyella and cashmere. She was never irritable or unhappy. On the rare occasions when she spoke sharply even Philip, who was sometimes difficult, did as he was told. He adored her. Caroline loved her, as children do, without thinking about it. But as she grew older she began to feel vaguely frustrated with her mother's continual placidity, her tolerance of minor misdemeanours, her informal standards of behaviour. When their father was out, which was most of the time, the children ate their meals in the kitchen. But when he was there they ate in the dining room off the second-best china, on chairs that were not quite high enough crammed into the small space between table and wall. 'Sit up straight, Carla,' said her father. 'Sit up like Princess Anne.' And: 'Don't gulp your tea, Philip.' Philip squirmed in his chair. Caroline sat absolutely still with her back very straight, feeling like Princess Anne. She went through a phase of taking very small bites when she ate, so that it took her almost half an hour to consume a slice of bread. 'You should chew your food a hundred times before swallowing,' said Dr Horvath. 'It facilitates digestion.'

'*Do* be careful,' said his wife, 'or dinner will never be finished. Caroline is such a literal child.'

When she had tea with her friends, she would hear their parents remark: 'What beautiful manners that little girl has!' She was always very careful when she went out to tea. Quite early on she realised that there were certain essential differences between her family and the families of other children, differences which had to be concealed. For example, her parents had separate bedrooms. Other people's parents, she discovered, shared the same room, with a single vast bed like an old-fashioned four-poster. She had peeped into one such room, unbelieving, and seen it for herself, a bed four or five times the size of her own and covered in quilted satin the colour of the dress she had worn as a bridesmaid. (Ivory, her mother called it.) Afterwards, she tried to discuss the matter with Philip, but he did not seem to think it was important. The things Philip considered important were always so unpredictable. At night, she knew, her mother often went to bed before her father came in. She took to sitting up very late, alone in her darkened bedroom, waiting for his return, with the window left open so the cold air would keep her awake. She heard her mother going to bed on the floor below, the running of taps in the bathroom, the soft final click of the closing door. Much later, her father's footsteps, coming quietly up the stairs. But her mother's door never opened. Caroline felt obscurely disappointed in her, as though she had failed him in some way, though she could not explain how. When she heard her father's door close she fell asleep almost immediately. Frequently, she forgot to shut the window, and she would wake in the morning to find the rain streaming in over the sill and the room as cold as ice.

Caroline worshipped her father. When she was very small, and they went to church together, she thought it was all for his benefit, the candles and the prayers and her blue Sunday

15

dress. He never joined in the hymns, although he had a good voice, because they were sung to him. Later, when he came less often, she heard the vicar say that the Holy Ghost was with them, and she saw her father's phantom, hovering like a genie above the altar. She thought he had so many god-like qualities, it took her a long time to dispel this illusion, and even then a metaphysical God somehow never became real to her. Dr Horvath was often absent, and her mother used to say, 'When he comes in, we'll ask your father,' as though appealing to absolute authority. At home, he would shut himself away in the inner sanctum of his study, writing something called a Paper, while Caroline hid on the stairs, waiting to catch a glimpse of him as he came out. She never approached him unless he asked for her. Once Philip hugged him, impulsively, and she saw how he unfastened his son's arms, very gently, and set him at a proper distance. Other children hugged their fathers, she knew, but they were ordinary mortals. They had rough red jowls or prickly beards and many of them smoked evil-smelling pipes. Her father never smoked and his face was smooth and beautiful, the skin stretched taut over his skull as though it could never sag or wrinkle, the cheekbones jutting out so sharply it seemed there was no flesh on them at all. Subtle blue shadows emphasised his pallor and there was a faint cleft between his brows, like the statue of Alexander shown in the big Classical Art book. His hair was very fair, his eyes like pale sapphires. Even after a long day in the surgery his clothes were always elegant and unruffled. None of his patients ever committed the sacrilege of being sick over him. Sometimes Caroline thought it must be wonderful to be really ill, to have his whole attention, to feel the cool still touch of his hands on your forehead. She tried to imagine unusual diseases for her and Philip to catch, but they only managed chicken-pox and measles, 'flu, diarrhoea, and the common cold, none of which was of particular interest to their father. 'He's a specialist,' Caroline's mother explained. 'He only cures people who have very special things wrong with them.' Caroline hoped her cold would develop into pneumonia (she called it pee-neumonia), and then felt guilty because it would waste her father's time. In fact, she always recovered quickly from any illness. It was Philip who languished, fretful and sickly, driven into a fever

16

by the most insignificant streptococcus. But Philip seemed quite happy to be nursed by her mother.

The marriage ended in August, a few weeks before Caroline's seventh birthday. They came back from a holiday in Devon to find Dr Horvath had moved out. Afterwards, Caroline could never remember her mother showing any violent distress, but Margaret Horvath was not the sort of woman to give way to emotion before her children. Philip found her weeping, once, but she stopped when Caroline came in. Caroline felt shut out, although she hated to see her mother cry: crying was unsuitable in a parent. 'I don't see why,' said Philip. 'My first Mummy cried a lot.' As far as she could recall, he had never mentioned his real mother in that way before, and Caroline was both shocked and frightened at this new evidence of adult instability. Perhaps her own mother had become like Valerie, an undependable creature, capable of any weakness. She visualised them coming and going in her father's life like the little wooden figures who emerge from a weather-house when the sun shines, and disappear at a cloud. Maybe she, too, was just passing through. Her father was the only person who did not change, the one steadfast theme in a world that was in flux. When she learned that she would no longer be living with him all the time, she felt as if she had gone down to the seaside to play with her new beach ball, but when she got there all the sea had run away.

After a few weeks, Caroline and her mother moved into a brand new flat in Knightsbridge. There was wall-to-wall carpeting even in the bathroom, a huge modern kitchen, a five-storey fridge. Philip went to live with his father in a house in the country, with a Welsh nanny called Blodwen and a big garden and a dog. (He sent them a drawing of the dog.) If there were scenes, neither Caroline nor Philip ever knew. In her school holidays, she went down to Cheyney to stay with them. At other times, Philip came to Knightsbridge, but these visits were less successful, since for some reason he always seemed to end up crying and clinging round her mother's neck. He cried with unusual frequency and abandon for a ten-year-old boy.

17

'What does he cry about, Mummy?' Caroline asked once, after he had gone.

There was a strange look on her mother's face, a softened, unhappy look, left over from when Philip had been there. But she only said: 'He misses us, Carla. That's all.'

'*I* don't cry,' said Caroline, 'and I miss him, too.' And I miss Father. But she did not say it; she never said it. Somehow, she sensed that her love for her father was the one thing which must not be mentioned. She knew now that there was another God above and beyond him, but that knowledge only made her own private religion more special, and more fiercely precious to her. She nurtured it like a dead bulb in the dark, believing passionately that one winter's day it would come to flower. But she did not cry for him, not even at night. Her new bedroom had pollen-yellow walls without stars, and she lay in bed gazing up at the ceiling, dreaming, endlessly, of her next visit to Cheyney. 'Are you asleep, Carla?' her mother would say, looking in on her way to bed. (She never used to before.) Caroline did not answer. There was nothing to stay awake for now. As long as her mother never realised how she missed him, how lonely she felt, without her nightly vigil. When Margaret Horvath looked at her daughter there was no unhappiness in her face, no painful softening. Her eyes were affectionate, her smile bright and practical. But Caroline was an undemonstrative child and she did not confide. Perhaps, instinctively, she knew how much it would hurt.

At school, Caroline's work improved, to the surprise of her teachers. 'Divorce usually upsets the child,' Miss Quentin (Arithmetic) said to Miss Sands (English), 'but Caroline's classwork is definitely better. She seems so much more alert than last term. She always used to drop off during long division.'

'Perhaps her father had affairs,' said Miss Sands, vaguely. 'He was a very good-looking man. Perhaps he'll be struck off the register. . .'

'Nonsense!' said Miss Quentin.

Caroline was good at her school work and had the usual number of friends, none of them very intimate. Margaret, thinking she must be lonely without her brother, had pinned Philip's drawing on her bedroom wall, but after a couple of days Caroline asked her to take it down. 'I don't like it,' she said. She did not know why she found it so disagreeable, picturing Philip in a wild green garden, playing with a strange dog. It was not as if she disliked dogs, after all. One of her friends had a spaniel which she was very fond of. In the drawing, Philip's dog was a curious yellow-brown colour, with a thick neck and a drooping, wrinkled face. It did not look like any dog Caroline had ever seen. She knew it was wrong to mind about it so much, since Philip loved it and it kept him company, but she could not help wishing he had no one to play with at all.

On her first visit to Cheyney, Blodwen collected Caroline from the station in the doctor's car. When they arrived at the house the dog came out, barking. Caroline thought it was the ugliest dog she had ever seen. 'It's not ugly,' Philip said, hurt. 'It's a boxer.' The house was large and rather dark inside in spite of the tall windows. The heavy Victorian furniture which had looked so cramped in Kensington fitted comfortably into the big gloomy rooms, still bare of curtains and littered with the flotsam of unpacking. The carpets, laid down by a previous owner, were at once dark and faded, worn thin by the scuffing of endless feet. There was a bathroom downstairs next to the surgery and another one upstairs with an astonishing green bath and a hot water tap that coughed and spat and blew out steam. The loo was in a room by itself and raised on a kind of dais, with a rather unnerving picture of a fish inside the lid. Philip thought it was beautiful but Caroline said severely that loos weren't supposed to be beautiful. In the corridor outside hung the 'Landscape with Serpent' which had dominated the living room in Kensington, looking oddly diminished against the pale stretch of wall. 'Where's Horace?' asked Caroline. But Horace had been put away.

She slept in Philip's room, on a camp bed under the window, because the radiator didn't work in the room that was to be hers. In the night she woke to hear a child crying, somewhere in the darkness of the garden, and she realised without any particular surprise that the house must be haunted. 'It's only an owl,' Blodwen told her, the next day. 'Philip was frightened too, at first.' Caroline felt disappointed, although her mother had told her there were no such things as ghosts. She had seen the child so clearly, a pale face peering through the twisted briars, feet that left no print in the soft mouldy places, small hands parting the wet grass. At the bottom of the garden there was an old font, relic of some long-dead collector of such things. Caroline decided the child had been christened in that font and, dying young, had returned to haunt it. She did not know why. The story became so real to her she almost expected to hear other people talk of it, the daily help, or the man who came to prune the trees: 'Poor little thing . . . so *young*. . . They say, at night, if you listen. . .' She often heard the voice, outside her window, but it never sounded like a bird. She did not tell Philip. It was the first time she had ever had a fantasy all to herself, and she was afraid to bring it out into the daylight, in case it should fade away.

Caroline loved the house at Cheyney. She loved the wet tangled garden and the draughty corridors and the strange country noises and still stranger country quiet. She loved going home to the flat in Knightsbridge afterwards, to the central heating and her mother's cooking (Blodwen was a very bad cook); but she never thought about that. When Philip grew old enough for boarding school he spent the occasional weekend with them, during term-time, and Margaret spoiled him a little, though she tried not to. 'Don't you miss Cheyney?' Caroline would ask. But Philip said he liked listening to the traffic at night and eating her mother's treacle tart. Blodwen had been succeeded by a procession of foreign au pairs, none of whom could make treacle tart. He didn't bring them any more pictures of Cheyney or the dog. He was becoming withdrawn and moody, getting older, Caroline thought, vaguely hurt, unwilling to believe that either of them could ever reach the end of childhood. 'What are you going to be when you grow up?' they had asked him, in class one day. 'A Man,' he said. 'My father says, I'm going to be a Man.' And he blushed, painfully, when everyone laughed. Dr Horvarth had talked to his art master after his first term and learned without surprise that he had no particular talent. He spoke to Philip carefully on the subject of growing up, of choosing a suitable career, of taking his place in society. His son's face was pale and unresponsive. Whether the doctor

20

thought of consulting Margaret, whom Philip still obstinately continued to love, no one ever knew. She had no rights. He came to London every week, to his Harley Street surgery, but as far as Caroline was aware after the separation her parents never saw each other again.

When she was ten her father re-married. The marriage took place in a Registry Office and Philip was allowed to go to the reception and drink his first glass of champagne, but her mother kept Caroline at home, saying she had a temperature. Caroline could never remember if it was true or not. The new wife was called Ursula, Ursula Cloud, and there was a ready-made baby sister called Melissa. Dr Horvath adopted her formally and had her surname changed and although Caroline knew they were not really sisters it was some years before this knowledge meant anything to her. Ursula's first marriage was never discussed and gradually the little world of Cheyney forgot that Melissa was not the doctor's own child. Looking back, Caroline thought how strange it was, that her father, who was not especially fond of children, should go to so much trouble to acquire them and stamp them with his ownership. Melissa was not a particularly attractive child. At three, she was chubby and well-grown, with rough dark hair and a wrinkled mouth and chin, rather like (Philip said) a little piglet. Caroline tried to love her, but his new school seemed to have changed Philip and he was merely scornful. It was difficult to love Melissa. Given a book, she would scribble on it; given a toy, she would pull it to pieces. She cried, angrily, when she could not get her own way (Ursula could not control her and rarely bothered to try). She had a one-eyed teddy bear which she seemed to enjoy torturing although Caroline decided she was really fond of it and wondered, sometimes, if she was fond of anyone else. Only Dr Horvath had any influence over her. If he came in during one of her screaming fits she would fall silent immediately, pursing up her little mouth as though someone had drawn it tight. It was a long time before Caroline realised how much she feared him.

When she was four, Melissa conceived a passion for Philip which was not reciprocated, and which inspired her to make herself even more tiresome than usual, following him around (he said) like a puppy that wants to go out, and whining for attention. At that stage, Caroline found it almost impossible to love her, or even to make the attempt. 'She's not much like her brother and sister, is she?' neighbours would say, forgetting there was no genetic reason why she should be. 'Such a pity. . .' She grew into a plain child of no specific intelligence, demanding affection with a too evident eagerness which adults found vulgar rather than winsome. Philip and Caroline took after the doctor, and were incapable of appearing either winsome or vulgar. They were both tall, over-thin, with their father's delicate bones and watercolour tints of complexion and hair. Philip's school work was erratically brilliant; Caroline's consistently good. Philip was sensitive, sarcastic, vulnerable, blushing uncontrollably whenever he least wished to show emotion; Caroline was aloof and polite, and she never blushed. In her blue school uniform with her long straight hair pinned back from her face she looked like a modern version of Tenniel's Alice, a demure, beautiful, colourless child. She might have been vain, if she had ever thought about her appearance, but her mother did not encourage vanity. Even in puberty, when other girls of her age were shortening their skirts to the thigh and padding their 'A' cup bras, she only looked in a mirror to study her face for a spot, or to see if her hair needed washing. Margaret worried sometimes that she was almost unnaturally clean. When she was older, Caroline decided that her bones were sufficiently well-arranged for her own personal standards of presentability, but she would have preferred to be dark. She never consciously compared herself with Melissa. But one day, when her step-sister said viciously: 'I'll cut all your hair off so you won't be pretty any more. Then Philip will hate you!' Caroline was uncomfortably aware of gratification.

She never knew exactly what happened to Ursula Cloud. After the marriage, Philip did not come to Knightsbridge any more and she paid fewer visits to Cheyney. It was not that she loved it any the less, but she was growing up, growing away, and there were so many other things to do. When she went there, Ursula made her welcome, in her way, but she had 'moods'. They started quite soon after the marriage. She was an untidy young woman, indifferent to bedtimes and mealtimes, with a passion for reading long Russian classics where she was invariably confused by the long Russian names. The first time Caroline saw her she was standing on a step-ladder repainting the kitchen ceiling, wearing an inadequate green apron over her cashmere sweater. 'You ought to change your clothes, dear,' said Mrs Bunce, the daily help. 'Cashmere's expensive and having a bit of money doesn't mean you should waste it. Old Joe would've done that painting for you, if you'd asked him.' Ursula said: 'I like doing it,' but she got down off the ladder and went upstairs, forgetting, on the way, why she had gone. If Caroline had been a very little older she would have liked her, but she still thought as a child, in stereotypes, and she disapproved. She did not know if her father was fond of Ursula. She could remember him kissing her own mother, once or twice, on the cheek, a cool, friendly sort of kiss; but she never saw him kiss Ursula. Looking back, she could not even recall him touching her. At first, when Ursula had moods, Caroline thought they were just a part of her general erratic behaviour. She would sit around in a dressing gown or her old grey slacks, with her hair coming over her face, talking at great length about things Caroline did not understand. She told stories without endings and once drew on the mirror (like a baby, Caroline thought, shocked) with a tube of lipstick. A week or so later, after she had gone to bed, Caroline went down the corridor for a drink of water (Ursula always forgot about night drinks) and heard crockery smashing in the kitchen and her father's voice, not loud, but incisive and very cold. It frightened her, hearing her father sound like that, and she went back to bed, although she did not sleep for a long time. In the morning, she asked Philip what it was all about. But Philip was fifteen now and only laughed, unpleasantly, although she was sure he knew. She thought of telling her mother, when she returned to Knightsbridge, but somehow the idea of having to describe the incident to her made Caroline feel uncomfortable. She had not deliberately overheard anything but she was conscious of being an eavesdropper, of having committed some indefinable treachery, both to her father and Ursula, in hearing what was not meant for her. To tell another adult (she still could not think of Philip as grown up) would consolidate that treachery. In the end, she pushed the incident to the back of her mind, trying very hard to pretend it had never happened.

She did not see the last weeks of the marriage. Years later, Philip told her about the vomit on the living room carpet, and the pile of broken Dartington, and Ursula lying in a heap on the floor, with the whisky bottle pressed against her cheek. They took her away in an ambulance, under sedation. She never came back. 'Poor bitch,' said Philip. 'Poor silly bitch. She was extraordinarily stupid: did you know?'

'Poor father,' said Caroline. She still did not understand.

2

Caroline never expected her mother to marry again. She did a little voluntary work and sat on one or two women's committees, doing the sort of things that women's committees usually do, but she never went out in the evenings or got her hair permed and only Caroline sent her flowers on her birthday. She was in her forties now and a little plumper but (Caroline thought) not much changed. She wore no particular make-up and her skin was good. Caroline loved her, of course, but her mother's practical mundane attitude to life still vaguely irritated her. They talked about Caroline's progress at school, and cordon bleu cooking, and clothes. They did not talk about sex. Caroline was uncommunicative by nature and she never discussed anything serious with her mother. Perhaps that was why Margaret found it so difficult to tell her. She invited Harry to lunch on Christmas Eve, with roast beef and Christopher's burgundy and a pendant Caroline had never seen before on the bosom of her best dress. 'This is Harry Gibb, Carla,' she said. 'We're going to be married.' When Caroline did not say anything, she added: 'I thought you were old enough now not to – well, not to mind.' Caroline said: 'Of course not,' much too quickly. She knew it was unreasonable to feel this sense of repulsion. At fifteen, she had never been in love, but most of her friends were enjoying their first adolescent agonies, and it seemed curiously distasteful to picture her mother, a plain, middle-aged woman, subjected to those painful transports. Her father's very remoteness had made his re-marriage more appropriate: so might a king re-marry, out of duty or royal prerogative, when his queen died or failed to produce an heir. But although she had once thought of her father as the rock on which to found her existence it was her mother who had always been there, staid, dependable, unchanging. Insensibly, Caroline had come to believe that she never *would* change. Now, though she could not pinpoint the occasion, she remembered suddenly seeing her mother cry, and she had to fight against a sense of disorientation. Perhaps, after all, this was a marriage of convenience, such as older women, divorced or widowed, sometimes made when their children were growing up and they began to be afraid of loneliness. Perhaps all her mother felt was a sensible degree of affection, a desire for companionship and security. Horrible to think of her, in the panic of approaching old age, snatching desperately at the first available man. But she could not possibly be in love with him. Her face was pinker than usual and she drank quite a lot of the burgundy. The best dress, which she had not worn for a while, was a little too tight and went into creases above her thighs. Caroline thought angrily how undignified she looked, and disliked herself for noticing.

The marriage took place in April. Margaret wore a dress of pleated chiffon with a matching coat and hat. Caroline wanted to wear her new sea-green crêpe from Biba but her mother said please, green was unlucky, so she wore her suit instead. It was pale grey and looked, she thought, like something at a funeral. There were very few people at the Registry Office. Afterwards, they went to the Ritz and Harry's friends became jocular over a liberal supply of champagne. Harry, Caroline decided, was exactly the sort of person to have jocular friends. He had plenty of money and the champagne was good, Dom Pérignon; but Caroline did not drink much. She was trying very hard to pretend she liked him. He was in his early fifties, a big, unhealthy-looking man with a Midlands accent and a craggy, greyish face. The flesh sagged on his broad frame like loose stuffing in a pillow. He had blue eyes with red rims and there were broken veins in his cheeks and forehead: Caroline concluded that the greyish hue was because he never shaved properly. She found it difficult to imagine that some women might find his cragginess and greyishness attractive. She was doing *Hamlet* at school, for 'A' level, and she could not help comparing her father to Harry, Hyperion to a satyr, the refined, handsome face against the ageing, coarsened one. 'Comparisons are odorous,' she told herself, but it was no good. After the marriage they moved to another, even larger flat in Knightsbridge. Harry asked her about her school work and her boyfriends and ruffled her hair when she had just brushed it and hugged her, clumsily, at all the wrong moments. He said things like 'I know we're going to be friends' and 'I want you to think of me like a second father'. He offered to buy her a car. At last Caroline wrote to Cheyney. 'I'm going there for the holidays,' she told her mother, adding, in a half-hearted attempt not to hurt: 'I expect you'd like some time to yourselves. It must be a bore, always having me around.'

'Carla –'

'I'll stay here in term-time, if I may. I don't really want to board.'

'Of course, but – '

'Thank you, Mummy. Please tell Harry how grateful I am for – for his being so kind to me. It's just that. . .'

'Why don't you tell him yourself, dear?'

'No,' Caroline said, unhappily. 'You tell him.'

She had not been down to Cheyney for more than a year. When she saw the house again she found herself looking at it quite differently, as if she were seeing it for the first time. It seemed smaller, as though she had grown and the house had correspondingly shrunken, no longer a huge, rambling mansion but an ordinary sort of house with a gabled roof and a couple of chimneys, rather dark from the shadow of the trees at the back. Even the wild green garden, tidied up, over the years, by the efforts of Old Joe and his aides, had dwindled to a dripping lawn, a shrubbery, a bed of begonias. There was aubretia growing out of the font. Caroline found herself wondering if the ghost had gone away. Inside, the front room had been refurnished for the benefit of the patients:

dove-grey carpets, velvet curtains, radiators. There was a very sophisticated flower arrangement on the table in the hall. 'Why do you look so strange?' said Melissa, who was taking Caroline to her room, carrying a lightweight shoulder-bag as a concession to being helpful. 'There isn't anything *new*. It was all like this last time.' 'Was it?' said Caroline. Sure enough, the 'Landscape with Serpent' had gone, to be replaced by a hunting scene in pale watercolours with very little mud. Only when she looked closely could she see the blood, red as cherries, dripping from the jaws of one of the hounds.

Downstairs, in the kitchen, they found the new au pair. 'This is Francesca,' Melissa said. 'She is very stupid and speaks no English at all.' Francesca nodded and smiled helpfully. She had enormous eyes in a thin brown face and a body that was both small and attenuated, like a tropical insect. 'She's from Brazil,' Melissa added.

'Can she cook?' asked Caroline, thinking of Blodwen.

'Oh no. But she's very good at arranging flowers.'

Beside the back door, there was an empty corner where the dog basket used to be. The boxer had been put down six months ago. Philip had mentioned it in a rare letter: cancer of the uterus, he said, but there had been no suggestion of a hysterectomy. Caroline asked her sister when Philip was coming home but she did not seem to know. He was staying with a friend, she said. Richard Somebody. He often stayed with Richard Somebody in the holidays. Caroline was conscious of something, disappointment or hurt; she had been looking forward so much to seeing Philip. It was difficult to talk to Melissa; she was too young. She sat at the kitchen table scowling over her homework, a blank map of New Zealand, smudged with erasures, on which she was supposed to mark the principal towns. When she discovered Caroline had done geography she said: 'Good – you finish it,' and went away. I don't like her, Caroline thought. She's my sister and I don't like her. But of course, Melissa wasn't really her sister. She remembered Ursula, standing on the step-ladder in her green apron. Ursula had died abroad two or three years ago, Asian 'flu turning to double pneumonia, her resistance weakened by alcohol and undernourishment. The kitchen ceiling had been repainted again, Caroline noticed, but she could not remember when. She knew she ought to feel sorry for Melissa but somehow she could not.

They dined formally around eight in the large dining room, which was cold. Caroline thought the table had shrunk until she realised a leaf had been removed. Francesca was, if possible, an even worse cook than Blodwen: the lamb was underdone and the rice pudding had set in a solid lump. 'She can make Brazilian things,' Melissa explained afterwards, 'but she's hopeless at English cooking. I think she doesn't understand the recipe books.' Caroline, who was doing a Spanish 'O' Level, decided that at the least she could help in translation. She had forgotten how accustomed she was to her mother's roast beef and Moulinexed cakes. Dr Horvath did not seem to notice what he ate, merely pushing most of it, indifferently, to the side of his plate. Like many people of little appetite, Caroline remembered, he had always been extremely fussy. Perhaps it was her imagination that he had grown thinner. In the bad light he hardly seemed to have aged at all and she found herself thinking with a queer wistful pang of the days when she believed he was a god. In those old memories, too, he was sitting in a bad light, like a de la Tour painting; evidently he had a predilection for it. She waited, uncomfortably, for him to ask her about Harry Gibb; but he did not. Perhaps he was too courteous to display curiosity; perhaps he felt none. Anyway, Caroline was relieved. She did not want to be disloyal to either of her parents. Over coffee, her father asked about her school work, though not her boyfriends, and whether she had any ideas about a career. He did not ruffle her hair or hug her. When he poured himself a small, pale brandy, from a bottle with an unassuming French label, he offered her one too. Caroline knew it must be a good brandy if her father drank it and she screwed up her courage to enjoy it. She was not very fond of brandy.

Dr Horvath considered her without either enthusiasm or disapprobation. She was the kind of daughter he had wanted: quiet, well-mannered, sensible, evidently with the rudiments of taste. He assumed she would go to university and then find herself a niche in publishing or on the production side of television. It was all very suitable. She was even quite good-looking, if devoid of distinction; he did not admire teenage girls. There was a wholesomeness about her which he found faintly distasteful, as though she had never had sex, never masturbated, never been drunk or stoned or sick on the living room carpet. He could imagine her getting up very early in the morning and walking up to the golf course to look at the dawn. When Ursula took to solitary drinking his fastidious soul had been revolted by the physical and emotional manifestations of alcoholism. But those scenes had left their mark. He had never thought about Caroline very much but suddenly he found himself wondering if she would ever grow up, becoming corrupted and a little wiser after the manner of human beings, or if she would always be the sort of girl who got up to see the sunrise. He must remember to ask her, at breakfast, what she thought of the view.

'What view?' asked Caroline, the next day.

'The dawn,' he said, 'from the golf course.' And he added, perversely: 'You should climb up there some time.'

Philip came home about a week later. Caroline was happy to see him but not as happy as she had expected; it was a long while since they had last met and at first he seemed to ignore her almost completely. He had changed, she thought, out of all recognition, grown and yet somehow diminished; he was no longer just an older brother but a young man, like and unlike the other young men she had met, both more real to her and more unreachable. For the first time she realised he was beautiful. His hair had darkened to a colourless shade somewhere between brown and blond; his eyes were deep-set under tapering brows, not blue like her own but a pale watery grey faintly veined with green. His skin was fair and too delicate: there was a cluster of spots on one cheek and a cold sore at the corner of his mouth, the leftovers of adolescence. He should have looked like her father, Caroline decided, but there was something in his face that was not quite right. Something to do with the droop of his mouth and the unhappy sarcasm that tinged almost everything he said. After a few days, when he began to talk to her, she found herself thinking how vulnerable he looked. I am older than he, she thought, meaning: I am stronger. He had the face of someone with little courage, little faith, no hope; an actor of potential

brilliance who knew he would never get beyond the bit parts.
As children they had always been very close, but that
closeness seemed to have altered with adolescence, though
she could not have said in what way. It was as if the traumas
of their shared childhood had marked them with a common
brand, setting them apart from humanity, and now at last
they were becoming aware of their own differentness, of the
hidden scars which held them together. We are two halves of
one whole, Caroline told herself, with all the solemnity of a
vow: the strong and the weak, the cold and the passionate.
It was a delusion that never wholly left her.

When he asked, she told him about Harry Gibb. It did not
seem to matter, telling Philip. 'That generation never grow
up,' he said after a while. 'Father's getting married again too;
did you know? He hasn't said anything, not yet, but it's
obvious. It's been four years now since he put himself and
some unsuspecting female through his own particular version
of hell. I suppose he feels it's about time.'

Caroline said sharply: 'Don't!'

'Don't!' Philip mimicked. 'Don't what? Do you go to
church, Carla? Do you believe all that rubbish? Honour thy
father and mother, no matter what they do. Hypocrisy is the
foremost of the Seven Deadly Virtues: Hypocrisy, Conformity,
Status, Brains and Balls, Bacon and Eggs. You still think you
love him, don't you? You're so innocent and hopeful. Shall I
tell you the truth about Father?'

Caroline said: 'No!' before she could stop herself. There
was an awkward silence.

Presently, she asked: 'Who is he going to marry this time?'
(So silly, she thought. As if he were Henry the Eighth.)

'Celia,' Philip said. 'Who is Celia, what is she, that all
our swains commend her? Right author, wrong play. You'll
understand when you see her. Unless you're very stupid.'

She came to lunch the following Sunday. Dr Horvath said:
'Celia, my daughter Caroline,' and, as an afterthought: 'This
is Celia,' but he did not say anything about getting married.
Mrs Bunce had come in to cook the lunch since roast beef and
Yorkshire pudding was too far outside Francesca's experience.
Beforehand, they had sherry in the living room. Only Dr
Horvath seemed completely relaxed, his silence effortless, his
eyes focusing on some other plane where they, and perhaps

even Celia, had no existence. Philip lounged, awkwardly, studying the visitor with his head a little on one side. Melissa fidgeted. Caroline sat on the edge of her chair, trying not to feel uncomfortable. We're all watching her, she thought suddenly. Like wild animals watching the advent of some bizarre new creature, unsure whether it is edible or dangerous. She imagined Celia surrounded by a ring of eyes: Philip's cool gaze, Melissa's sullen unwavering stare, her own eyes, slanting and blue as the eyes of a Siamese cat. But Celia hardly looked at them at all. She looked at her sherry glass, at the doctor, at a speck of fluff on the carpet. When she spoke, her manner was brusque and uncertain. Caroline thought she was one of the most sexless women she had ever seen, with her square shoulders and square jaw, her hair cropped close against her skull. Her brows and lashes were sandy; so was her skin. Even her clothes were masculine: tailored jacket, tailored shirt, cuff-links. 'She's really quite handsome,' Philip said, disparagingly, 'if you like handsome women.'

'I don't believe it,' said Caroline. 'He can't possibly want to marry her. She looks like a man.'

'Exactly,' said Philip.

Caroline never knew when she first realised the truth. The idea germinated in darkness, in her subconscious, creeping into her waking thought in unguarded moments, then pushed aside, hastily, to linger unwanted at the back of her mind. There was no sudden shock of revelation, no frantic denial. She had accepted it, unconsciously, before she even came to think about it. Childhood memories, things half-forgotten, fragments of a jigsaw-puzzle that had never – quite – made a picture, all these appeared in a different perspective, as if through a new lens, fitting together with a kind of hideous logic. 'When did you find out?' she asked Philip, long after. It was nearly midnight and they were sitting in his room playing records, with the volume turned up because Dr Horvath was out. They had been talking about something else but Philip knew what she meant.

'I didn't "find out",' he said. 'I just knew. Perhaps it was instinct. At school, there was a boy a few years older than me: blond, good-looking, frightfully good at sport. There was some trouble with another boy in my class. The parents made a fuss and he had to be expelled. I had rather a thing about him myself. You should have seen him on a cricket pitch.'

'Did he look like Father?'

'Not really.'

Later, she said unexpectedly; 'It must have been terrible for him. Father, I mean. Wanting to be normal, to be happily married, to have a family, and never being able to make it work. Having to live with failure, every time. . .'

'Bullshit!' The anger in his voice startled her. 'Oh yes, he wanted all that. He also wanted a big house, a Mercedes, a garden, a dog.' His sneer was overdone, distorting his face. 'He doesn't like dogs; he just thought he ought to have one. He doesn't like wives, either. It's a question of status, of social standing: keeping up with the Sinclair-Joneses. His wives aren't usually very pretty – have you noticed? – but he hasn't married a bad cook yet. Ursula was wonderful with sherry trifle until she took to drinking the sherry. And Celia's got some kind of culinary degree. It'll make a change from Francesca, won't it? We ought to be thrilled.

'If they're pretty, he's afraid they'll expect too much. Perhaps he thinks it's only pretty women who like sex. After all, he comes of a naïve generation, hungover with Victorian morality and Edwardian immorality. I don't know which is worse: both eras were revoltingly coy. There's no such thing as immorality nowadays, but Father doesn't know that. None of his generation do. He still believes that if you *look* respectable it doesn't matter what the hell you *do*. Appearances alone are important.'

Caroline said, unhappily: 'You're being horribly unfair.'

'Am I? Why should you stand up for him? Do you imagine he loves you? Don't kid yourself. You're just another bit of the furniture, like his wives, who have left him, or his dog, who is dead. Why do you think he wants me to go to Cambridge, to get a good degree, to become a doctor or a lawyer or a chartered accountant? Because that's what upper middle-class sons are supposed to do. And behold me, the model of filial obedience, fulfilling his every wish. Next term I shall go up to Cambridge. I shan't do much work, but they say it isn't necessary. Do you know how much I dislike myself?' He shook the last cigarette out of a crumpled packet and lit it with an unsteady hand. 'I wish I had some dope.'

'Does it do any good?' asked Caroline.

'Not really,' said Philip. 'Anyway, I don't like it. Look at us, Carla. How beautifully we behave! Doesn't it make you sick? With our background, we ought to be delinquents. I ought to be a junkie and you ought to be a tart. Or vice versa. Have you ever had sex?'

'No,' said Caroline. 'Have you?'

'No,' said Philip. 'Yes. It depends on how you look at it.'

'What do you mean?'

'It happened,' Philip explained, 'last time I stayed with Richard Willoughby Grant.'

'What happened?' asked Caroline.

'Sex,' said Philip. 'With Richard.'

In the autumn, Philip went up to Cambridge and Caroline went back to school. Dr Horvath married Celia at Christmas. Caroline did not know quite why this wedding upset her so much less than her mother's marriage to Harry Gibb. It had a quality of unreality, resulting partly, perhaps, from her newfound knowledge of her father, partly from the quick-change emotions of growing up. 'Take it lightly,' said Philip, who was taking it hard. 'Drink too much.' Celia wore a powder-blue suit with an elaborate corsage instead of a bouquet. She had a good figure, Caroline noticed with surprise, broad-shouldered and long-legged, like a model or an athlete. When they toasted her, she blushed, a deep, unexpected blush that flowed right down her neck and inside her silk shirt. Afterwards, the happy couple departed for a brief, dutiful honeymoon somewhere in the West Country. Everyone assured them they would be snowed up. 'I do hope,' said Caroline, who was feeling unnaturally carefree, 'I don't have to go to any more parental weddings.' Melissa drank too much champagne when nobody was looking and Francesca had to take her home. Caroline followed soon after, supporting Philip. He had lost his tie and his hair was wet with sweat or liquor. We're both frightfully drunk, she thought. Everybody's drunk. She felt idiotically decadent.

Half way down the road, Philip was sick. He swore

horribly, between paroxysms, propping himself up against a lamp-post. When they got home, Caroline put him to bed. She wondered if she ought to undress him but although he was her brother she did not quite like to. She had never seen a naked man. Eventually, she compromised, taking off his shoes and socks and undoing most of his shirt buttons. There was a soft triangle of hair in the middle of his chest but otherwise his skin was very white and smooth. He looked younger and somehow more vulnerable than ever, lying there with his mouth open and one arm extended, like a child caught in a restless dream. There were dark smears under his eyes and a scab on his chin where he had picked a spot during the speeches. She had a sudden vision of him ageing, hideously, like the picture of Dorian Gray, while her father remained eternally young. Then he turned over, mumbling, and looked up at her through half-shut eyes. 'Carla. . .'

'It's all right,' she said, adding, practically: 'Do you want to be sick again?'

'No.'

He caught her wrist and pulled her down on the bed beside him. She said: 'Shall I get a blanket?' but he shook his head. It felt very natural, lying there in his arms. A long time passed when she thought she must have slept, although she could not remember it, because suddenly it was night beyond the window and the light had shrunken to a dim yellow circle around the bedside lamp. Philip was looking at her with a queer glazed expression, as though he could not see her properly at all, as though he could only focus on one tiny detail at a time, an ear-lobe, an eyebrow, a mole at the base of her neck. Presently, he began to kiss her. She knew she ought to stop him, but she could not. He kissed her, not like a brother or a lover, but like a man who is thirsty, sucking at stones for drink. His arms tightened around her and he pressed his body into hers; she could feel his erection, hard against her thigh. She had never felt an erection before. She ought to resist him but she was trembling inside like someone on the edge of a fever. Her very bones felt soft. He was breathing quick and short now and biting at her lips. Then his whole body went rigid, so that for a moment she was frightened, and the rigidity broke into shudders, racking him like sobs, and there was a patch of wet stickiness soaking through onto her leg. 'Sorry,' he whispered, when he had caught his breath. 'Sorry. Sorry. . .'

She stroked his hair, absently, for a little while. Then she said: 'Why?' Once, long ago, it would have been wrong, but since she learnt the truth about her father her old standards of right and wrong had become meaningless. She was a child no longer, following adult rules: she had grown up and found a new innocence, devoid of artificial morality. 'Why?' she repeated.

There was a slight sound, as though the door, which was not quite shut, had fidgeted on its hinges. Glancing up, Caroline saw the white of an eye rolling in the gap. Then there was a laugh, cut off short, and the door banged. Footsteps ran down the corridor.

'I wonder how long she's been there?' Philip remarked sleepily. 'What fun for her!'

'Melissa?' asked Caroline, without any particular surprise. It was strange, she thought, how little it mattered. Nothing seemed to matter much now.

3

After Caroline left school she followed Philip to Cambridge. He was in his third year now and had abandoned much of his earlier notorious behaviour, no longer hanging round the Stable or the Scaramouche, dressed in skin-tight trousers, flirting with elderly men and picking up young ones. From time to time she would hear stories, most of which she discounted: he ate marijuana fudge for breakfast, smoked opium, took snuff; he had a four-figure overdraft: he was screwing his lecturer, his lecturer's wife, the captain of the cricket team, Zuleika Dobson. He had tried to commit suicide by hanging himself in his fishnet tights. Once he came to see her, and she thought how tired he looked. The flesh seemed to have shrunk against his skull and the shadows under his eyes had become lines. He told her he was trying to work again but seemed to have lost the ability to concentrate. 'I might as well get the bloody degree,' he said, 'though God knows why.' She made him tea with three sugars and plenty of milk (she was one of those rare students who never ran out of milk) while he sat, looking out of the window across the grass. He did not tell her much more. Perhaps he felt it was unnecessary. Her room, he thought, was like herself, a cool, quiet place, intensely private. There were a few pieces of Chinese pottery, not valuable, but very delicate, a few books, a woodblock print of a woman playing a mandolin, simplified down to the essential outlines. On the window sill, there was a bottle of white wine from the college cellars. Later, she offered to open it, but he said he had to go. He kissed her goodbye, on the cheek. 'I'll come back,' he murmured vaguely, 'some time.' After he had gone, Clive came round and sat in the most comfortable chair for nearly two hours, complaining about his tutor. She did not tell him about Philip's visit. Clive despised Philip. He said he was indolent, feckless and immature, all of which Caroline found unanswerable. Clive was mature and sensible and hardworking. He was not particularly good-looking (in a man, she felt, looks should be unimportant), but he was extremely intelligent and utterly self-assured. She knew that one day, probably when he got his Ph.D., he would want to marry her. She did not think she wanted to get married just yet. She was no longer stunned by his intelligence and assurance and there was her own career to consider, although she was not yet sure what she wished to do. Something in journalism, perhaps, or the BBC. She saw herself on the editorial staff of a superior magazine, in the production team for a topical documentary, even reading the news, in her clear, unfaltering voice, her poise unshaken when the autocue broke down or someone passed her a piece of paper saying the Prime Minister had been shot. But all that was a long way ahead. In the meantime, she worked hard and did many of the things that students usually do. She went punting in the summer and drank champagne for tea and sat under the magnolia outside the University Library, reading Anaïs Nin. Once or twice a week, she let Clive make love to her, but that, like Anaïs Nin, was not very exciting. 'Do you mean,' strangers would say to her at parties, with varying emphasis and unvarying astonishment, 'you're really *Phil Horvath's* sister?' She half-hoped, half-feared he would come to see her again before he left, but he did not.

When she went home for the long vacation Philip wasn't there. 'He's moved to London,' Celia explained, uncomfortably. 'I'm afraid there was a disagreement.' She wouldn't say any more. Caroline learnt what had actually happened when she visited her mother in Birmingham. Harry had moved there after Caroline left school, to a house in Edgbaston which was larger than Cheyney and unexpectedly pleasant, set well back from the road and surrounded by trees and immaculate stretches of lawn. They had two cocker spaniels, a resident au pair, a solarium, a wine-cellar. 'I'm getting interested in wine,' Harry told her. 'I've been in Paris a lot lately on business; they know what's what over there. Here: try this.' Caroline sipped a vintage claret and said what she hoped was the right thing. Even now, she was still not completely at her ease with Harry. 'Haven't you seen Phil?' her mother asked her. 'I would have thought, with both of you in Cambridge. . .'

'I haven't seen him,' Caroline said. Almost as if Cambridge were a village, she thought, not quite amused.

'He wrote to me,' her mother went on, 'I'm not sure why; he hasn't written to me for ages. Perhaps he felt the need to tell someone. It seems he's decided he wants to paint after all. Your father won't hear of it, of course. There must have been a row: Phil didn't say much, only that he's never going home again. So melodramatic and extreme, poor boy, but perhaps he'll grow out of it. I told him to come here but I doubt if he will. I don't know if he's very talented –'

'He isn't,' Caroline said flatly, biting her lip.

'– but obviously he needs to get it out of his system. If only Stephen could be a bit more understanding. Apparently, Phil's living in Covent Garden, with some squatters: it doesn't sound very comfortable. He says he's looking for a flat. There's a bit of money from one of his mother's aunts and now he's twenty-one he can do what he likes with it. I do hope he'll be all right.'

'Couldn't you talk to Father?' asked Caroline. But she knew in advance what the answer would be.

She did not see Philip until the next long vacation. It was an unnaturally hot summer and she left college early, missing the May Balls, and stayed over in London on her way down to Cheyney. Philip was sharing a flat with two other people, a black homosexual clarinettist and a balding young man who worked in the City and liked to think he was artistic. It was a nice flat except for the kitchen, which was ill-equipped and far too large, so no one ever did the washing up, merely moving it from one stretch of draining board to the next as another pile accumulated. Philip's room was untidy and badly lit, which concealed the untidiness. Above it, there was a small attic with a skylight which he used as a studio: it was very cramped, Caroline thought, with boxes and canvases stacked against the walls, an empty easel in the middle, an old piano effectively blocking the door. ('Dave plays the piano as well,' Philip explained.) On the table, there was a jam-jar half-filled with murky water, a bottle of turpentine, several paint-brushes, and a palette which looked as if it had never been cleaned. Caroline sat down on the piano stool. 'Do you really want to see my paintings?' Philip asked. 'I'm not very good, you know.' He said it, not like someone being modest, but as if it was the truth.

Caroline said: 'Yes,' knowing she would not have to be polite. She often told polite lies, but not to Philip.

He showed her about half a dozen paintings, though there were more (unfinished, he said) piled face down under the table. There was a still life, a surrealist lampstand, two or three portraits of the coloured clarinettist, a meaningful picture of snails crawling across a chessboard. They were all drawn with a vague disregard for accuracy or symmetry and somehow none of the colours was quite right. The greens were too acid, the purples too pink, and there were glints of yellow where there should have been glints of white and brownish-black shadows where there should have been black-ish-brown ones. Caroline thought of saying: 'Your ideas are good,' but she was not quite sure it would be true. Only the last picture made any particular impression on her, and even then she did not know why. It showed a shining hairless head with very few features against a background of bright blue sky. It reminded her of something she had forgotten, which was perhaps what she liked about it. 'That one's the best,' she told him. 'It must be something you've seen. You paint better when you're painting things you've seen. It's when you try to be symbolic and obscure that it doesn't work. Those snails look like Nature Art wrapping paper.'

Philip smiled, rather tightly. 'I know what I want to paint,' he said. 'I can see it inside my head. Unfortunately, it doesn't seem to come out the same on the canvas.'

'Why do you do it?' Caroline asked.

'Why not?' he retorted. 'Because I want to. Because Father doesn't want me to. When I got my degree, he still had hopes of my becoming a good little chartered accountant; did you know? I nearly did, too. I'd never have had the guts to do this if it hadn't been for Aunt Helena's money. I haven't got much guts, I'm afraid.' He sneered at himself, Caroline thought, as though he were posing for a self-portrait. The Artist Looking Into His Own Soul. She wondered if he really felt things deeply or if, as with painting, he merely *wished* to feel things deeply, and tried and failed over and over again.

'I don't really understand,' she remarked, 'why Father should mind so much. It's not as if he disapproves of art. The house at Cheyney is full of paintings. And he doesn't just buy known artists who are going to appreciate, he buys what he thinks is good.'

'Exactly.' Philip almost laughed. 'Father wouldn't mind at all,' he said, with an odd note in his voice, 'if he thought I was any good.'

In the evening they went to a dingy cinema to see *Belle de Jour* and had a meal in a restaurant somewhere in Soho. 'The food's wonderful,' Philip said, 'but you'll have to pay for it.' Caroline's grant came from her father, but she had an additional allowance from her mother which she never used because she knew it was really Harry who paid it. She was not particularly extravagant and her bank account was always in credit. Philip, no matter how large or small his income, was invariably broke. Caroline bought the meal on her Access card and they walked for a while in search of a taxi. Between the street lamps there were dark, quiet places, alleyways and shadows. Noise exploded suddenly from a chink in a doorway. Briefly, wistfully, she thought of Cambridge, the sunlight on the river, the willows, the beautiful grey buildings, old in tranquillity. If she married Clive, she might never have to leave Cambridge. She did not really like London, she decided, although she had lived there half her life. It was a restless, unhappy city, overgrown and unco-ordinated, a city of strangers. Not a place to be alone in, she thought, and a faint, cold shadow brushed the corners of her mind. . .

In the taxi, Philip asked her: 'Are you still going out with that physicist?'

'Computer science,' she murmured automatically. He had only met Clive once, very briefly, in a bar, and she was surprised he had remembered. 'Yes. Yes, I am.'

She could not see his expression in the dark but his voice mocked. 'You're the perfect daughter, aren't you? Suitably behaved, suitable ambitions, suitable boyfriend. What a pity Father hasn't even noticed.'

'I don't want to be a good daughter or a bad daughter,' Caroline said softly. 'I want to be myself.' But she was not at all sure she knew what she meant.

She arrived at Cheyney the next day in the late afternoon. There was a strange car drawn up in front of the house with the driver's door open and a young man in an old school blazer loading two large suitcases into the boot. Presently, Celia came down the steps, carrying another, smaller suitcase and a leather shoulder-bag. When she saw Caroline she stopped and looked, for a moment, completely blank.

'You're early – aren't you?' she faltered, in a voice so unlike her usual cool monotone that Caroline was shocked. 'I – I wasn't expecting you.' Behind the surprise, Caroline thought, her face was lit up, transformed, her cheeks pink, her short hair happily dishevelled. She was wearing bright blue eye-shadow and a blue shirt with most of the buttons undone. The sun had burnt a deep red V on her chest. 'I thought,' she continued rather helplessly, 'you would be going to parties and things.'

'It was too hot,' Caroline explained.

'Perhaps it's just as well you've come,' Celia said at last.

'I expect you've guessed: I – I'm going away. You can tell your father. I haven't left a note.'

'I'll tell him.'

Suddenly Celia smiled, an unaccustomed, cheek-splitting smile that showed all her gums, as though she knew she should not be smiling and at the same time could not help herself. 'This is Geoff,' she said. 'I'm going to marry him.'

He had rabbity teeth under a dense moustache and an air of pre-war dash. At any moment, Caroline felt, he might say: 'Bung ho!' She wondered if the old school from which the blazer originated had ever formed a part of his education. 'I hope you'll be frightfully happy,' she found herself saying, with unexpected sincerity. Perhaps it was because of the smile which still hovered irresistibly on Celia's lips.

'Thank you. Thank you very much.' She bundled into the car, almost losing her shoe. 'There's a casserole in the oven: it wants about another hour. And there's salmon mousse and a pie in the fridge. I've done the potatoes.' As they drove off, she leaned out of the window and called out something about lettuces which Caroline did not catch. Then she was left alone at the gate, looking up the steps to where the front door stood open on the empty house. She thought of Valerie, who had killed herself, of her mother's painless clinical separation, of Ursula, throwing her guts up on the cold grey carpet. And now Celia, eloping improbably with an emblazered young man: 'I've done the potatoes.' She was conscious of an idiotic desire to laugh.

Her father came in around seven: she was in her room, but she heard his quick footstep and the closing of the study door. She went downstairs and knocked, softly, hesitating a moment before she went in. He was sitting at his desk by the window. The sun had gone down behind the house and the room was already rather gloomy: his head stood out in a featureless silhouette against the last of the daylight. Suddenly, horribly, she found herself wondering if the books which lined the walls were really volumes of medical wisdom, if the Victorian print of a male nude with all his ligaments unravelled was there for purely scientific reasons. I wish Philip would leave me alone, she thought, helplessly. The study was like any other: piles of correspondence, green-shaded desk lamp, the smell of old leather armchairs. She closed the door quietly and went over to her father. He looked preoccupied, she thought, the cleft between his brows accentuated, his pale eyes gazing, as always, through her or beyond her rather than at her. Perhaps it was a trick of the light, but for the first time she seemed to see a web of tiny lines, just under his skin, drawn by elfin fingers with a very fine pencil, and needing only a hint of pain, a feather-touch of tragedy, to bring them out. 'He must know about Celia,' she told herself. 'He must have noticed she isn't here.' There was a sheet of notepaper in front of him and he had unscrewed the cap of his fountain pen. 'What is it?' he asked her.

She said, abruptly: 'Celia's gone.' She wanted to say she was sorry but something in his face stopped her.

'I see.' He did not ask if she would be coming back.

'She was going,' Caroline explained, 'when I arrived.' She did not tell him about Geoff; presumably Celia (or her lawyers) would write. 'She said, she'd done the potatoes.'

'How thoughtful of her!' Unexpectedly, he smiled, a faint, tired smile, as though he was really amused. In that moment, in spite of everything, Caroline felt she loved him quite painfully. If he had only been able to talk to her, even if it was about something else, if he had only been able to stop being a god and a father and become a fallible and unhappy human being. For just five minutes of real conversation, she thought, she would have done anything, no matter how terrible or how trivial, to spare him hurt.

He said: 'Is Melissa home yet?'

'No.'

'Then just make something light, for the two of us. I'm not very hungry.'

At dinner, he asked her about college, though not about Clive, but he did not sound really interested, and anyway, it was too late.

Melissa came in when Caroline was going to bed. 'Where have you been?' she asked, hearing herself sound eldersisterly. 'It's late.'

'It's not eleven yet,' Melissa scoffed. 'Anyway, Father won't know unless you tell him. Has Celia gone yet?'

'Yes.'

42

'I knew she would. She's got a boyfriend somewhere: I heard her talking to him on the telephone. His name's Geoff. He must be pretty wet, wanting to go out with Celia. Perhaps he's a queer. Perhaps he dresses up as a woman and she dresses up as a man and they do it that way. Do you like my badge? It says: If you're close enough to read this, you're too close. I'm going to pin it on my knickers.'

This, Caroline decided, was a conversation she could do without. She said: 'You shouldn't listen to other people's telephone calls.'

'Why not?' Melissa sat on the bed, looking at Caroline sideways, sly-eyed. She was wearing a dark red lipstick which made her look younger than ever and prematurely dissipated, like a grotesque cherub. Her legs and arms were thin but her stomach stuck out like a child's. It was as though she had stopped growing somewhere just short of maturity, and the dumpy, overgrown little girl had become the awkward, under-sized adolescent without any specific physical development. 'We have a little sister and she hath no breasts,' Philip had quoted of her, derisively. Poor Melissa, Caroline thought; I ought to be kinder to her. She often wanted to be kind to people but it wasn't a quality which came easily to her; she had tried too long to maintain her own aloofness, her inward isolation. Perhaps Father should do something, she reflected. Something drastic. Like sending her to Roedean. Caroline had been at school with a girl who was sent to Roedean, in a desperate attempt at rehabilitation, after being found in bed with her judo instructor. Caroline had no idea if it had done her any good. She visualised Roedean as a cross between a convent and a prison, where Melissa's natural and unnatural urges could be held in check, forcibly, at least for a few years. Someone had told her that her former classmate, on leaving school, had gone to a redbrick university and slept with the entire rugger team, but she did not really believe it.

'Do you think,' Melissa was saying, 'if I did exercises, it would develop my bust? Geraldine Hacker has a much bigger bust than me, and she does weight-lifting. She told me, she read about it in a health magazine. Only her mother won't let her wear a bra yet, and she flops all over the place in netball.'

'It's fashionable to be flat-chested,' Caroline pointed out.

'Yes,' said Melissa, unanswerably, 'but it isn't sexy.'

Caroline remembered herself at thirteen, wearing a sensible brassiere carefully selected by her mother and feeling about as comfortable as a lunatic in a straitjacket. 'You ought to go to bed,' she said wearily. 'I'm tired even if you're not. Go to bed, and tomorrow you can use my make-up. If you promise to throw away that lipstick you're wearing, I'll give you one of mine.'

Melissa got to her feet, white-faced, her mouth screwing itself into a vicious little pout. 'If I go to bed!' she snapped. 'If I'm a good little girl! I'm not a child any more, to be bribed with presents. I'm grown up now. I'll go to bed when I like.' In the doorway, she hesitated, as though struck by a sudden thought. When she turned the sly look was back on her face. 'You went in to see Philip, didn't you?' she said. 'Is he any good?'

'Any good?' Caroline repeated blankly. For a moment, she wondered if her sister was talking about painting.

'You know,' Melissa said, with a curious little giggle. 'In bed.'

4

A year later, as everyone expected, Caroline graduated with a 2:1 and left Cambridge. She went to Birmingham. She had already enrolled for a secretarial course, starting in September. 'With secretarial skills,' her mother had said, predictably, 'you can get in anywhere.' She had done a lot of thinking, in those blank moments during revision when the words started to run into each other and her brain emptied. For once in her life, she did not want to go home. 'Home', since the recent divorce, had become meaningless: the corridors were empty of all but pictures, her father was never there, and Melissa spent most of her time with unknown friends, invading Caroline's room at odd hours of the night to pour out unwanted confidences or childish malice, as though she could not make up her mind whether she loved her sister or resented her. I can't help her, thought Caroline, I can't help either of them. The new au pair, an Austrian, cooked well but had an unfortunate fixation on Wienerschnitzels, which Caroline did not like. In Birmingham, there would be no emotional demands, no Wienerschnitzels. She was still uncomfortable with Harry but she thought, for her mother's sake, she could try to get on with him. And although Birmingham was an alien city whose streets breathed carbon monoxide and whose inhabitants spoke with Birmingham accents, she found the Midlanders friendly, the sunsets (owing to pollution) spectacular, and at least it was smaller than London. London was vast and infinitely more perilous. And in London there was Philip. She did not want to see too much of Philip, though she did not analyse why. The thought of being with him gave her a curious thrill, part excitement, part fear, which her reasoning mind told her she ought not to feel. It was a thrill which she savoured, in spite of herself, even as a child savours the thought of unwrapping a particularly intriguing present, knowing that once the gold paper has been discarded and the contents revealed the pleasure will never be quite the same. Perhaps the element of fear in that secret thrill was in part the fear of disappointment. When she considered it logically she told herself that she and Philip were brother and sister, they loved each other, nothing could change that. He would always be there. She had all the time in the world to be with him.

A fortnight after she started her course Clive came for the weekend, and proposed, tastefully, in the Botanical Gardens. 'He's a very nice young man,' her mother said. 'Rather conceited, of course, but then most men are.'

'Plenty of brains,' Harry remarked cryptically. Caroline wondered if it was meant for a compliment.

'I don't want to marry him,' she said. 'I thought I would, one day, but I was wrong. I suppose I might get married, but not to Clive. Not ever.' She did not know why she was so sure. Only that it was so. After Clive had gone, she expected to find herself missing him, in the way one misses something familiar and dependable, but she had very little leisure. By the time she had adjusted to her new routine and could lapse into a daydream over her shorthand, he had receded into the past, a closed episode, no longer relevant. Caroline never dreamed about the past.

She moved to London the year after she finished her course. Jobs were scarce, particularly for someone with no experience, and she had been unable to get anything more exciting than an insurance office. The female staff talked about hairdos and *Crossroads* and the rising cost of living; the male staff talked about sex and football and the rising cost of living. In between, they talked about insurance. Caroline decided that insurance salesmen have to justify their existence by convincing themselves that insurance performs some useful function in civilised society, offering, perhaps, the promise of Heaven and a secure after-life which the tentative modern religions no longer supply. 'We'll have to get you into Sales,' said the manager, calling her into his office one day. Had she ever thought – I mean, really *thought* – about the need for insurance? Did her family have any, for example? He personally had life insurance, car insurance, house insurance, private health insurance. If anything were to happen to him (except, of course, an Act of God) his wife and two-point-six children would be All Right. Did her father know that if he paid only 10p a week, tax-deductible (magic words!), on their special new policy, in the year 2050 he would collect thirty thousand pounds? If he died before that date . . . Caroline forbore to point out that if they had not all been wiped out by nuclear war long before then the pound would almost certainly have devalued to a level where thirty thousand would be little more than expensive lavatory paper. She said she would think it over (it seemed to be expected) and escaped. 'You're wasted in that place,' Harry told her. 'Why don't you let me help? I've got plenty of friends who'd be glad to employ a bright girl like you.' Caroline shook her head, pressing her lips together, and the next day Harry did not say anything more. She wondered if her mother had spoken to him.

By the time the letter came from Philip, she had almost made up her mind to write anyway. Apparently, the black clarinettist was leaving, moving in with his boyfriend; if she was really bored with insurance the room would be free in January. 'There'll be more opportunities in London,' her mother said. Caroline said yes, there would be. She had a feeling, unusual for her, of being swept along by some irresistible current; yet she was only following a sensible course of action, suggested by circumstances: there was no reason for her to fight against it. The thought of living in London again still illogically troubled her, but she told herself she had been in Birmingham long enough to readjust to the traffic and the crowds. She wrote to Philip, handed in her notice, and began to pack up her things. In the New Year, remembering the big awkward kitchen, she made a firm resolution not to do all of the washing up all of the time. Her mother, who had lately become a health food enthusiast, gave her a book on high-fibre cooking; Harry gave her a cheque for a hundred pounds which she would have liked to refuse but did not know how. He offered to drive her down but although she had quite a lot of luggage she said she would prefer to go by train. Even after living in the same house with him for over a year she was not quite sure what they would talk about, all the way down the M1. 'Have it your own way,' he said shortly. And then: 'I have to come down next week – business. At least let me bring those suitcases, love. You won't want everything all at once.'

'Thank you,' Caroline murmured. She felt very ungracious.

In Philip's flat, the kitchen looked even worse than on her previous visit; Caroline wondered if the black clarinettist was the only one who ever did any washing up. She surveyed it with a feeling of undeserved guilt which instinct told her would soon become all too familiar. In the evening, she made a half-hearted attempt to train Philip, but it was useless. 'You'll do it, won't you?' he said with a faint, sweet smile. 'It's so lovely to have a woman about the house!' (She thought of Melissa, years earlier, with her geography homework: 'Good – you finish it.') The balding young man who worked in the City had been replaced by a slender, asexual youth who shifted stock all day in Woolworth's and spent his evenings at the nearest ice rink trying to be another John Curry. 'He wobbles,' said Philip, 'in his treble spin. I've seen him.' The flat seemed to attract failures, Caroline reflected. An artist who couldn't paint, a skater who couldn't skate, a young man behind an office desk who believed he had a soul. Perhaps she, too, was a failure. What, after all, had she ever done?

'What happened to Leonard?' she asked. The balding young man had been called, unfortunately, Leonard.

'He threw himself under a tube,' Philip told her. 'Only nobody noticed.'

'Don't talk nonsense.'

'It's not nonsense,' Philip said. 'It was the rush hour.'

She never found out what actually happened to Leonard. The ice skater was called Steven but he had changed it to Stefan (he was that type) and most people called him Stef. He was slightly in awe of Caroline and washed up quite often if forcibly encouraged. He had a pale, city-bred complexion and his usual expression was slightly pained: she wondered if he were in need of a high-fibre diet. He did not seem to have either a boyfriend or a girlfriend but he was much attached to a pair of tropical fish which he kept in a tank in his bedroom. ('It uses too much electricity,' Philip complained, regularly.) Stef had the largest bedroom, on the same floor as the kitchen and living room. Philip, Caroline, and the bathroom were upstairs. Caroline said she would do Philip's washing up if he would clean the bathroom, but she usually did that for him, too, although not when Stef was around in case he felt she was discriminating. Philip, she decided, seemed to think he had done his share of the domestic chores by introducing a sister into the flat, rather as if he had just invented the vacuum cleaner. She felt used, but she could not be really angry with him. He was one of those people for whom everyone always made allowances. 'You can't expect me to clean things,' he would say, unanswerably, 'when I never notice if they're dirty.' He worked hard, or appeared to, spending long hours shut up in his studio. Caroline went in every two or three days to collect the backlog of coffee mugs: the room smelt of turpentine, cigarettes, and cheap marijuana, and the air was thick with smoke a week old. Sometimes, she wondered how Philip could see to draw. When she entered, he always stopped what he was doing and covered it up, waiting for her to go. There was never anything on the easel. Frequently, he stubbed a cigarette out in his palette. After she had gone out, she imagined him still sitting there, playing with a paint-brush or a piece of charcoal, and doing nothing, for hour after hour.

In the evenings, he went out with one or other of his girlfriends. When Caroline first came, he took her to the theatre a few times (if she paid), to various pubs and wine bars; but as soon as she began to make friends he left her alone. He had two regular girlfriends: Hazel, who had expensive clothes and rather large teeth and whose father (Philip said) was one of the few rich aristocrats left in Britain, and Deniece, who had antique clothes and small, pointed teeth and who was supposed to be a drug-pusher. Philip often drew Deniece, usually without her antique clothes. She was ugly but interesting-looking, with bleached hair and enormous haggard eyes in a pale masculine face. When she was posing, she would wander downstairs naked, oblivious to the cold or to the presence of Caroline and Stef. She was so thin her breasts had shrivelled and the ribs stuck through her flesh like bars. 'She's wonderful, isn't she?' Philip said. 'Straight out of Belsen. She goes around like something that has been dead a long, long time, seeking living men to batten on. A skeleton with the appetite of a succubus. And what eyes! Do you know, even in orgasm her expression doesn't change? Her upper lip just twitches a little, in a kind of snarl. I've often imagined Father coming like that.'

By now, Caroline had learnt to change the subject. 'I like Hazel best,' she said. 'She's nice.'

'I know,' said Philip. 'She's far too nice for me. If she wasn't so rich, I'd have finished it months ago. She's terribly clinging, too; the nice ones always are. And oh, so grateful every time I bring her on. This is real, Philip, this *means* something; no one else ever made me feel this way. Poor silly creature, it's time she got hurt and corrupted like the rest of us.'

'You shouldn't tell me these things about your girlfriends,' Caroline said. 'It's obscene.'

'Obscene!' Philip laughed, horribly.

'Sex is private,' Caroline persisted. 'People's feelings are private. Talking about them to someone else – making fun of them – is the worst kind of treachery. It's an offence against human dignity.'

'They can talk about me,' Philip said. 'I don't care.'

49

Caroline looked at him with sudden detachment. 'You would care,' she said coldly, 'if I did.'

She knew it was important to be detached. Sometimes, when she saw him sitting in his studio in a haze of cigarette smoke, his eyes screwed up into tight little balls of pain, she wanted very badly to put her arms round him, but something always happened to change her mind.

It was some time before Caroline found work. The job market was already shrinking and in the first week she decided she was completely unemployable, her experience inadequate, her typing inaccurate, her shorthand hopelessly out of date. Could she use a word processor, a switchboard, a telex (Caroline hated the telex)? Did she speak Serbo-Croat? Did she think she could identify with bathroom fittings? In the second week, she turned down three offers, two insurance companies and a retailer in need of a personal slave. What do you *want*? asked the girl in the agency, evidently bewildered. Timidly, Caroline mentioned publishing (she didn't dare mention the BBC). Heads were shaken, eyebrows raised and then dropped. Apparently, everyone wanted to work in publishing. In the end, Caroline decided to temp until a permanency came up which she really wanted. After two months' erratic employment she was lucky: sent to fill in for a sick copy-typist at a well-known publisher's she ran into an acquaintance from Cambridge, and when the copy-typist was discovered to be pregnant Caroline stayed. On the way home, she was so elated she bought a packet of real coffee-beans, forgetting they did not have a grinder. 'I've got a job!' she called out to Philip, who was painting Deniece (or so he said) in the bedroom. Later, he came downstairs to congratulate her. 'I shall write to Father,' she said. 'I've only written once since I came to London.'

'Bugger that,' said Philip. 'When do you get your first pay-packet? We'll celebrate.'

'We could celebrate tonight.'

But that night Deniece was giving a party. 'All dope, no dignity,' Philip explained mockingly; it wouldn't be her scene.

'Another time,' he said.

* * *

Caroline thought Philip would forget about celebrating (he often forgot things like that) but he did not. 'We'll go to a cocktail bar,' he said, about a week later. 'Do you like cocktails?'

Afterwards, Caroline could never remember very much about that evening. They started on tall, pastel-coloured cocktails tasting of fruit and fluff and crushed ice, and progressed to small, dark, syrupy cocktails tasting of cough mixture and benzine. To finish, Caroline had a dim recollection of something called a Zombie, which made her feel like one. The bar was round with high spindly bar stools and at some point in the evening she remembered leaning forward too far, almost overbalancing, and Philip putting his arm round her shoulders to steady her. Later on, they danced, close together, on a very small dance floor. She rather thought the music was fast but they danced very slowly, shuffling round and round in the same little circle, while all about them sparsely clad bodies gyrated furiously and random arms and legs described wild, meaningless gestures. 'I couldn't dance like that,' Caroline thought. 'The floor wouldn't stay put.' She was not too happy about the state of the floor anyway; she knew it ought to be perfectly solid but it seemed to be tilting slightly as she shifted her weight from foot to foot. She clung tightly to Philip, who did not tilt, at least not yet, and closed her eyes, pressing her face into his shirt. He smelt of warm body and warm skin, of sweat and cigarettes and Hazel's cologne. Long after, she could still remember that smell. Other men's closeness would bring it back to her, unwanted, with a pang of old, old longing. She had never before been so conscious of the smell of another human being, of blood beating, skin breathing, hair growing. Whenever Clive started to sweat he would take a shower immediately, vaguely irritated by the functional details of his body. He showered two or three times a day and his skin barely even smelt of skin. At the time, Caroline had approved of this. Perhaps, she thought, smells, like feelings, were secret things, to be shared only with the people you love best. She did not think she had ever loved Clive.

'What are you thinking about?' Philip murmured, his mouth against her ear.

'Clive,' said Caroline.

'You need another cocktail.'

This time, they were sitting on cushioned benches, against a reasonably solid wall. The cushions were red, or perhaps it was the light. The cocktails were definitely blue. 'I'm bloody drunk,' Philip said. 'Kiss me.' She shook her head automatically, but he did not seem to notice. His arms felt unexpectedly strong, thin, hungry arms like the arms of a beggar or a starving man. Afterwards, she remembered she had sensed the same kind of desperation in his kisses, the very first time he kissed her. 'Your face is all muddled up,' he murmured, feeling blindly for her mouth. 'Like a Picasso.' And then: 'What are we celebrating, anyway?'

'I don't know,' said Caroline.

Outside, the cold air gave her an illusion of clear-headedness. They walked for a while, unsteadily, through a network of side streets lined with blank windows and dark doors. The street-lamps cast a dull, white sheen on the wet pavement, like artificial moonlight. Caroline watched her feet, treading in the moonlight, her feet and Philip's feet, side by side. The clearest memory she had of the whole evening was of watching her feet. Presently, they came to a main street with shops and neon-signs and traffic. 'Where are we?' Caroline asked.

'No idea,' said Philip. 'Let's get a taxi.'

When she woke up the next morning he was lying in her bed, his bare leg almost touching her own. He lay on his stomach, heavily asleep, face crushed into the pillow. For a while, she did not move, recuperating quietly after the initial wrench of opening her eyes. Her insides felt horribly unstable, as though at any moment they might dematerialise and leave her with a yawning vacuum in her middle. After about half an hour, she got up and went into the bathroom. The cold water on her face made her feel much better and she drank two glasses of it although she knew you should never drink water from a bathroom tap. Then she went back to bed. Downstairs, she could hear Stef, with the radio turned on full. 'Stef,' she thought. 'He'll know. He'll know I'm here with Philip.' But it did not seem to be very important. She hated the idea of having to pretend, of lies and intrigues and cheap deceptions. She knew really that her mother, if she found out, would be shocked and distressed, that her father, perhaps, would never wish to see her again, but such reactions seemed remote and improbable, less real than dreams. She had a feeling of completeness, of an oracle fulfilled, a long suspense now over. 'I could lie here,' she thought, 'for ever. Nothing more can happen to me.' Years after, when Philip was long dead and almost forgotten, her heart would still go cold, remembering that ineffable delusion.

If Stef knew, he never said anything. A curious side-effect of the relationship was that Philip stopped complaining about his angelfish, and perhaps Stef was too grateful to wonder why. Once, Caroline tried to imagine him writing an anonymous letter to her father, clutching the pen, clumsily, in his left hand and wearing his big sheepskin mittens to prevent fingerprints, but the idea was so ludicrous she almost laughed. 'Why worry?' said Philip. 'Father wouldn't do anything, even if he found out. Only think of the scandal.'

'I'm not worried,' Caroline said. 'It's just that sometimes I feel I *ought* to be.'

Later, she asked him, child-like: 'Is it wrong?'

'Not for you,' he whispered, inside her, his whole body riven with complicated shivers of pleasure. 'Not for you.'

They slept together nearly every night. Often, Philip did not want to make love, merely wrapping himself round Caroline and talking himself to sleep with his face in her hair. The first time, he was embarrassed and tried to apologise the next morning, blushing painfully as he used to when he was a child. Caroline looked blankly at him. 'What does it matter?' she said. 'I thought sex was supposed to be fun, not something you have to do every night, like putting the cat out.' (In her last year at college, Clive's flatmate had had a cat.) In spite of his behaviour in the past, Philip was not, she realised, very highly sexed. Perhaps he had been trying to prove something, like the psychiatrists always said. In any case, she did not want to speculate. These days, she tried very hard not to think about her father. Her own sexuality was something about which she was still very uncertain: her physical needs had become so entangled with her emotions she could not separate the one from the other, and a certain note in Philip's voice, a secret joke, a shared look, meant as much to her as all their lovemaking. She thought that maybe she too had very little need for sex, requiring more the things of the spirit: emotional fulfilment and a quiet mind. Sometimes, when she held Philip in her arms, she felt a sweet, sharp pang deep in her abdomen, but whether of hunger or rapture she did not know. He still went out with Hazel and Deniece from time to time, and when he came in, for some reason, he always wanted to make love. Hazel was completely unsuspicious but Caroline felt Deniece watching her, when she was not looking, with cold baleful eyes. Whenever Caroline was there she invariably took her clothes off and sat around in the living room, pallid and incongruous, like a statue of something unpleasant. Caroline did not mind about Hazel but she would have liked to ask Philip to finish with Deniece.

5

Philip never painted Caroline. Much later, she wondered if it was because he knew he would never do it well enough, and failure, under the circumstances, would be a kind of sexual impotence. She did not know if she minded. He still painted Deniece now and then, impelled, so he said, by the fascinating patterns of her ribs, but the pictures grew more and more surrealistic and disjointed until in the end nothing remained of the original figure but a stepladder of greenish bones climbing out of a mottled background. 'They're getting worse,' Caroline said. 'There's no focus, no line. Just a chaos of paint on a canvas. Why don't you try something more –' she searched for the right word ' — more representational? "Still Life with Cucumber." Something like that.'

'Very phallic,' said Philip.

'It would be good for you,' Caroline insisted. 'Discipline.

I thought artists were supposed to need discipline. I could buy the cucumber on my way home tomorrow.'

'I can paint a cucumber,' Philip said coldly, 'from memory. It isn't very challenging.'

'You could cut it in half,' Caroline suggested.

'Don't worry,' Philip snapped. 'I've decided what I'm going to do next. Failure: a self-portrait. An unsuccessful picture of an unsuccessful artist. You are a constant source of inspiration to me; did you know? When it's finished, you can tell me why it doesn't work. It'll be like one of those competitions in magazines: a hundred and one deliberate mistakes. Pity you can't win a toaster.'

'You asked me what I thought,' Caroline said, suddenly furious. 'That picture's no good and nothing I say will make it any good. Anyway, I won't lie to you. I won't ever lie to you. Don't you know how important that is?' She went out, stumbling against the piano and banging the studio door. Downstairs, she found that she was crying. But she could not wish the words unsaid, no matter how hard she tried.

Two weeks later, Philip called her up to the attic. 'My self-portrait,' he said. 'The Artist at Work. What do you think of it?' It showed a small spirit lamp with a little blue flame (Philip had one), and behind it the vague shadow of a figure on a cardboard-coloured wall. But there was no one there. Beside the lamp stood an empty mug, a paintbrush, an ashtray full of cigarette-ends, one of which still glowed just a little too red. A thin stream of smoke rose from it, bisecting the picture. There were no greens, no purples, no glints of yellow. The perspective was distorted but effective. Caroline stood looking at it for a long time, not knowing what to say. 'You see,' said Philip, 'I can paint quite well, when I want to.'

'You talk as if your bad pictures are deliberate,' Caroline whispered.

'Perhaps they are,' he said, trying to be enigmatic, she thought, putting on an act. 'After all, no one gives a damn, do they? Least of all me. Sometimes, I get halfway with a painting, and then I make one small mistake, and I can't make the effort to correct it, I have to ruin the whole thing. Or else, I only have half an idea, and the other half never develops. That's the difference between me and Hockney, or Kokoschka, or Matisse. I am only half a genius.'

'I don't believe a word of it,' said Caroline.

After Philip died, when she was alone in London, she could never bear to look back on those last few months. It was not that they were specially happy: that was what was so unbearable. They argued a good deal and made it up in between and wasted precious time on fruitless anxieties and recriminations. (Time was an item which had never seemed precious to her, until it was too late.) Oddly enough, it was Philip who was conscious of guilt. For Caroline, her love was as natural as a spring wind, the inevitable consequence of a shared heredity and shared experience. She had avoided it, for a while, because she knew avoiding it was useless, because it was in her nature to hold back, particularly from the things she wanted most. As a child at parties, she had always refused to eat cream buns, afraid of appearing greedy, or finding the cream less melting than anticipation made it. Philip, she remembered, had usually eaten too many, and been consequently sick. She did not really understand what it was that made sex, or cream buns, so fatally tempting, and so inimical to his system. She could not have imagined, even if he had tried to explain, the loathsome, secret pleasure that writhed in his loins, knowing he was making love to his own sister. Later, when orgasm was over, the memory of it would return like an aftertaste. Caroline, he thought, was in some ways curiously innocent, a changeling from another dimension, with other rules, for whom everyday morals are meaningless. But he was aware of sin, that voluptuous, old-fashioned conception; he had resisted it all too briefly and given in all too sweetly. Sometimes, straddling her body, his legs wrapped around hers, he saw her as a creature made of sunlight, wholesome and ethereal, while he was the accursed, misshapen spirit who had seduced her from the upper air. And the worst thing was that the more he struggled not to see it, the more the image excited him.

In the summer, Caroline went to France for a week, stopping at Cheyney on the way back. She still thought of it infrequently as home, although it was so long since she had been there, and the emptiness which followed Celia's departure had remained. Strange, she thought, that Celia, whom none of them loved or wanted, should have left such a void behind her. In an undefined way, she expected her father to have changed, as though her affair with Philip, about which he knew nothing, should have eaten into him like a canker, destroying the tenuous illusion of his beauty. Perhaps she felt guiltless because, unconsciously, she had transferred her guilt to him, blaming him at last for his betrayal of the god she once believed in. The sins of the children shall be visited upon the fathers. But when she saw him again, sitting in his study, he looked no different. After dinner, he offered her a brandy, and she remembered with an old familiar ache the first time he had done so, when she came down from London after her mother's re-marriage. She almost fancied it was the same bottle, the liquor scarcely sunken in seven years. They talked, politely, about her job, a play she had seen, French food and wine. They did not talk about Philip. He loves Philip, she thought, wretchedly. If he didn't, he would ask after him, like he asks after me. She had come to realise that he did not, perhaps he could not, love her, but she still believed that he cared for his son and (like most parents) what he wanted for him was the happiness and security he himself had never known. On an impulse, she began to talk about painting. 'I've bought that,' her father told her, indicating a picture on the far wall. 'Julian Bell. What do you think of it?' There was a faint derision in his voice, as though he doubted her ability to judge, but she did not notice.

'It's good,' she said. 'Much better than most of Phil's pictures.' (She looked straight at him, when she spoke the name, but his expression did not alter.) 'The trouble is, he starts well, but then he seems to lose heart, or interest, or perhaps he just can't concentrate any more. Lately, he's done one or two things which I think might be good, though I don't know very much about it. There was something he called a self-portrait, and an old soup tin with some orange peel and stuff. He seems to like –' she sought for a word '– debris. I wish you would look at them some time.'

'When he brings them to me,' said Dr Horvath, without interest.

'He won't,' Caroline said, unable to stop herself, knowing,

even as her voice broke, that it would be fatal to show emotion. 'You know he won't.' It was the nearest she had ever come to confiding in him, but when she saw his face she could not go on. The next day, in the train, she bit her lip at the notion, afraid to hope he might remember what she had left unsaid.

He came to the flat later that year, on a grey October day. Caroline never knew what made him do it, if it was for his own sake, or for Philip's, if it was love, or merely the cold acceptance of responsibility. She imagined him hailing a taxi in Harley Street, giving their address, on an impulse, instead of Victoria Station. But she knew he was not a man who ever gave in to impulse. When Philip saw who it was he looked at her, for a moment, with hurt, accusing eyes, as though he realised this was something she had wanted, maybe even engineered. Father and son shook hands, politely on the doctor's part, reluctantly on Philip's. Caroline made tea. She had Earl Grey, which she knew was her father's favourite, but he drank it as though he did not even notice. She thought, hopelessly: they hardly know I am here. She felt like a character in a play who walks on and off at the back of the stage and doesn't get to say anything at all. She had dreamed, sometimes, of bringing her father and Philip together again, of making Philip understand that he at least was loved. And now here they were, face to face, and she was quite helpless: there was nothing she could say or do to affect the dénouement. They did not talk much. Of the two, Dr Horvath was the more relaxed, sitting in the best armchair with his long legs crossed. Philip propped himself against the mantelpiece, looking suddenly and horribly like a distorted image of the older man, the colours dingier, the poise ungraceful, the beautiful face marred with bitterness and vulnerability. He responded sullenly to his father's cold inquiries and smoked a great many cigarettes. It's all Philip's fault, Caroline decided, with unexpected anger. He doesn't even try to understand. She offered more tea but nobody wanted it. Presently, Dr Horvath asked to see the pictures.

Caroline did not follow them upstairs. She took the tea things into the kitchen and washed them, very diligently, under the running tap. For a minute, when her father said: 'Let me see your work,' she had felt wildly hopeful, but she stifled the feeling almost immediately, afraid, in that sensitive atmosphere, that thoughts, like words, might be overheard. She stared out of the kitchen window, at a view of rooftops and high walls and someone else's back garden. When she looked down, she found she was washing the same teacup over and over again, her fingers rubbing automatically at non-existent stains. She put the cup in the rack and switched the tap off. The last mutterings of the plumbing gradually died away and a silence fell in which everything seemed to stop breathing. The silence of the city, Caroline reflected, no longer hearing the familiar hum of traffic two streets away, thinking of country silence in the garden at Cheyney, a silence of birdsong and the rustling of trees. A sparrow hopped on the window sill, pecked a crumb, flew away. There were birds in London, she thought, but they did not sing. And she remembered with an inexplicable chill how she had once been afraid of coming back to London, afraid of finding herself alone in those silent crowds. She waited in the kitchen for a few more minutes, but nothing happened. Then she went back into the living room and helped herself to one of Philip's Gitanes, smoking it, very slowly, without flicking the ash, until half the cigarette was burnt away.

When her father came downstairs he was carrying the self-portrait. 'This is good,' he said. 'I should like to show it to a friend of mine. If you can produce some more work of this calibre there may be the possibility of an exhibition...' Caroline said goodbye and touched his cheek, automatically, in a brief substitute for a kiss. (She did not know it was the last time she would ever kiss him.) Even now, she did not dare to look happy. After he had gone, she turned to Philip. 'What's the matter?' she said, searching his face. 'It has worked out, hasn't it? You might even get an exhibition. Aren't you pleased?'

'Pleased!' To her horror, she saw he was almost crying. 'Why couldn't you leave things alone? I don't *want* his exhibition, can't you understand? I don't want anything from him. I don't want his friend or his opinions or his bloody financial support. Don't you know what he'll do with that painting? He'll hang it in his private surgery and he'll say: "My son did that." He'll say it in that cool, casual way, like it doesn't matter to him, and all those rich, smug, psychosomatic people will be frightfully impressed. "The integrity of it!" they'll murmur, "the self-loathing! the disillusionment! You must be so proud of him." I don't want him to be proud of me, can't you see? I don't want him even to think of me or speak my name. Isn't it enough that I owe my whole existence to him, that every time I look in the mirror I see his face, his image, no matter what I do to make it different?'

This is so horrible, she thought, it can't be happening to me. She stammered: 'You don't mean these things – you can't mean them. Don't you *want* to be a success?'

Philip hardly heard her. 'You did this, didn't you?' he said. 'You sold me to him. I trusted you and you sold me to him. I doubt if you even collected the standard thirty pieces of silver. You just did it out of idiotic sentiment, out of your pathetic sense of duty. Did you think I would be grateful? Did you picture him, clasping me to his bosom like the prodigal son? After all I've said to you – '

At least, thought Caroline, Stef hasn't come back. At least there's no one here to hear us. She said in an unreal voice: 'He loves you. He doesn't love me very much, but he loves you.'

'Love,' Philip retorted, 'as Joan Baez once said, is just a four-letter word. You never learn, do you? I suppose you thought you could use me, to get *him*. You couldn't live with him, so you lived with me. You couldn't screw him, so you screwed me. And in the end you gave me to him, like a priceless gift, out of your great love and the generosity of your heart. You gave him everything, didn't you? You gave him my freedom, such as it was, my little integrity, my very soul. I painted that picture for you – did you know? – and you gave him that, too. You leave me with *nothing*.' He was holding her by the shoulders, his fingers pinching her flesh. His face shook. 'Are you pleased with yourself, Carla? Do you like what you have done?'

He's dramatising himself, she thought. He doesn't mean it. He'll be reasonable tomorrow. She said: 'I can't talk to you when you're like this. I'm going out.' She pulled herself free of him and ran upstairs to get her coat. When she came down again he was standing by the window with his back to her.

Suddenly, she was angry. She went out without speaking to him, slamming the door. In the street, she did not look back. Afterwards, it always seemed to her the worst thing, that she had not even said goodbye.

That night, Caroline came home around ten, having spent the evening with an old school-friend whom she had not seen for several years. They had a lot to talk about but Caroline's attention wandered and she excused herself as early as she could. When she approached the house, the first thing she saw was a crowd of people standing in the road, evidently absorbed in something which she could not see. Beyond, there was a brightly coloured vehicle with a flashing light on top, strung with ladders and tentacles of hose. A man in a helmet was struggling to make himself heard over the wails of the siren: 'Back! Get back!' The crowd jostled and re-formed a little farther off. There must be a fire, Caroline thought, with the vague incuriosity of someone who is rarely interested in other people's disasters. Funny, I can't see anything. She tried to make her way round the crowd but people kept bumping into her and someone said: 'Here – stop pushing!' Then the man in the helmet again: 'Stand back, miss. It isn't safe to get too close.' But Caroline didn't move at all. She was looking at her own house, the house where she had lived for almost a year. She had seen burning houses in films or on television, with the walls caving in and flames bursting from the windows. But the windows were shut and the outer wall still stood, so that if she had not known she might never have guessed there was anything wrong. Then she saw the smoke, thick dark smoke laden with filth like an obscene fog, pouring from the gap where the roof had been. Behind the upper windows the light was a murky red. Presently, one window (it must have been her bedroom) shattered, and flames leapt eagerly through the gap. Just like in a film, she thought, almost gratified, stupid with shock. She looked round for Philip, to take his hand, but she knew beyond doubt, beyond hope, that he would not be there.

After that, everything became very confused. She remembered saying: 'I must go in. I must go into the house,' and someone who knew she lived there trying to comfort her, stroking her hair, though she hardly felt it. She was quite calm and perfectly rational. She had to get into the house and save Philip's paintings: that was all that mattered. Nearby, a cockney voice commented: 'They say it started in the attic. There was an old biddy downstairs, in the basement flat, but they got her out.' So it's too late, Caroline thought, stupidly. There's nothing I can do. She wondered how on earth she was going to tell Philip. But of course, she wouldn't have to tell him. She wouldn't have to tell him anything ever again. . . Much later, she remembered a figure running towards the house, and the firemen coming back with something that struggled and screamed. 'My fish! My fish! I must get my fish!' Suddenly, she found herself imagining them, swimming round and round, while the water grew hotter and hotter, and little coils of steam rose from the surface, and the glass began to disintegrate. There they would be, flapping about on the table, until all their rainbow colours turned black. At the thought of the angelfish she began to cry a little, it seemed so pathetic, and someone who lived down the road brought her a mug of cocoa.

No one knew exactly how the fire started. At the inquest, they produced Philip's painting, with the detail of the spirit lamp. Caroline had to get up and say that he had such a lamp in his possession. 'I gather he was an artist,' said the coroner. 'Possibly he used this lamp to heat wax, for Batik work.' (His daughter did Batik.)

'I think,' said Caroline, 'he lit his cigarettes with it.'

They brought in a verdict of accidental death. A doctor who had once attended Valerie Horvath spoke about the possibility of inheriting suicidal tendencies, but the evidence was dismissed as inconclusive. It was pointed out that the attic had been full of highly inflammable material: canvas, paper, hardboard, wooden shelves and furniture. An inspector claimed that the house had failed to conform to the current building requirements for rented premises and should have been pulled down years ago. A policeman suggested that Philip had been under the influence of drugs and asked to call a Mrs Deniece Lamprey (Caroline was surprised at the Mrs), but she had already left the court. Philip's own doctor testified that he had not been a drug addict and the alleged activities of his alleged girlfriend had no bearing on the case. The coroner gave a short lecture on the evils of smoking. Caroline tried not to imagine Philip, after she had gone, shutting himself in the attic, dribbling turpentine and methylated spirits on the piano, the table, the crooked shelves, holding a match to his latest canvas until the flame began to eat into the picture. Perhaps he had rolled himself a joint first and sat, smoking, looking at his work, with who knew what thoughts going through his mind. Dr Horvath had stood up in the witness box and admitted, reluctantly, that he and his son had had a minor difference of opinion over the question of Philip's career which had subsequently been resolved. Philip had no reason to kill himself and had never been a suicidal type. Looking at her father's face, unmoving and very pale, Caroline thought: He *knows*. He knows it isn't true. But afterwards, when they talked, he did not mention the fire at all.

Philip was buried the next day, in the cemetery at Cheyney. There was a coffin but nothing very much inside it, or so Caroline understood. Hazel was there, in black, which did not suit her, and weeping inelegantly into an expensive handkerchief. Stef arrived, late, looking even more pained than usual, but perhaps he was still pining for his tropical fish. Deniece did not come. The vicar uttered conventional religious platitudes in a suitably ecclesiastical voice, the congregation droned, inevitably, 'Abide With Me', and Caroline stood in the front row, neither speaking nor praying, staring tearlessly at the altar. 'It's just like the insurance man,' she thought. 'If you're good, if you pay your dues, you will have everlasting lilyfields and a halo and a harp. Philip has cashed in the great Insurance Policy of Life. . . Only Philip wasn't good. And I'm not good, either. I'll never be good.' In the cemetery they stood around the grave, shamefacedly, like people at a cocktail party who do not know what to say. The wind bit. Ashes to ashes, intoned the vicar, and dust to dust. Dinner for worms, Caroline said to herself, thinking that was what Philip would have said, if he had been able. Through a sudden blur she saw her father, looking like the archangel Gabriel in Bible prints when she was a child. The archangel Gabriel in a smart black suit, watching, indifferently, as those who had not paid up on their insurance policy made their way down to Hell. He ought to have changed, she thought, remembering the elfin lines she had once seen, as though through thin tissue, under that beautiful façade. He ought to have aged ten years in three days. But there was no anguish in his face, no loss, only a hint of anxiety carefully concealed. She had a sudden recollection of her mother crying, unbearably, when she was seven or eight, of Philip saying: 'My first Mummy cried a lot.' There was a pain inside her too sharp for tears. Beside her, Stef whispered awkwardly: 'Are you all right?'

'Yes.'

The last handful of earth had been thrown on the coffin and the mourners turned away, trying not to look relieved. Later, when the grave was filled in, the flowers would be arranged on the top like an ornamental salad. Caroline took her father's arm (it seemed to be expected) and walked away with him towards the car, cold at heart.

PART 2

STEPHEN

6

After Philip's death, Caroline stayed with Angela Teviot, the old school-friend whom she had met on the night of the fire, until she could find more permanent accommodation. She had been invited up to Birmingham, but there was her job to think of (she was the senior secretary now), and anyway, she was afraid to talk of Philip, afraid of her own weakness, of her desperate need to confide. Sometimes, she was glad that her mother, in bed with 'flu, had been unable to attend the funeral. Harry's letter (semi-legible and unexpectedly long) said that she had been deeply distressed by the news and had suffered severe post-influenza depression. He would have come himself, he wrote, but he had not liked to leave her. Thank God, Caroline thought listlessly, remembering his enormous floral tribute with an instinctive shudder. She supposed she was getting inured to Harry, but she could not have borne his tactless sympathy or the encouraging hand-squeeze he would have felt impelled to give her at some stage during the proceedings. At least she had been spared that. She thought she had never really appreciated the difficulties of her relationship with Philip, until he was no longer there. She cried little, in case, in the temporary release of tears, she should cry too much. She hardly spoke of him. In the mirror, she saw her reflection growing paler and thinner, and she forced herself to eat meals she did not really want. Sometimes, walking down the grey winter streets, she thought: I'm alone now, I'm alone in London, like I always knew I would be. She imagined the city stretching away on every hand, the roads and alleyways, avenues and crescents, each packed with houses, jammed shoulder to shoulder, where the rooms were piled one on top of another like children's bricks, and in each room a separate human being, and in each human being a separate core of loneliness. It all seemed so hopeless. There is nothing anyone can do for anyone, she decided, without originality. But it was too late now for the lesson to be of any use.

She spent Christmas in Birmingham but Harry's sister was there with her family, so there was very little time for private talk. In the New Year she moved into another flat, with a friend of Angela's who spent most of her time abroad (they both worked for a travel company). When she was in England, Glynis lived with her boyfriend, under circumstances of extraordinary discretion for fear of affecting his divorce settlement. In a way, Caroline found it a relief to be by herself. Angela's company was entertaining but very tiring. She was a tall girl, needle-thin, with a pretty, bony face rather like a vivacious horse and long hair unexpectedly streaked with grey. She ascribed this at various times to some rare, unnameable illness which had nearly carried her off in her early teens, to an unhappy love affair at the age of twelve, and to a genetic mutation of enormous, though baffling, scientific significance. (She had joined Caroline's school in the fifth form, and her hair had been grey and her stories colourful even then.) She talked as easily as some people breathe, her conversation being fluid and frequently meaningless and having, Caroline sometimes suspected, very little to do with her underlying processes of thought. Her position in the travel company was said to be based on her ability to talk any opposition to a standstill in a variety of languages, including fluent French and Italian, ungrammatical Spanish, and vulgar Portuguese. She made Caroline sandwiches with quark and wholemeal bread which she said were very nourishing and offered her endless cups of tea. Caroline fed the sandwiches, unobtrusively, to the cat, who did not want them. After she moved in with Glynis, Angela visited her regularly, once with two volumes of Proust (Caroline could not read Proust), once with avocados and champagne. 'Edgar bought the champagne for me,' she explained, 'but I told him I only like Bollinger so I said I'd give it to you. Anyway, it's been in the fridge for far too long so it's probably ruined. I'm afraid I'm dreadfully snobby about wine. Let's open it, shall we?' When Angela had drunk most of the champagne, she went home. Caroline, who had not had any alcohol for a long time, was feeling very strange. After Angela had gone she thought about crying (she had so few opportunities to cry), but there did not seem to be any point. I want to go *home*, she said to herself, without any real idea of what she meant. (Home – Cheyney, the doctor, Melissa.) She had not written to her father since the tragedy. Probably, she reflected, viciously, he hasn't even noticed. She was aware of some other feeling, sharper than the pain she had been stifling for so long. Looking down, she saw that her hands were clenched, so that the nails dug into her palms. I hate him, she thought wonderingly. I *hate* him. She had never hated anyone in her life.

It was Angela's suggestion that she should go to Greece. 'Special discount: employees' friends and family only. Honestly, Carla, you can't turn it down. I haven't been myself but they say it's simply heavenly. All that sun and warm sea.'

'You go,' said Caroline.

'Darling, I'd love to, but I'm *far* too busy. . .'

When she got back, Caroline felt different, somehow more relaxed. She still missed Philip so much she did not even dare to think of him, but the sun had got into her blood stream and for a little while it stayed there. She had dinner, two or three times, with an attractive young man in the Publicity Department who had been asking her for months. She spent a weekend in Birmingham. ('You look better,' her mother said. 'My poor darling. You and Phil were so close.') She wrote to her father. It was difficult to know what to say, with this terrible new bitterness welling up inside her. Or perhaps it was an old bitterness, old as childhood, too long thrust to the back of her mind. She had to throw away the first three attempts. The fourth she sealed and sent off, without thinking too much about it. A month or so later, she met her father for lunch, in his club.

'I haven't seen you for a while,' he remarked, making small talk. 'How is your job?'

'Fine.' She felt compelled to elaborate, although she knew he wasn't interested. 'I'm getting involved in editing now. They give me obscure 500-page novels by admirers of Tolkien or Dostoyevsky and tell me to turn them down tactfully. I suppose it's useful experience.'

Her father said surprisingly: 'I rather like Dostoyevsky. The Russians have such an interesting sense of morality. Not like Dickens, who was incurably bourgeois.'

Once, thought Caroline, I would have been so happy to hear him talk to me like that. We are having a literary discussion. We are *talking*. . . She said only: 'It doesn't sound quite the same in the language of the 1980s.'

Later, she asked after Melissa, but her father had little to say. 'She's left school,' he explained. 'She re-sat three of her 'O' Levels but failed and would doubtless fail again. She seems incapable of sustaining intelligent thought for more than five minutes, if as much. I'm afraid she takes after her mother.'

Caroline swirled the gin round her glass so that the ice cubes knocked together and said nothing.

Towards the end of the meal a young man came up to their table and spoke to her father. Close to, Caroline saw he was not quite as young as he appeared. He called the doctor 'Stephen' and gave him a curious sidelong smile. 'My daughter Caroline,' said Dr Horvath. She had the feeling he was not quite pleased. After the young man had gone, she found herself wondering, for the first time, what sort of men he liked. For no particular reason she thought of a yellow-eyed Greek, smiling an infinitely knowing smile in the cool gloom of a beachside bar.

The following year, in September, Caroline went back to Greece with Angela. They had decided on the holiday some months ago. 'You *must* come,' Angela insisted. 'You know you had a marvellous time last year. Besides I don't want to go on my own.' Caroline slept badly these days and, lying awake in the early summer dawn, she would find herself making nebulous plans, strange fancies born of loneliness and insomnia, in which, once or twice, she saw Ulysses' face. She began to remember odd things he had said, careless remarks thrown up in the flotsam of conversation. 'I would sleep with a fat old woman if she made it worth my while.' (His voice, in her mind, sounded dispassionate and matter-of-fact.) 'Or even a fat old man. Why not? I am young and beautiful, and if they wish to pay me for their pleasure, what is the harm in it? I am contributing to the happiness of humanity.' But he was joking, of course. It was the kind of thing people said, without meaning it, when they would shrink from the actual act with revulsion. Anyway, he had probably left the island by now, moved on to Athens or America or wherever beautiful young Greeks go to become rich and sophisticated. . . In the mornings, Caroline did not think about her plans. She told herself that by day they would appear nothing more than the chimera of a sleepless hour, devoid of potential reality. But perhaps she was afraid to think about such things in a clear light, in case her thoughts, too, became clear. She paid a brief visit to Cheyney and found that Melissa had become a punk, with her hair spiked and dyed black and tight, shapeless trousers clinging to her thin legs. Dr Horvath hardly seemed to have noticed, except when he looked her over, with vague distaste, as she came in to lunch. She's still afraid of him, Caroline thought, watching her face. He has the influence: why doesn't he use it? Perhaps he just doesn't care any more. He's written her off, like an experiment that went wrong, or a crossword clue it isn't worth the trouble to resolve. . . Later, Caroline tried to talk to her, but it was no good. 'What shall we talk about?' said Melissa. 'Philip?'

'No,' Caroline said with an effective finality that surprised her. 'That has nothing to do with you.' She could feel herself hardening inside, her unlove for her sister deteriorating into dislike, contempt, and other, still more ignoble emotions. She fought against them, but she could not change herself. Possibly something of this showed in her face; anyway, Melissa stared at her for a moment, half nervous, half insolent, then flung herself out of the room, shouting an insulting remark when she was too far down the corridor for her sister to hear it.

Left alone, Caroline went into the hall. Under some strange compulsion, not quite curiosity, she tried the door to her father's study. It was not locked. She entered quickly, closing the door behind her, and switched on the light. A familiar smell assailed her nostrils: old leather, old books, wrinkled words, ageing, or so she imagined, like people, the capitals bent double with rheumatism, the letters stumbling off the page and curling away into dust. Perhaps, she thought, they are just for show, like so much of her father's outward personality. Perhaps they were dying of forced inactivity, unread. If she had time, she would look at them. She went over to his desk and began to go through it, coldly, thoroughly, like a professional in a spy film. She did not know quite why or what she was looking for. She scanned address books and diaries, noted places, dates, times. One drawer was locked and she was almost relieved when she could not find the key, though she did not try to imagine what might be inside. Maybe it was just correspondence. Afterwards, she was vaguely surprised to feel no pangs of conscience. Melissa had gone out (she had heard the door slam) so she knew she would not be disturbed. She stood for a while glancing through the books, which had always seemed tacitly forbidden although nothing had ever actually been said. There were several old medical textbooks, probably very valuable, Swinburne's verse, Oscar Wilde, translations of Ovid and Plato. There was what appeared to be a complete set of Arthur Conan Doyle. Caroline was still half expecting some horrid revelation from those thin, closely-printed pages, but she found only a part of a letter, mostly about the weather, from someone called Paul, and a dried flower in a folded piece of paper with a Latin name scrawled across it in unfamiliar handwriting. In many of the antique textbooks the pages were uncut, so she thought maybe her earlier fancy had been right. When her father came in from his dinner party ('Monica Anstey,' said the diary, '8.00 pm. Spinal curvature and Pekinese dog'), she was sitting in the living room watching television. 'Did you have a good meal?' she said, with automatic politeness. She was wondering how he would look, whether it would mean anything to him at all, if she asked him: 'Who was Paul?'

She had thought, when in Greece, she might be able to forget her father. Last time, the very differentness of the landscape, the sun-bleached earth, wind-gnarled trees, opal sea, made her feel dream-like and relaxed. Her problems, even her sorrows, belonged to England, to grey streets and grey skies. But nothing is ever the same, coming back. She lay on the

beach, half listening to the complicated saga of Angela's latest
love affair, her mind moving restlessly behind her closed eyes.
It took her a while to accustom herself to the leisurely pace
of life on the island after the frantic rat-race of London, and
for the first week she felt both exhausted and bored, sleeping
fitfully and waking late, still dizzy with tiredness, to the
sound of Angela flooding the shower and someone else cursing
blithely as the water leaked into the kitchen. Down on the
beach she stretched out in the sun, for hour after hour, as
though nailed to the rock. It was nearly the end of the season
and the shrubs along the cliff-top had shrivelled to a skeletal
webbing of twigs, brittle as rice-paper. Rubbish – bottles and
cans, crumpled wrappings, orange peel and apple cores –
overflowed the wastepaper bins and piled up in the hollow
beside the path. Debris, thought Caroline inconsequently,
remembering Philip. She and Angela smoked constantly to
keep away the wasps. For some reason, she waited several
days before going into Ulysses' bar, afraid, maybe, that he
would not be there, or that, finding him, she might start
saying things that would have been safer left unsaid. Perhaps,
after all, he would hardly remember her: hundreds of English
girls must pass through the village every year, many of them
equally tall and slender, tanned the same rose-beige, with
sun-lightened hair. When she stood in the doorway and saw
him, leaning on the bar reading a newspaper, she felt
suddenly uncertain. But he remembered her.

That evening, after dinner, she came back with Angela and
a few other friends. It was someone's birthday (Caroline never
found out if it was the busty redhead or the courier or both)
and Ulysses gave them champagne on the house. Angela got
drunk and became, if possible, even more vivacious than
usual, taking a succession of embarrassing photographs with
a microscopic camera which might well have been designed
for a master spy. She caught people pulling faces, blowing
bubbles, spilling drink, the busty redhead falling out of her
T-shirt, Ulysses giving the courier a birthday kiss (if it was
her birthday), Ulysses with his arm around Caroline. He was
attracted by Angela, Caroline realised, by her liveliness, her
thin elegance, her clear sophisticated voice. Rather to her
surprise, Angela was equally attracted by him. 'You can see,'
she said on the way home, 'he is very intelligent.' Angela's

73

men were usually much older than her, cultured, well off. Her current boyfriend was a Canadian in his late forties, twice divorced, with a handsome face tanned to the colour and texture of leather, greying temples, and a body kept in condition with squash and daily exercise. 'The strong, silent type,' Angela had once remarked, languorously. Caroline often wondered if it was his body she loved or the presents he always brought her and his unerring taste in theatres and restaurants. Sometimes, she thought Angela wondered, too. She liked men with a sense of style, a discriminating palate, an American Express card, but she was not mercenary at heart and she spent long hours sitting on the beach trying to work out if she was really in love with Michel. It was unlike her, Caroline reflected, even to notice a young man more or less her own age whose principal asset was a beautiful face. The next morning, in the bar, she told him, not without malice, about Angela's remark.

'I *am* very intelligent,' he said indignantly. 'She is a woman of perception, this Angela. I speak four languages: Greek, English, Italian, German. I run this bar. I make love to many women, and marry none of them. To do these things, you need brains.'

Caroline shrugged dismissively. 'I don't want you to be intelligent,' she said. 'It isn't necessary.' She might have added: It isn't necessary for *me*. But she did not want to say too much. In any case, she did not really think he would come.

When she had gone, Ulysses picked up an apple which his mother had brought for him and sat outside, eating it, staring broodily across the harbour. He was very bored. It seemed to him he had spent the whole season gazing at that same blue stretch of water, watching endless bikini-clad figures trailing up and down the path to the beach. One semi-naked body looks very much like another, in the end. There was nothing to do but eat and drink, sleep and screw, or get into occasional fights with the other locals, usually over a girl who was not really worth it. Most of the time, he leant on the bar and dreamed, following in his mind some white-winged yacht that went sailing past the harbour, to a quiet, secret cove where a solitary villa hid behind the olive trees, with cream-coloured telephones in every room and a woman sunbathing on the terrace, dressed in nothing but a solitaire diamond as big as a peach-stone. Soon, it would be winter, the clouds would roll down over the hills, violent rainstorms would tear at tree-root and mountain-root as though trying to wash the island into the sea. One of his friends was going to Germany, another to New York. But his German was poor and he could not afford the fare to the States. He thought of England, which he had once visited. He retained a vague memory of smoke-filled rooms and tepid beer; of ice-blue skies, knife-edged winds, sleet; of London, that huge, dirty, noisy whirlpool of humanity, the lights of Piccadilly and the shadows of Soho and the Park Lane traffic jams where every second car was a Rolls Royce. London was glamorous, dangerous, exciting. He was not afraid of danger. He was afraid of safety, familiarity, of marriage to some doe-eyed local girl, settling down and growing old, like one of his uncles (his father was dead) who spent the whole day sitting in the sun and cackling at all the briefest bikinis. He did not want to grow old. Better to have fun and die young, quickly, never knowing wrinkles and rheumatism, impotence and indignity.

He finished the apple without relish and tossed the core to a stray dog which was sitting nearby scratching for fleas. A blonde girl walked past, waving a greeting, and his mind moved automatically to Caroline. She had annoyed him that morning, as she often did, with her gentle mockery, her assurance, her instinctive assumption of superiority. But these things which annoyed also attracted him. She and Angela, he decided, were the only girls in the village worth talking to. He thought of a film he had seen recently, on his cousin's television, where a beautiful woman planned her husband's murder with the aid of his chauffeur. The actress had not been a type he admired, over forty, with a fleshless attenuated figure and Oriental eyes, but he had been fascinated by her cold duplicity, the feline smile with which she beguiled her victim. That was only a story, of course. But there had been something a little like that, a sort of aloof calculation, in Caroline's expression, when she sat at the bar making plans. Ulysses had no wish to rank as a mere chauffeur, yet he could not help fantasising about the possibilities of such a role. He told himself that if he went to England, it would be for the lure of variety and glamour, for profit, for adventure, for anything but Caroline's cyan-blue eyes and unreachable smile. Now, knowing her better, he found it still more difficult to picture her letting him touch her, letting him run his hands down her long narrow body, over her breasts, between her thighs, into the little entrance which he could never imagine violated or even moist and sweet with desire. He knew there must have been someone, naturally; she was twenty-five or six and she did not look innocent, only infinitely cool. Perhaps she had merely submitted, without passion or interest. He did not dare to believe she would ever submit to him. But sometimes, dangerously, he dreamed of somehow acquiring a hold over her, a mysterious influence that would compel her to come to him, reluctantly, softened and stimulated in spite of herself, giving her body, not in indifference, but in hatred and lust. He tried not to dwell on that image, or not for more than a moment: the very thrill of anticipation felt unsafe. After all, he reasoned, as coldly as he could, it was not as if he loved her: he had never been in love and frequently doubted its existence. Why should sex with Caroline be any different from sex with any other woman? She had two legs, two arms, two breasts, a hole in the usual place. If – if – he fell in with her plans it would be for strictly practical ends, not for any chimera of undreamed sensuality. He enjoyed the pleasures of the senses, but (so he assured himself) he had not let them rule him. He could not be such a fool as to become entangled in some fantasy of conspiracy and revenge, for a chilly English Persephone who had never eaten a single pomegranate seed.

She did not actually tell him what she wanted him to do. It was he, at the last, who put it into words, watching her face for a moment of flinching from the truth. But she merely looked thoughtful, and her eyes, when she raised them to his, held something that was almost satisfaction. It occurred to Ulysses that his unsubtlety pleased her.

'It sounds very melodramatic, doesn't it?' she said lightly, or as lightly as she could manage. 'And I am not – really – a melodramatic person.' With a curious detachment, she found

76

herself wondering at the unsuspected depths of her capacity for passion – a cold, hungry passion that was stronger and deeper than any warmer feeling she had ever known. Yes, she thought, I suppose I *am* being melodramatic, and she might have been amused, in a wry kind of way, if the idea had not hurt. Or perhaps it was the amusement which hurt her.

Ulysses was studying her face like a child with a book that is too advanced for him. 'No,' he said. 'But you are full of hate. It is bad for you, to hate like that. You should learn to love a little.'

Caroline shrugged noncommittally. 'Maybe afterwards,' she said. (To Ulysses, it sounded almost like a promise, or the hint of a promise; but he was looking for promises.) 'One thing at a time.'

'Have you ever loved anyone other than your brother?'

'Boyfriends, do you mean?' She did not want him to guess too much. 'I expect so. They didn't really matter, though. Philip and I were very close.'

A little later, he asked her. 'Why should *I* get involved in this?'

'No reason.' Caroline smiled a queer certain smile. 'You would do much better not to.'

'But?'

'But nothing. You told me once it was the kind of thing you would do. I always thought it was only talk.'

'How rich is your father?'

'Well off.' She was very nearly sure of him now. 'Rich enough to afford a gigolo.'

'So that is what you think of me!'

'No,' Caroline said with gentle regret. 'I think you are just like everyone else. There are no more gigolos. It's a lot easier to earn an honest living than a dishonest one, particularly nowadays. I don't blame you.'

'You think you are so clever, don't you?' Ulysses said sharply. Even her insidious manipulation fascinated him. He wanted to ask her if she would lie with him, as a part of the contract, but it was a question he never asked until he was sure of the answer. Instead he said: 'We would be – partners?' It was nearly what he meant.

'If you like to put it that way,' Caroline replied, noting the vocabulary of the Western with the edge of a smile. She had no intention of allowing him equal status, but she did not feel it was necessary to say so.

It would be so easy, Ulysses thought, to understand too much from that empty statement. It would be so easy to imagine, behind that fleeting, sphinx-like smile, the riddle of her feelings, the unasked question, the answer. He knew he was deceiving himself, letting her deceive him, but his mind had become fixed on the thing he desired with all the wanton greed of the morally deficient, and he could no longer visualise that greed endlessly unsatisfied. He told himself that her father was wealthy, that winter lay heavy in the islands, that faith moved mountains. 'I'll think about it,' he said.

Caroline, blinkered by her own fantasies, did not know or care what he understood.

7

October. The terminal at Gatwick Airport was full of people with the pinched faces and damp footwear of an English winter. Arrivals, incongruously tanned, emerged from Customs pushing trolleys top-heavy with baggage and bemoaning the sun they had left behind. Caroline stood at the barrier waiting for the flight from Athens, which was late. She was not particularly surprised; on both her trips to Greece the flights had been delayed. The Greeks had not yet invented radar and Air Traffic Control was rumoured to exist only in the imagination of a little man pushing paper 'planes around a draughtboard. She thought about lighting a cigarette but decided against it: it would be rather like smoking in the street, she felt, a habit she had always disliked. Beside her, there were a few other people waiting for the same flight: a little old woman in a headscarf with a brown, wizened face, like a pickled walnut, two families, and a tired-looking young man in a chrome yellow T-shirt bearing the legend 'Aegis Holidays'. Waiting, Caroline reflected, destroys rational thought. She wished she had a book. The old woman was knitting something indescribable in vivid scarlet wool; the father of one of the families was making an apathetic attempt to control his younger offspring. She tried to concentrate on her present anxieties but her thoughts drifted, aimlessly, backwards in time to lost days, lost opportunities, lost love. It was nearly two years now and she knew it ought not to hurt so much. Time was supposed to heal such things, to supply new faces, new loves, in place of the old. She was young and resilient: a week of tears, a month of Hell, and she should be able to get back to the business of life. But she had never cried much, never been conscious of suffering. Only an emptiness inside. A fortnight earlier, she had seen from a bus the back view of someone who looked like Philip. The same length of hair, the same faded jeans, the same walk. As he disappeared round a corner she found her pulse was racing and a surge of useless panic was rising inside her. For the first time she was aware of pain, not a dull, stifled ache but real pain, sharp and immediate, as though those two long years, the slow hours, the lonely nights, the endless, faceless days, had passed in the blink of an eye. The shock had worn off but she was unchanged, or so she thought. She had no particular qualms about the future, no doubts. Her only fear was that Ulysses might change his mind. 'I'll never be good,' she told herself, as she had told herself at the funeral, vaguely conscious that what she was doing was wrong, at least by normal standards of conduct, and sometime, somewhere, she would have to be held responsible. But it did not matter now. Over the tannoy, a clipped female voice announced the arrival of the 'plane, an hour and twenty minutes behind schedule. Caroline looked at the clock and tried to work out how long it would take for Ulysses to disembark and collect his luggage.

If he was there.

A week later, Dr Stephen Horvath emerged from his Harley Street surgery into a chill grey evening and hailed a taxi. He was going to his club. He always dined at his club on Thursdays, not so much out of habit but because he was a methodical person, preferring a flexible routine to the muddle of an open schedule. The food at his club was not very good, but then nor was the food at home. And at home, there would be Melissa. Whether she sat through the meal in sullen silence or whether she volunteered some tentative remark which she half hoped, or half feared, would shock him, he would be equally irritated and bored. He sometimes wondered how he could ever have been so misguided as to adopt Melissa. He had known nothing of her father (a mistake) and cared less. At the time, it had merely seemed an ideal way to acquire an extra child without the disagreeable preliminaries which had been necessary for Philip and Caroline. There was something so very respectable and bourgeois about having children. They grew up, they went to university, they had careers and marriages and more children of their own. If you had children, no one ever wondered what you did in bed at night. Childless couples were immediately suspect: they were self-absorbed, too much in love, over-age Romeos and Juliets, impotent, frigid, lesbian, homosexual. Worst of all, they never looked worried and run down like everyone else. Stephen Horvath had been proud of his children, at first, even though he experienced a faint twinge of distaste at the sight of their swollen pink faces and dribbling mouths. Still, that was perfectly normal; only eccentric fathers wished actually to hold their sons, throwing them up in the air for all the world like beach balls or talking to them in babyish gurgles which would teach them little about intelligible speech. Those fathers, he reflected, were probably the ones who had phantom pregnancies and labour pains, who got up in the night while their wives slept to warm milk and sterilise bottles, who knew how to change nappies. He left all that to Valerie, and later, Margaret. He had no wish to infringe on female territory. He intended that his children would do all the things children were supposed to do: play with Lego and Spirograph, dolls and train-sets, read E. Nesbit, the Famous Five, *The Water Babies*, go to church and Sunday school and sing in the choir. He wanted them to be quiet and well-mannered, to say 'Please' and 'Thank you', to shine in class. His son Philip would grow into an intelligent, well-educated young man who would get a good job and eventually marry a nice girl, so that the female patients who flocked to his private surgery in the vain hope that he would break the Hippocratic oath could say to him: 'Of course, dear Dr Horvath, he takes after you.' Instead, Philip had turned out weak, tiresome, sexually unpredictable, intelligent without application, artistic without talent. There had been times when he had dreaded to hear one of those women murmur, in the phantom voice of his hopes: 'Of course, dear Dr Horvath. . .' Now, Philip's 'Self-portrait' hung on the surgery wall, and the women looked sympathetic and longed to press his hand, and their husbands said the picture was 'not bad', and 'tough luck', and cleared their throats. It was quite a good painting, he admitted privately, probably a fluke. He wondered sometimes, without ever consciously framing the thought, if Philip had been afraid because he knew he could not maintain the same standard. In looks, Philip had resembled him, but in character he took after Valerie, Valerie who had been oversexed, over-demanding, devoid of courage or self-respect. Valerie who had killed herself. Stephen Horvath knew he had done his best for his son. He had gone to the flat on that fatal day, persuaded partly by a cynical estimation of Caroline's sincerity if not her judgment, partly by an expensive lunch with an art dealer called Charles Lefèvre who was an old acquaintance of his. He had been prepared, under certain conditions, to forgive if not to forget. Fortunately, there had been no scenes, though he had been afraid Caroline might give way to emotionalism. And then the next day it was all over. 'A sense of space,' said Charles Lefèvre. 'Not much else. Self-conscious.' It seemed like a suitable epitaph.

At the club, he selected a table in the corner and ordered Lancashire hotpot. He did not particularly like Lancashire hotpot, but nor did he like steak-and-kidney pudding, or haddock with tartare sauce. At the next table, a smart woman in tweeds was talking to a well-known cancer specialist and chain-smoking cigars. Women were allowed in the club these days, as guests or even honorary members, presumably as a result of the new laws. He was not a misogynist, or so he told himself, but he did not really approve. It was simply that he was not very interested in women. Of his two daughters, Melissa bored and disgusted him, Caroline merely bored him. It was odd that the faults he had deplored in Philip – sexual irregularity, a predilection for soft drugs, the inability to hold his drink – were the same faults that he wished, perversely, to find in Caroline. If only she were less transparently sincere, less thoughtful, less untouchable, less serene. Sometimes, he would picture her coming home, having been beaten up by an unsuitable boyfriend, her hair streaked with vomit, her pale face distorted with bruises and swellings. He wanted to see her sobbing, hysterical, helpless. He used to smile at himself for these irrational fancies, remembering how he had abhorred the scenes with Ursula, redolent of cheap whisky, or Valerie, with her warm, feminine odour of closeness and tearfulness and bed. He did not think about his ex-wives very much, but when he did, it was with a certain relief. He thought about Margaret the least because she had caused him the least amount of trouble. Celia, he felt, had deliberately deceived him: he could still visualise her face as he had seen it on their honeymoon, hurt, reproachful, ugly red with shame. She had been an ugly woman, he reflected; she should have been more grateful. He had offered her a comfortable house, status, a generous allowance, more than many far prettier women would ever possess. But it had not been enough. When she left, he decided he need not marry again. He was getting older; people might well believe he was disillusioned. At dinner parties, he was still placed beside unattached women who regarded him soulfully over the digestifs, but his response was mechanical. It was no longer necessary to wonder, with an elusive shudder, what their bodies were like under their clothes, how their fingers would feel, exploring his most intimate organs, whether they were passionate or tepid, eager or discreet. He missed good cooking, he supposed, pushing a residue of meat and potato to the side of his plate, but it wasn't important. When the waiter returned he requested coffee in the bar, in order to escape the smoke from the tweedy woman's cigars.

Just after Celia left, when he first started dining at his club every week, he would have a post-prandial cognac in the bar and catch a train home, not too late, sitting in a first-class compartment reading a newspaper, or a medical journal, or sometimes a book. It was some six months later that he began going to the Charioteer. He had heard about it from Charles Lefèvre but they never went together and he deliberately chose to patronise it on Thursdays because he knew Charles usually spent Thursday in Paris. He had to give the art dealer's name, as a reference, but although Charles must have been contacted and was doubtless aware that he had become a regular, neither of them ever referred to it. He told himself it didn't really matter, going somewhere like that, because he invariably went alone, and only to look. He had always had a horror of such places, of the men you met there, white, paunchy men with fluttering fingers, eternally young men whose faces were painted like pre-war film starlets, viper-thin youths in skin-tight trousers which revealed athletic muscle and flagrant virility. He was afraid to communicate with such men, to touch or be touched by them, to be drawn, irresistibly, into the sordid circle of their lives. When he went to the Charioteer, he sat at a table by himself and spoke to no one. Once, a young man with red hair came and sat opposite him, trying to initiate a conversation, but he did not respond. The next time, someone who might have been the manager joined him for a discreet interval and bought him a drink: a gesture of recognition, perhaps. After that, they left him alone. He usually drank mineral water since the wine was dubious and the brandy inferior. He never stayed beyond midnight. The day after, when the memory of the place still lingered in his mouth like an ugly savour, he would tell himself that it meant nothing, he was only an onlooker, he could break the habit any time. But a week later, he always went back and sat at the same table, sipping his Perrier, watching the habitués of a world he avoided with a cold, disinterested gaze.

That evening, as usual, the Charioteer was a little too empty, a little too quiet. The busy nights, so he had heard, were Friday and Saturday; there was rarely much of a crowd on Thursdays. He preferred that, despite an uncomfortable feeling of being conspicuous, since he was less likely to have trouble with drunken strangers who did not know he wanted to be left alone. He recognised most of the people at the bar, without ever having said hello, and presumably they recognised him. (He never paid much attention to the couples at the other tables.) There was the red-haired youth, a plump businessman in a tight suit, two or three sloe-eyed Neapolitans. He found himself thinking, not for the first time, that they looked more like animals than human beings, ill-assorted animals only waiting for an unwary moment to fall upon their companions and devour them. The Italians were definitely reptilian; the plump businessman was a clumsy, blubbersome creature out of its element, an elephant seal or possibly a dugong; the red-haired youth, who was already becoming paunchy, resembled some kind of marsupial: Squirrel Nutkin, he thought, with a vague recollection of a story which had frightened Caroline as a child. They were talking to another young man whom he had not seen before. Also Italian, he decided, though fairer and not so thin. A mixture, perhaps. He was built like a slenderer version of Michelangelo's David, graceful without effeminacy, ostentatiously muscular. His hair, raggedly curling, was streaked blond from some foreign sun. He wore white jeans stretched taut around the crotch and a clinging T-shirt. A cat, thought Stephen Horvath, studying him with his usual detachment, a cream-fed domestic cat who slipped through a chink in the doorway, late at night, and roamed the alleyways in search of fights and dustbins and sex. At that moment, the young man looked up. He did not, like most of them, let his gaze wander leisurely round the room, surveying the talent, lingering thoughtfully on the empty chair at Dr Horvath's table. He looked straight at him, as though he had read his mind. Stephen was somehow shocked by the crude, sensual beauty of that dusky face, so different from the austere symmetry of his own features. For a minute, he returned the stare, coldly. Then he looked away. He knew it was only a matter of time before the young man came to join him.

In fact, the newcomer did not approach his table for nearly an hour and a half. Stephen had almost ceased to expect it, and the brusque words of dismissal which had been forming in his mind momentarily eluded him. The young man sat down, without asking, in the vacant chair. Not an Italian, thought Stephen, not quite. He was looking into large, almost lashless eyes the colour of twelve-year-old whisky. There was an uncomfortable jolt somewhere in the vicinity of his abdomen, the kind of jolt he had not felt for a very long time and would have preferred not to feel now.

'Buy me a drink.' The accent was marked but not overdone.

'I never buy drinks for slags,' Stephen retorted frigidly. The unaccustomed crudeness sounded, to his ears, both awkward and brutal. 'I suggest you try your luck elsewhere.'

The young man smiled, a limpid triangular smile with a hint of suppressed cruelty. His lips were shapely and unfeminine, not the thick, pouting lips of so many like him. 'Then let us talk,' he said. 'They tell me you are a doctor.'

'I don't talk to slags, either,' Stephen snapped. '*They* would do well to mind their own business. So would you.'

The smile widened. 'Then let's screw.'

Abruptly, Stephen Horvath got to his feet, picked up his coat and briefcase, and walked out. Halfway down the street he knew he was running away.

The following week, he went back to the Charioteer filled with a definite sense of anticipation. He knew it would have been wiser not to go. He had told himself, over dinner, that he would ring for a taxi from his club and go straight to Victoria. He had even marked the article he intended to study on the train. But he was well aware that none of these plans would materialise. He ate with unaccustomed appetite although the food was no better than usual. In the bar, he ordered a double brandy with his coffee and lingered, talking to an ear, nose and throat specialist, waiting to miss the train he had timed himself to catch. He had not felt like this for many years, this sweet, slightly sick thrill of expectancy, this pleasurable discomfort. He saw himself rejuvenated inside, suffering, incongruously, from the tremors of a lost youth. He had rarely allowed himself to feel young, even in his twenties: youth led inevitably to folly, folly to exposure, exposure to ruin. His face, unmarked by pain and ecstasy, lust and love, had scarcely aged, remaining fixed in the same emotionless mould. But now he was seized with a terrible fear that these few hours of fatal anticipation would age him irrevocably, transforming him in an evening into a haggard, demon-ridden old man. In the gentlemen's cloakroom he glanced briefly in the small mirror; but he was unchanged, though very pale. Back in the bar, the ear, nose and throat specialist offered him a lift, and he heard his own voice declining, politely, coldly: 'I have an appointment elsewhere.' He told himself, firmly, that he was only going to look: there was no reason to suppose the young man would come back. Besides, why should he change his habits for an importunate stranger? It was ridiculous, undignified, the way he had run out the previous week, almost as though he was afraid. He paid off the taxi, as always, outside a small pub some fifty yards from the entrance to the Charioteer. He was uncomfortably conscious of his heart beating and the sweat on his temples. When he went in, he installed himself in the usual place. He did not look round.

The young man was there. This time, it was twenty minutes before he looked at the doctor, a long, still look: two hours before he came and sat down. Stephen had already prepared words of rejection, only to discard them with impatience when the young man made no move. Now, looking into the beautiful foreign face (Spanish? South American?), he knew this was why he had been coming to the Charioteer the last few years, for this moment, this meeting. He had denied his body too long and now it was too late. The young man sat with one elbow on the table, his chin in his palm, and Stephen found himself looking at the rounded muscular forearm, the skin faintly velveted like the skin of a bee, and longing almost unbearably to touch, to caress, to dig his fingers into that firm resisting flesh. He knew that behind those yellow eyes was the soul of a prostitute, greedy, treacherous, and cruel, but the knowledge only excited him. In bed, it would arouse him all the more, driving him to hurt and be hurt, to loathe and be loathed, to submit, with luxurious self-abasement, to the power of someone who was everything he despised. He imagined them wrestling, naked, on a wide bed, his white cold limbs writhing ineffectually against the strength of that sun-warmed, sun-browned body. When he managed to speak he was surprised to find his voice without a tremor. 'I told you last week –'

The young man intervened as though he knew the dismissal was meaningless. 'Shall we have a drink this time?'

Stephen heard himself ordering two Pernods in the same cold, unshaken voice. Too late, he realised he had betrayed a knowledge of what his uninvited guest liked to drink. But if the young man was gratified he did not show it.

Over the drinks, they talked little. Stephen made a mental review of the standard questions – What country do you come from? How do you like England? Have you many friends in London? – and deliberately refrained from asking any of them.

86

If his companion wanted conversation, let him do the talking. But the young man evidently considered the customary preliminaries unnecessary. He sat back, apparently relaxed, and drank his Pernod, looking round the room, from time to time, with the automatic watchfulness of a professional in a crowd of potential clients.

Once, Stephen inquired: 'Have you been coming here long?'

'Last week and then this week.'

As though, Stephen thought, he was looking for me. Perhaps it was dangerous to imagine such things. He knew a sudden, idiotic impulse to say: You came here two weeks to find me; I have been coming here five years, waiting for you. Folly! That way lay fatalism, destiny, doom: all the delusions of emotional involvement. What he felt was not emotional, merely physical, utterly, overwhelmingly physical, like a dyke bursting, letting in the tide, at last, across a wide flat bay, while reason and restraint were swallowed in the quicksand. . . One night, he told himself, only one night. After that he would be his normal self again, passionless and controlled, this sudden onrush of mindless need drained away.

The young man finished his drink. 'Shall we go?'

They took a taxi. Stephen paid, fumbling in his wallet with unsteady fingers, outside a hotel of whose existence he had long been aware without ever having had occasion to use it. Then they were face to face in a room with satin-striped wallpaper and an amber-coloured quilt on the bed. The young man came very close, without touching him, waiting for him to make the first move. Stephen was past hesitation now, past thought. He let his hands slide very gently over the slim hips, down to the crotch. After a minute or two, he drew the young man nearer, palpating his buttocks, feeling the muscles straining under the taut jeans, gripping the flesh, his hands become claws, his nails driving through the stiff material. . . And then, just as he had imagined, they were falling together, falling into the quicksand, wrestling, naked, on the wide yellow bed.

Afterwards Stephen lay on his back, staring up at the ceiling, in the habitual attitude of all exhausted lovers. But it was a very long time since he had last been a lover, and he was unaware of being commonplace. The bedside lamp cast an illusory glow of warmth across his pale features. The young man studied him, carefully, as though seeking some other face, some other essence, behind that cold, still mask. Presently, Stephen said distantly: 'You may stay all night, if you wish.'

'I intended to.'

Later, almost as an afterthought, Stephen asked him: 'What is your name?'

'Ulysses,' he said.

8

That night, Caroline had dinner with Matt Hennessy, the young man in Publicity whom she had dined with occasionally the previous year. Matt was dark, good-looking, and chronically broke, so they had a cheap meal in a grubby Italian restaurant and spent most of the evening in a wine bar. Caroline quite liked him, she decided, but her mind was on other things. In the morning, she went to find Ulysses at the Greek restaurant where he was staying with friends. The restaurant was closed but a round, smiling woman served them with coffee and toast and a pot of Sainsbury's jam. She did not appear to speak any English at all. 'She has been here ten years,' Ulysses remarked, 'and all she can say is "hello" and "thank you". But she likes England very much.' Caroline thought he looked hopelessly out of place in London, with his brown skin and sultry, feral beauty, like an exotic animal escaped from the zoo. He did not smile. He gave her one swift, clear look and then concentrated on his coffee.

'I assume,' Caroline said presently, 'it went off all right?'

'Of course.'

'Did you make any further arrangement?'

'At first, he said he did not want to see me again. He tried to pay me, but I would not take any money. That worried him, you understand. If he had been able to pay me, then he might have felt that the whole thing was over; he could go away and forget it. Anyway, at the last minute he changed his mind and asked me for tomorrow. It was no problem; I knew he would. It is all much too easy. Caroline –' He hesitated.

She asked him, seriously: 'Are you having qualms of conscience?'

'No. Maybe. I don't know. It is just – he is not a nice man, Caroline. I have met other men like him, men of forty – fifty – years old, who wanted me; some of them offered me money. But he is not quite the same. Perhaps he has been bottling it all up for too long, and now he has gone bad inside. Perhaps he was born that way. He is beautiful to look at, beautiful and almost young, but underneath, he is not a young man any more. His heart is stiff and old and his mind is going rotten. His beauty is like a deformity, a sixth finger or an extra nipple, something which does not belong. When I made love to him, his face changed – distorted – as though the ugliness behind it was beginning to come through. Soon, he will be an old man, and I do not think I wish to see it.'

Caroline said numbly: 'What – what did he make you do? No, don't tell me. I don't want to know.'

'It is nothing definite. Just the way he touches me, the way he – anyway, it does not matter. He is afraid, Caroline, and I don't like that. When I am close to him, I can smell his fear. I think he has been afraid for a long time.'

'I want him to be afraid.'

'You don't understand. He is afraid of *himself*. All these years he has hidden behind this safe respectable mask, and now even he does not know what his thoughts and feelings are really like. Are you so sure you want him to find out?'

'So you do have a conscience.'

'Don't be stupid. I am not a mere weapon, a robot you can programme to do whatever you want. I am a human being. Like most human beings, sometimes I have a conscience, sometimes I have not. In this case, I think it is not my conscience which troubles me. I have told you, I don't like your father and I don't care what happens to him. But I care what happens to me.'

'Don't you want to go on with it?' Caroline said coldly.

The look on her face reminded him, uncomfortably, of her father, a cool, arrogant look, the look of a lion-tamer eyeing a recalcitrant lion. In physical terms, the animal is far stronger than the man. But the end of the contest is always a foregone conclusion: the lion will obey. . . Ulysses gave his head a quick shake, as though to dispel the fantasy. 'It is as you wish,' he said at length. 'I only wanted you to think a little about what you are doing – for your own sake as well as mine.'

'I *have* thought,' said Caroline, remembering long sleepless nights, empty days. 'If you think too much about these things, you never get anything done.' She had an idea Ulysses was trying to divert her, to mislead her somewhere she had never had any intention of going. Half unconsciously, he had reached for her hand, and was uncurling the fingers from her palm. She drew it away carelessly, as though she had not noticed. 'We have a long way to go,' she continued. 'Eventually, I hope, he will bring you to Cheyney. In the meantime, I want you to be seen with him in public as much as possible. Make him take you to the best restaurants, the places where he has been before, where there will be people he knows and who know him. The list I gave you is almost certainly incomplete, but it should do for a start. If he takes you anywhere too quiet and subdued, complain about the food, or the décor, or whatever. Anyway, you must know how to do it.'

Ulysses gave her a brief, gleaming smile. 'You talk,' he said, 'as if I have had practice.' There was no smile in his voice.

Two weeks later, Ulysses was dining with Stephen Horvath in a restaurant in Covent Garden. The interior was cleverly designed to look small and dark although actually it wasn't. Corners opened into corners, bewildering the less experienced waiters and people returning from the loo. Rows of pillars and half-finished partitions divided the room into sections, creating an illusion of mirrors where in fact there were none.

Ulysses caught himself looking at his reflection only to find it was somebody else. At intervals, just to add to the confusion, there were real mirrors, long, narrow ones fitted into the pillars. There was also a good deal of concealed lighting, lying in wait in Gothic alcoves, under bizarre lampshades, or behind hollow panelling. The food was very expensive and very good and Ulysses, who had a healthy appetite, had already accounted for quite a lot of it. Stephen ate with his usual restraint. He thought perhaps it was the extra element of anticipation which had made him so hungry, that first time, a voracious, sensual hunger which he had not felt since although every time he arranged to meet Ulysses he knew the same sick thrill of pleasure and apprehension, the same desire to run away. When they first started dining together in public he had felt even more insecure, prickling with nerves, unable to make even cursory small talk or to swallow a mouthful. But they had not met anyone he was acquainted with and gradually he had learnt to relax. One day, he knew, it would happen. But he had ceased caring any more.

They had reached the coffee-and-brandy stage when a tall man wearing a raccoon-skin coat passed their table in the wake of the head waiter. When he saw Dr Horvath he paused.

'Stephen.'

'Charles.'

Charles Lefèvre let his eyes wander over Ulysses without apparent comment. His smile broadened. It was a smile that held understanding, appreciation, even a hint of malicious satisfaction. Welcome, it seemed to say. Now, you are one of us.

Stephen's face did not change. It was ironic, he thought, with wry humour, that it should be Charles, of all people. If he had thought about it at all he would not have been surprised. He felt as if he were part of a pattern whose significance was as yet unclear, heading for a pre-ordained destiny on a road he had chosen, long ago, with some trivial, irrevocable act, buying a ferry-ticket, leaving a letter unanswered. (He had met Valerie on a ferry.) But it was all nonsense, of course. Life was a string of random chances, without meaning or final purpose. Fate (like God) was a delusion of the credulous. He had offered lip-service to religion because he considered it a necessary part of the image he wished to create for himself, but it meant nothing to him. Only now and then he had the feeling that some malignant god was watching him, laying traps for him, waiting, with infinite patience, for him to fall.

Charles, though talking to Stephen, was studying Ulysses like a horse-dealer inspecting a particularly handsome stallion. Ulysses stared back insolently, without interest. He was so patently bored Stephen felt a wary sense of gratification.

'I'm meeting Monique,' Lefèvre was saying, indicating a table a little way off where a very smart, very ugly woman was sitting drinking dry Martini. 'Business, I regret to say. Otherwise I would suggest you joined me for a drink. Perhaps another time? With –?' He half turned towards Ulysses, who had stopped looking at him and was reading the label on the empty wine bottle.

Stephen said: 'Another time.'

Later, in bed, Ulysses asked him: 'Who was that man?'

'Charles? He's an art dealer, I've known him for many years, though not well.'

'He liked me,' Ulysses remarked, with a hint of complacency.

To his fury, Stephen heard his own voice asking, icily: 'Did you like him?'

'No.'

Afterwards, he found himself wondering what Ulysses had really thought about Charles Lefèvre. He was not given to speculating about other people's feelings very much, except where they were directed against himself and might possibly threaten his security in some way. He did not think he was particularly self-centred, no more than most men; merely uninterested. He had never, for example, wondered what Charles thought when he began frequenting the Charioteer. Perhaps he preferred not to know. Charles, at least, would not expose him. Other people's feelings, whether critical or approving, had never been important to him, until now. He had told himself, at first, that Ulysses was only a prostitute, without relevant emotion, just so much meat in a butcher's window. In bed, he sensed the Greek despised him, which he found exciting. But as he spent more and more time with him Ulysses' behaviour appeared increasingly incomprehensible. He would watch the people round him with a detached

92

professional eye, but he did not flirt, and Charles' all-too-evident admiration did not seem to interest him. Most young men, Stephen reflected, would have responded, attracted by the sumptuous raccoon skin or merely to make their escorts jealous. Possibly Ulysses considered such tricks unnecessary. There was a sureness in his attitude to Stephen which the latter found at once agreeable and disturbing. This constant refusal to accept payment troubled him, too. Sometimes, he imagined the end of the affair, after an unspecified period of time: himself, pale and taut, standing behind his study desk; Ulysses, storming from the room. A moment later, a small man in a discreet suit came in and placed in front of him an account that ran into six figures. 'Your bill, sir.' Stephen knew the daydream was nonsense but he did not like the idea of accumulating a debt. In a restaurant, Ulysses would order the most expensive dish on the menu, but he never took any money and became angry when Stephen tried to insist. 'I do not want to be paid,' he had said. 'What do you think I am?'

'A prostitute.' Stephen's voice was contemptuous. Contempt was an emotion which came easily to him. Somehow, he sensed he had an advantage, and he intended to press it. 'A fanny boy. A slag. Call it what you like.'

The yellow eyes became fixed and hard. 'If you ever say those things to me again,' Ulysses whispered, very gently. 'I will hit you.' Fingers, so much stronger than Stephen's own, clenched on his arm. He knew a moment of purely sensual terror at that wanton strength. Then abruptly Ulysses released him. 'Sometimes,' he snapped, viciously, 'you are *very* stupid.'

Stephen did not use the word love, not even in his inmost thoughts. He knew he was not in love and he found it impossible to believe that Ulysses, with his compulsive greed, his insolence, his curious flashes of pride and temper, could feel any sustained emotion above the belt. When he thought about it at all, he decided the younger man must be drawn to him with a need which paralleled his own, something more than purely physical, so basic that the language of men had no word for it any more: the slave's need for the whip of his master, the captive's need for torture, humiliation, subjection. There were so many moments in bed when, fulfilling his own desires, he sensed other desires fulfilled. He had never thought of trying to please his partner in sex: before his first marriage, he had been too young, too nervous, too inexperienced: with his wives, he had not considered it necessary. He could still remember his instinctive disgust when he caught Ursula reading a book called *The Female Orgasm*. But he grew to like the idea of pleasing Ulysses, of knowing him aroused and satisfied, of feeling those strong fingers tracing the contours of his face, moulding the flesh against the bone, while the sphinx-like ochre eyes watched him with curious fascination. It gave him a sly sense of power. He despised Ulysses for the same things he needed so much: the beautiful animal body and healthy animal appetite, the prostitute's cunning and total disregard for civilised mores. But in those moments of insidious euphoria after coitus he would find himself talking, talking as he had rarely talked before, giving himself, he thought wretchedly, for a pleasure he had scarcely missed in years. What was the need to give, after all? It was only necessary to take, and be silent. Giving, pleasing, confiding, these were the dangerous weaknesses which would take him down and down, to a lonely old man sitting by himself at a table in the Charioteer, paying for his entertainment. (And where are you now? mocked a voice inside him. You are old, yes, even you, under that mask of frozen youth. Old, desperate, used. . . But he would not listen.) He was afraid to continue the way he was going and unable to draw back. He tried not to think what he would do, if Ulysses said he was going home for Christmas.

It was in the same Covent Garden restaurant, shortly after, that they first encountered one of Stephen's patients. He had been unwilling to go back there after the meeting with Charles Lefèvre, but Ulysses said he liked the place and withdrew into a savage fit of sulks which Stephen found both exasperating and irresistible. After all, the food is good, he told himself. It is only your own cowardice which keeps you away. You fool: it is too late now to be afraid. In a moment of jealousy, bitterly regretted, he accused Ulysses of wanting to meet Lefèvre again. 'It's a pity Charles doesn't go there very often,' he heard himself saying, and he did not know if the contempt in his voice was for himself or for the young man who had reduced him to this.

But Ulysses did not even trouble to be indignant. 'They do a very good Tournedos Rossini,' he said simply. 'I like Tournedos Rossini.'

The night they met Mrs Willoughby Grant, Stephen was watching him eat, fascinated, almost aroused, by his cursory table manners and obvious greed. He would have liked to see Ulysses with the leg of some prehistoric animal, dripping blood and liquid fat, his sharp white teeth tearing off huge mouthfuls of half-cooked flesh. Stephen himself was eating fish, pale and boneless, in a pale sauce. He toyed with it, touched his fork to his lips, replaced it beside his plate. The wine was below standard, and the waiter had removed it, with profuse apologies, returning subsequently with another bottle. Stephen tasted it without comment. He had just seen Mrs Willoughby Grant.

Of all his patients, he reflected, she was the one he would least have wished to see. She was not, fortunately or other-wise, one of the many women (married and single) who came to his private surgery with thriving constitutions and still more thriving imaginations in the hope that one day he would say, just like the doctors on television: 'And now, please take all your clothes off.' Mrs Willoughby Grant, according to popular rumour, had never loved anyone but her undesirable son Richard, a former schoolfriend of Philip's who had matured (but not much) into a poor little rich kid desperately trying to climb down from the upper classes and bewildered to find himself passing the lower classes, climbing up, on the way. He had had a notorious affair with an ageing actor who got him bit parts in soap commercials, but his mother, either in sublime ignorance or self-deception or possibly both, con-tinued to transport him down to Chatters (the ancestral mansion) from time to time to meet a selection of hopeful débutantes. Richard was a willowy youth with a slack mouth and uninteresting eyes who probably took after his father and who could not inspire even a débutante with much enthusiasm. Jocasta Willoughby Grant, on the other hand, was a tall woman with a salient bosom – indeed, most of her features were salient – a tan the colour of broiled swede, and an air of shattering vitality. She went to Dr Horvath because he was fashionable, expensive, and because the few friends who had survived being at school with her all swore by him. In fact, there was very little wrong with her beyond the usual discomforts which afflict hard-riding women in the late middle age, but, like many very healthy people, she was terrified of illness and convinced the slightest hint of a backache would lead to her being crippled for life. Dr Horvath did not disillusion her: he merely sent her away with a firm belief in his professional skill and a prescription for some very expensive treatment. He had seen immediately that she was the kind of woman who would judge the efficacy of her cure by the gap in her bank balance. With people like that, he always put ten per cent on the bill as a matter of course. She was not the sort of woman he would have enjoyed meeting socially under any circumstances; now, beside his usual boredom, he sensed a faint, cold thread of apprehension. There had been abortive trips abroad to salvage the unfortunate Richard from the company of his degenerate friends, trips to the beaches of Marseilles, the backstreets of Naples, the gurus of Nepal. On one occasion, he was rumoured to have hidden from her in an enormous jar, like something in the Arabian Nights: on another, he disguised himself as a belly-dancer, and only his height led him to be unveiled. And on one of those trips, perhaps, she might have found Richard with a beautiful young man in tow, the kind of beautiful young man who was attracted to money and weakness, with wicked liquid eyes and skin the colour of old Amontillado. . .

'Dr Horvath!' She sailed across the restaurant towards him, trailing fluttering chiffon streamers of the sort that should only be worn by slender, ethereal women, but never are. Her voice, as might have been expected, was penetrating. She inquired perfunctorily after himself and his family (probably, he thought, she did not know about either his divorces or Philip's death) and proceeded to launch into a long description of the mysterious pangs endured by a friend of hers who had recently been in a riding accident. 'Mind you, nice soft landing. Cow-pat. Smelt a bit high, poor Dilly, but I daresay it was more comfortable than the path. Told her she ought to come to you.' (Stephen had a sudden urge to point out that he didn't treat people for smells, but he repressed it.) 'Oh no, Jocasta, she said, I'm sure I could never afford him.

Rubbish, I said. Your health comes first. Never mind the money. She fussed and complained all the way home, silly woman, but she hasn't done anything about it. I should have made the appointment for her myself.'

At this point, she registered the presence of Ulysses and broke off to stare at him with the fixed curiosity of those who consider themselves above good manners. Or was it just curiosity? Stephen wondered. Was she, perhaps, less ignorant and self-deceived than she appeared? Possibly, even now, she was searching her memory, trying to 'place' Ulysses. . .

'A friend of my daughter's,' Stephen murmured, at random.

'Of course.' Her smile showed huge teeth, like the wolf in 'Little Red Riding Hood'. 'Not married, is she? How old is she now?'

'Twenty-four or five,' he said, realising he didn't know.

'Time she was getting married.'

'Mrs Willoughby Grant,' Caroline said thoughtfully, two days later.

'That was the name,' Ulysses affirmed. 'A big hearty woman, with big teeth. The king of Englishwoman who comes into American films. I did not know they really existed.'

'Perhaps they don't,' Caroline said idly. 'People aren't always as stereotyped as they seem. She's crazy about her son.' She was remembering what she had heard of Richard Willoughby Grant.

'Like a female spider,' Ulysses said, 'who eats its children.'

'Female spiders eat their husbands,' Caroline corrected him. 'I'm not sure about their young.'

'What about you, Caroline?' He quoted, maliciously: 'Time you were getting married. When will you have a husband to eat?'

She wished he wouldn't keep making these irrelevant remarks. Perhaps he thought this kind of sexual banter was expected of him, an essential part of his image as the all-purpose Latin lover. Perhaps he felt it necessary to emphasise, to himself or her, that he was still heterosexual. She knew he found her attractive – she had even used that attraction – but she did not want to be reminded of it. That aspect of the situation had never entered into their bargain. Looking at him, she was shocked afresh by the coarse, physical quality of his appeal, the full, hungry eyes, the over-large features, the unsubtle, sensuous mouth. She half wondered how her father, the dedicated ascetic, could bear so to debase himself. But perhaps it was that very debasement which he found so irresistible. The mere thought of Ulysses holding her, caressing her, filled her with a sudden revulsion that was almost like excitement.

She said coldly: 'I shall never get married.' Even to herself, the statement sounded melodramatic and unnecessary.

9

Shortly before Christmas, Angela Teviot went to Canada. The glamorous Michel was returning there for at least a year (his job, Angela explained) and she decided, since she had missed him so much in Greece, that the consequent separation would be unendurable. Caroline recalled how she had bemoaned every morning that he was not there to bring her tea in bed, how she had sat on the beach in the sun, shredding at her emotions: 'I love him; I love him not. I love him. . .' Perhaps it's true, she thought; perhaps that's what love is. She found that although it still hurt a little, thinking of Philip, a thin, distant pain like a local anaesthetic wearing off, she could not remember any more what it had felt like to love him. Only vague images of improbable happiness which seemed, in retrospect, quite fantastic. She could not imagine ever feeling like that again. Maybe she was growing cynical, becoming one of those cool, successful women she had always admired, during her uninformed teens, women whose passions were few and disciplined and whose aims in life were invariably attained. (She had always pictured the boardrooms of the BBC dominated by such women.) Or was it, she wondered, with a sudden coldness of the heart, that she was simply not young enough to feel that way any more? She thought of Angela, sometimes, as immature, but perhaps immaturity was an essential concomitant of falling in love: immaturity, vulnerability, youth. She herself had matured, painfully, too early, growing a hard, brittle shell on the outside of her soul which let nothing out, nothing in. She would never feel young again. And for the first time, looking back, she was conscious of a vague regret for those years of desperate self-containment, the mistakes she had not made, the follies she had not committed. When had she ever let herself go, save with Philip? And what, after all, had that relationship really meant? He had never said he loved her. Reaching in her memory, she found that the harder she tried to remember, the more dim and unreal the images became, until instead of a great affair all she could recall was a brief sexual fling scarcely adequate for the name of experience. And that was all she had ever had. (Clive she had almost forgotten.) She told herself, savagely, that bitterness was useless; but it was bitterness which had bred revenge, and that, she supposed, was useless, too. Still, she could not turn back now. Whatever she had or had not done, it was to her father's account, and through revenge she would purge her spirit of all bitterness, all useless guilt. (Then what? whispered the wind, through the slats of the jalousie. What will you do, without your hate?) 'In any case,' she said to herself, with a strange little smile, 'I have given him his heart's desire. For the moment.' It was the first time she had ever been able to give him anything.

She took Matt Hennessy to Angela's farewell party and they both got very drunk on someone else's champagne. 'We're in the wrong business,' Matt remarked. 'Look at all these fledglings, just down from university, already preening themselves for directorships. The creases are still warm in their trousers. Whereas here I am, getting much too close to thirty, footloose, unsuccessful, and skint. I think I shall go into property speculation.'

Caroline said: 'There's no money in that now, either. Failure,' she added, 'is in the air.'

'Not for you,' said Matt. 'You're going to be a successful businesswoman: it's written all over you. Have some more champagne. Who brought it, by the way? Not that it matters.'

'Probably,' said Caroline, 'someone called Edgar.'

'Who's he?'
'I don't know.'

Towards the end of the party, she remembered to ask Angela about the photographs. It probably wasn't important, but she wanted to be safe. Angela, predictably, had forgotten. 'Yes darling, I know I promised, but honestly I've had so much to do. You couldn't possibly expect me to piddle about with something like that. Don't worry: I'll sort them out when I get to Canada and send them to you. I will really. I know I've packed them somewhere.'

'Are you sure?' Caroline queried doubtfully, unwilling to press the point.

'Darling, don't *fuss*. Of course I have. Anyway, Michel will find them for me: he's fantastically competent about things like that. Now, *please* don't spoil my party by going on about it. Well, honestly, what a commotion for a few holiday snaps! They probably won't come out anyway: I was frightfully drunk when I took them. I suppose you want the one of you with that Greek guy – what was his name? He was *madly* attractive. . .'

Caroline let it go.

They sang 'Auld Lang Syne' and 'We'll Meet Again' and someone (Caroline never found out if it was the unknown Edgar or not) produced more champagne. Angela opened her leaving present from her friends at work and wept copiously over one thousand sheets of expensive coffee-coloured note-paper, five hundred matching envelopes, and a mono-grammed Waterman fountain pen. Male ex-colleagues queued up to kiss her goodbye. Somebody put 'Lonely This Christmas' on the music centre. Matt said: 'What Greek guy?'

Caroline was thoughtfully dipping sponge fingers into her champagne. 'Nobody special,' she said.

As usual, she spent Christmas in Birmingham, dutifully playing the latest Christmas game, 'Jaws', with Harry's nieces, while he (and, in theory, his nephews) put up a train set round the living room. 'It's the new London to Edinburgh express,' he said, 'the fastest train in the world.' His youngest

100

nephew, Giles, pointed out that the new London to Edinburgh express had broken down in bad weather and anyway, the fastest train in the world was actually in Tokyo. Daisy, Giles' sister, shrieked: 'Your left leg's been bitten off!' and punched Caroline enthusiastically in the ribs. She found herself wondering why she was reminded so sharply of Melissa, and – yes, Clive. She had not thought of Clive for a long time. He had seemed so confident and mature when she first knew him but now, listening to Giles, who was still holding forth on Japanese technological supremacy with an air of pitying superiority, she realised Clive was just another precocious schoolboy who had never really grown up. Perhaps men didn't grow up, she reflected, contemplating Harry, flat on his stomach beside a minor derailment. Philip, for example: had he ever grown up?

'You're not concentrating,' Daisy said. 'You've got to concentrate or you won't have any legs left.'

'Sorry,' said Caroline.

In the background she heard Damian, Giles' brother, saying in even more superior accents: 'Anyway, that's all a load of bollocks. The fastest train in the world is in France. Everyone knows that.'

Ulysses stayed in London, with his friends at the Greek restaurant. Stephen toyed with the idea of inviting him to Cheyney, knowing it would be disastrous, or of suggesting they spent the holiday together at a hotel, somewhere he was not known. But he was not quite sure Ulysses would come. In the end, he made a date for New Year's Eve and went down to Cheyney on his own. The au pair had gone home for the week, leaving a note to say she would not be coming back. He did not really need an au pair any more, but he had continued to employ one, partly out of habit, partly just to have someone in the house all the time. Recently, there had been very little for her to do. On the days when he had his surgery in Cheyney, Mrs Bunce had said it would be no trouble for her to drop in, during the evening, and prepare his dinner. 'Perhaps Melissa ought to learn cooking,' he remarked, one day. 'I believe she does still live at home, doesn't she? It would be nice if she did something useful for a change.' But he did not make an issue of it. Melissa's culinary experiments, in her early teens, had not been encouraging. Lately, she had become involved with a group of squatters who had set up a kind of commune in a disused house just outside the village, and she spent most of her time there, smoking dope and having deep conversations. She did not move out. For all her uninformed left-wing views and vaunted scorn of the bourgeoisie she could not quite bring herself to abandon her home, with its well-stocked freezer, central heating and hot baths, for the discomforts and deprivations of squatting. She had never learnt to make a bed or even wash her own clothes, preferring to leave her soiled underwear in the sink, for the benefit of Mrs Bunce or the latest Brigitte or Anne-Marie. 'It's a pity the doctor doesn't take more interest in her,' Mrs Bunce told her sister-in-law, over the Christmas pudding. 'Still, she's not his own child, of course. He don't seem to think on it, but you can't tell. Took her in without a murmur, he did: no questions asked. There's not many men would do that. He's a lovely man, the doctor,' she went on, rendered loquacious by her husband's elderflower champagne, 'but vague, very vague. I sometimes think if you didn't put his dinner right under his nose he'd never eat anything at all. Pecks away at his food like a sparrow. He's clever, mind you, and a good doctor: when my back seized up he put it right just like that, and never sent me no bill either. What's more, there's never been anything wrong, though the way all the ladies run after him is something chronic. They come into the surgery, tarted up to the eyes and smelling like a perfume counter: Oh doctor – yes doctor – you're so good to me doctor. Well, you can't deny it's a temptation for a man. He's had a sad life, poor thing, what with Melissa's mother, who drank, and his last wife running off like that. She was a bit young for him, I know, but she didn't seem flighty. And then his son, dying in the fire. They say he was a genius. It doesn't seem fair, really: some people, everything seems to go wrong for them, like they're touched with tragedy. And he's such a *nice* man. . .'

Stephen had his Christmas dinner with the Ansteys, as he had done the previous year. Their elder daughter was home from Los Angeles with her husband and the conversation was mostly about the wonders of the New World. Stephen did not join in. Monica's ageing Pekinese, who did not like him, was curled up among the sofa cushions, watching him from under its greying fringe and growling intermittently like an old lady with bronchial problems. Once, he threw it a slice of meat, unobtrusively, but the dog rejected it. The turkey was well-cooked but he had even less appetite than usual: he told himself it was the sight of Sarah Jane, the prodigal daughter, eating and talking with equal voracity, which put him off. He could see the particles of meat and vegetable sticking between her teeth. When the Christmas pudding appeared, he said he was full. Sarah Jane had two helpings, morsels of dried fruit joining the chewed sprout and turkey round her large white incisors. He found himself wondering what Ulysses was doing, how soon he could get away, whether it had been worth so much effort, so many sacrifices, just to eat his Christmas dinner in a respected middle-class household listening to a conversation which bored him and drinking a poor quality brandy because Gerald Anstey was too mean, or too ignorant, to buy the best. He felt the same sense of anomie as the irascible Pekinese, who was ostentatiously burying the parson's nose in the midst of the sofa cushions. He tried to imagine how Charles Lefèvre spent his Christmas: in Paris, maybe, drinking Chateau Lafite in a discreet restaurant, with a friend. But Charles was an art dealer. Art dealers were expected to be unconventional, Bohemian, even immoral. He was a doctor, and doctors were supposed to be pillars of the community. His mother had always wanted him to be a doctor. They played charades, and he could hardly drag his gaze from Sarah Jane's teeth, exposed almost constantly in a bray of laughter or a gush of vocal enthusiasm. Presently, he ceased to see the rest of her at all, and there were only her teeth left, clacking away by themselves on the end of a stalk. 'You will stay to tea, won't you?' said Monica Anstey. 'So dreadful for you, going home to that huge empty house. And on Christmas Day, too.'

But he made his excuses, with automatic politeness, and escaped thankfully into the dingy afternoon.

Melissa had Christmas dinner at the squat: roast chicken and roast potatoes, cheap wine, Sainsbury's Christmas pudding.

103

It was an old house and the living room was large, low-ceilinged, with creeping draughts that found their way in despite the thick stone walls. There was a small open fire in the huge fireplace and they sat round it, close together, licking the chicken-grease from their fingers and passing the bottle round. Melissa kept her jacket on. Years later, when they moved into council houses and turned respectable, they would talk about this Christmas as one of the 'good times'. There was a Duncan, two Johns, an Anne who belonged to one of the Johns and a Stephanie who belonged to anybody. Duncan was an artist: the walls were covered with his poster-work, dramatic representations of the Apocalypse in black and orange, and virulent green abstracts that looked like studies in vegetable decomposition. 'My brother was an artist,' Melissa boasted. 'He committed suicide.' It was a throw-away line which somehow failed of its effect, possibly because she had thrown it away so often. My brother committed suicide, my mother was an alcoholic, my step-father is a homosexual. 'Do stop going on about it,' Stephanie had said, one day. 'Honestly, your family are so weird it's boring.' Duncan looked deep into Melissa's eyes, when he felt in the mood and told her: 'You've had a rough time, kid. You're all mixed up. Cool it' – advice culled from watching too many American T.V. programmes in the days when he lived with his parents. Melissa usually took her clothes off and cooled it. Duncan (sometimes) made her feel interesting, an unhappy, complicated creature who had been cruelly misused by her relations, Fate, and the unfeeling world. She hoped he would ask to draw her, but he never did. When she was much younger she had had fantasies in which Philip drew her, while she posed, patiently, usually in the nude, and he commented on the poignancy of her features and the perfection of her budding breasts. (Her breasts had been budding since she was thirteen but had somehow never come to flower.) Occasionally, in those fantasies, Caroline would come in, wrapped in a coat made from the fur of Dalmatian puppies, her pale face distorted with hatred and spite. And Melissa would sit there, unmoving, while Philip told her sister, in the annoyed, faintly bored voice which Melissa knew so well, that she was disturbing them, and she would have to go away. When Philip died, Melissa shut herself in her room for hours, nursing her grief like a sick animal, afraid that if her attention wandered even for a single moment it would slip away for ever. She took to masturbating a lot, indulging in bizarre sexual fancies where there was a rat between her thighs, nibbling her, or where she had been thrown into a snakepit in the dark and she could feel the snakes, climbing up her legs. It was difficult, having nobody to fantasise about. In real life, there was Duncan and his predecessors, but real life was no substitute for the warm, safe, closed-in world of her dreams.

Her father had given her a cheque for Christmas, quite a large cheque, like a bribe, she thought, because he wanted her to go away. (He never gave real presents.) She had bought some high quality dope and she produced it, in the afternoon, to share with the others. She was not naturally generous but she knew they had not really accepted her (Melissa never felt accepted anywhere) and she hoped to buy their approval, somehow, in exchange for her lavish gesture. But the gesture was too forced, too ostentatious, and they only resented her. 'If I had a big house and money, like you,' Stephanie said contemptuously, 'I wouldn't spend Christmas in a hole like this, eating burnt potatoes. I'd have turkey and bread sauce and a whole box of chocolates, and I'd sit in front of the telly all afternoon, with the electric fire on full. You must be pretty stupid, coming here.'

'I don't want all that,' Melissa said, unhappily. 'Those things belong to the privileged classes. I've rejected that whole scene.'

'No you haven't,' said Stephanie. 'You're too soft. You can't make up your mind what you really want so you just sit on the fence and suck up to everyone. You're not one of us.'

'Oh, leave the kid alone,' said Duncan.

In the early evening, Melissa went home. She had smoked too much, drunk too much, and eaten too many potatoes, and everything seemed to have coagulated in a tight, hard lump just under her waistband. But she could not quite manage to be sick. When she got to the house, her father was in his study (she could see the light under the door), but he did not call a greeting, although he must have heard her come in. She went upstairs to her room. Having emptied the wastepaper bin onto a corner of the rug and put it within easy reach of the bed, she lay down. The room was not precisely spinning but it showed a tendency to swing from side to side. She closed her eyes, wishing she could throw up, and throw up, over and over again, until she felt purged and empty and light as thistledown.

When the trains started running again, Caroline came back to London. 'We hardly ever see you these days,' her mother had said. 'I do hope you're all right, Carla. I was afraid you might be lonely without Phil. Have you got a young man at the moment?' Caroline said hastily that there was no one and promised to write soon. In the train, looking out at the snow-laden hills, she allowed herself to relax. Always, with her mother, there was that nebulous feeling of guilt, that inexplicable weakening, the insidious desire to confide. Yet she had never been in the habit of confiding. In her teens, she had hidden her various insecurities behind an aloof, unforgiving mask, showing her true face, whatever it might be, to no one; now she was an adult, assured, self-sufficient, whose problems concerned nobody but her, she found it strange that now and then she should feel this adolescent urge to break down, to talk and weep and be comforted. She could never do so, of course. The mere thought of her mother's face, if she learnt about the relationship with Philip, gave her a vague pain inside, the kind of pain that comes from failing the people you love. And she could not possibly discuss her father's behaviour: Margaret never spoke of her marriage, nor, Caroline recalled, had she ever so much as intimated that she knew the truth. 'Perhaps she *doesn't* know,' Caroline said to herself, unreasonably angry. What had Philip called them? A naïve generation. Perhaps her mother (and Harry) knew nothing of homosexuality, incest, passion, bitterness, revenge. These were things which she, Caroline, had discovered, all by herself, even as Eve, first of all women, had discovered sin, and calvados, and men. There was no point in thinking of her mother. Margaret Horvath had fallen in love again, late but not too late, married, lived happily ever after. She could not even begin to understand. Caroline turned her thoughts to the present and reviewed the progress of her plans. The doctor was meeting Ulysses on New Year's Eve but she would have to see him first. She hoped her father had spent Christmas by himself, in front of the television, watching endless re-runs of 'The Generation Game' and 'Blankety Blank'. Or maybe he would have dined with friends, bored, bored out of his mind by their banal conversation, their healthy normality, their seasonal goodwill. If he had gone to the Ansteys he would have had to play charades. They were the sort of people who always played charades. Possibly Sarah Jane, the Ansteys' uninspiring daughter, would be there (or wasn't she abroad?). As a child, Caroline had once or twice been compelled to go to tea with Sarah Jane, a dull girl a little younger than her who had a peculiar obsession with rabbits. She kept two live ones in a hutch in the garden and three toy ones, one pink, one pink-and-white, and one blue, in her bedroom. When she was older, with her rather protuberant teeth, she even grew to look like a rabbit. For a moment, Caroline visualised her father, surrounded, like a male equivalent of Alice, by pink rabbits and mad duchesses, watching, distastefully, while a dormouse fell asleep in the teapot. And all the while there would be the thought of a beautiful young Greek, eating round the edges of his mind. . .

'It's Christmas,' she had said to Ulysses, the last time they met. 'Make him spend money. Make him give you things. He's never given anybody anything.'

'What makes you think it will be different with me?'

'Of course it will. It's like sex: when you haven't done it for a long time, you go a little mad. He is beginning to go mad already. He'll give you anything you want. Gold cigarette-lighters, hand-made shoes, anything. You can always sell them later, if you'd rather have the money.' She added, uncomfortably: 'That's what you're in it for, isn't it? For the money.'

'Is it?' The yellow eyes considered her scornfully. 'I suppose I expect *him* to treat me like a prostitute, sometimes, but not you. It would be so much easier, wouldn't it, if you could pay me off? Both of you.'

'That was a very effective line,' Caroline said, 'with my father. But you forget, I've heard it before.'

Presently, she had asked him: 'What do you *really* want?' Even before the words were out, she had wished them unsaid.

His gaze wandered over her face so warmly, so intimately, it was almost like a touch. She felt herself held, against her will, as though in an invisible web of tension.

After a few moments he smiled, a mocking, satisfied smile, as if he was pleased he had made her ask. 'I will let you know,' he said.

10

Ulysses moved down to Cheyney towards the end of January. 'A new au pair,' Stephen told Mrs Bunce. 'A young man. Apparently, he came over here to teach but he couldn't get any work. A friend asked me to help him out. I don't know if he cooks or not so perhaps you wouldn't mind coming in to do the dinner, at least for a week or two.' He knew the story would not stand up for long. 'A young man!' Mrs Bunce repeated to her spouse, who wasn't listening. 'Well, really! Ever since they passed this Sex Act everything's gone topsy-turvy. The Wintons, over at Chigworth, what Mrs Puttock does for, they've got a male *nanny*. All I can say is, it don't seem like a good idea to me. The doctor, he won't notice much, and there's his teenage daughter in the house. Mind you, she's got a boyfriend, and I daresay they're carrying on like all the young people nowadays, but at least he's *British*. . .' Melissa, when she heard the news, guessed at once what it meant. Possibly it was instinct. She did not know why she should be so upset, only that she felt betrayed, even at this late stage, almost as though she had loved her father and he had chosen to reject her in this way. She told herself she would be cool about it, laid back, everyone was laid back about homosexuality, these days. But it was one thing to boast of the doctor's secret sins, privately, among friends, never quite sure if those sins were real or merely a monstrous fantasy grown from suspicion; it was something else when the

108

fantasy became reality and reality came to live in your spare room. She visualised the young man, as far as she was able to speculate, as someone slender and effeminate, with weedy hair. Nothing had prepared her for Ulysses. When she first saw him she thought, unbelieving, that she must have been wrong. Surely no one like that would waste his time with a perverted old man. (To Melissa, everyone over thirty was old, everyone over forty senile.) She was dazzled by his excessive good looks, his blatant sexuality, the cat-like grace with which he lounged around the living room. She would have taken to staying in for supper, if she had dared; but her father looked at her with a cool, unfriendly eye, and Ulysses did not look at her at all. When she saw them together, she knew they were lovers. The idea gave her a queer, squirming sensation in her abdomen, almost like physical excitement. She would have liked to spy on them, as she had done with Celia, with Philip and Caroline, to see them touching each other on the more intimate portions of their anatomy, to see Ulysses' zip, gaping, and a secret glimpse of his body. But she did not dare. As far as she knew, they hardly touched each other at all. At night, Ulysses had his own room, although once or twice, creeping to her door, she heard footsteps in the passageway. In bed, she began to imagine how he would look, peeling off his tight jeans, the muscles she had seen straining at his clothes entwined around her father's pale clammy body. She did not know if her father's body felt clammy, but his very pallor suggested dampness, the cold grumous touch of a corpse. In the morning, if she met Ulysses at breakfast, she would find herself blushing at the recollection of her nocturnal imaginings, a hot, excited blush which reached right down into her belly. She found it very difficult to think what to say to him. He never said anything to her at all.

At first, those people who heard of Ulysses' arrival seemed to accept him, with a lifted eyebrow, as further evidence of the doctor's tolerance and generosity. But Stephen knew it was only a matter of time. They would not forgive him, these people whom he had deceived: they would cut him in the street, strike him from their Christmas card lists, desert his hearthside and his waiting room. If he had been open, discreet but honest, he would have been less successful, but he might have survived. As it was, he would never survive the pitiless revenge of people who feel they have been made to look like fools, who have been hit, below the belt, on the tenderest part of their dignity: the women who worshipped his classic profile and apparent dedication, their husbands who thought him a good chap, one of us, white all through. He pictured them, gathered in their eau-de-nil drawing rooms, murmuring: 'Of course, I always suspected there was something wrong. . . When his last wife left him, I *said* to Gordon. . . Never quite liked him, you know. Nothing definite, just gave me a creepy feeling under the skin. Felt like that once in the Commandos, just before walking into an ambush. . .' He smiled derisively at the thought of them all, frantically trying to save face. Everyone anxious to prove that he, or she, had always known. Poor Monica Anstey would never live it down: she would have to fall back on the Pekinese as the sole example of family sagacity. He found himself wishing, sometimes, that it was all over, and he was left alone with his ruin. Perhaps he would go away, with Ulysses, losing themselves in some provincial crowd where he would not be known. Parts of the West Country were very pleasant, he reflected, trying to think constructively; the Midlands or the North would be a deliberate act of penance. As for work, there was always work for a doctor. If only he were not so well known among his colleagues in the profession. He ought to go now, cut his losses, before his patients began to look at him askance, searching for confirmation, and his next two dinner parties were cancelled due to bad weather, and the receptionist's boyfriend told her to give in her notice. But he stayed on, without courage or hope, waiting for the pattern which he had dreaded to be complete.

'I'll pay your rent somewhere in London,' he had said, when Ulysses talked of going home.

'I do not want to be "somewhere in london",' Ulysses replied. 'I want to be with you. It does not matter any more, nowadays. The English, they are very broad-minded. Nobody cares about these things. Why should I not be with you?'

Stephen murmured something about his career, the Medical Council, unspecified responsibilities. 'Bullshit,' said Ulysses, whose English was, when necessary, extremely graphic. 'You just want to go on treating me like a prostitute. You want me to wait around in some horrible little flat for

110

the occasional evening when you feel like a screw. As though I was a dog, hoping to be taken for a walk. What am I supposed to do with myself the rest of the time? Or would you rather not know? You make me sick. You talk all that shit about emotional commitment but you don't even want me to live with you. Well, don't worry: we are not committed. I picked you up when I wanted to and I can drop you when I want to. If I mean to go, there is nothing you can do to stop me.'

'Don't be a fool.' Panic made Stephen angry and impatient. 'Are you too stupid to see the truth? My livelihood depends on the people who come to my surgery, dull, self-righteous people if you like, but still necessary to me. When they see you, they will know I have lied to them, cheated them, used them. Can't you understand what that will mean? I *used* them –'

'All I understand,' said Ulysses, flatly, 'is that you are ashamed of what you are, ashamed of *me*. That's your problem. We are supposed to be adults, but you – you behave like a child who has wet his knickers and hides them under the bed. If that's how you feel, it's over. Why should I stay to be insulted by someone who can't even act like a man?'

Stephen said wretchedly: 'If I were married –'

'Are you wishing you had lied to me? I would have known. In bed, you would have told me the truth. You always do.'

There was a pause. 'Would you really – leave?' Stephen asked, his voice cold and bitter with the humiliation of his own need.

'Of course. How could you hold me?'

In that moment, Stephen knew Ulysses did not love him, did not want him, did not need him: he was there, without reason or resentment, only to destroy him, the instrument of that patient and implacable Fate whose existence Stephen had always denied. But he lacked the strength, or even the will, to resist. It was much easier to succumb, to take what he could while there was time, above all, not to look too far ahead. 'Very well,' he said dully. 'We'll go to Cheyney. After all, how should anyone realise. . .? I'll think of some story. Can you cook?'

'No. Why should I?'

'No matter.'

* * *

Afterwards, Stephen wondered why he had never thought of Melissa. Perhaps that was her particular tragedy, that she was essentially a person whom no one ever remembered, no one ever took into account. 'I don't want her here,' Ulysses said, the first time they were alone. 'She is in the way. Besides, she spies on us. She listens at doors, watches through keyholes. Perhaps that is how she gets her pleasure. She is so unattractive no one would want to give her pleasure any other way. How did you come to have a daughter like that?'

'She isn't my daughter. She's adopted.'

'Then you can send her away. There is no blood-tie and you are not fond of her; how could you be? She is over eighteen. Your wonderful British Social Security will look after her. Or you could give her some money for a flat, if you are afraid of what people will say. That is what always worries you the most, isn't it? What people will say.'

'I can't send her away.'

'Why not? Do you love her?'

'No.'

'Then why not?'

'Because –' Stephen hesitated, miserably, loathing himself, loathing Ulysses '– because of what people would say. Because of how it would look. Everyone would know –'

'About us?'

'About us. Anyway, I've brought her up as my daughter; I can't just abandon her, not yet. She is immature and not very stable. She might conceivably take an overdose, just to make a dramatic gesture. Even if I rented a flat for her it probably wouldn't answer: she'd turn it into a pig-sty in a week and the landlady would have her ejected. I can't do it; you must see that. I know you are sublimely indifferent to public opinion, but do you really want to provide dinner-table small talk for a pack of commonplace busybodies? Imagine how happy it would make them, discussing your probable habits, doubtless with their mouths full. Nothing so exciting has happened in the neighbourhood in years. Is that really what you want?'

Ulysses shrugged, indifferently. 'I want *her* out,' he said.

'She won't spy on us,' Stephen went on. 'Not if she knows I'm watching her. As a child, she was always afraid of me, and I haven't noticed that she has acquired any more courage since. I will see to it she spends less time at home.'

'Then she is all the more likely to come in, unexpectedly, when we don't want her. I thought we were going to be private down here. Make her go.'

'We *are* private,' Stephen said, half desperate, half exasperated. 'I told you, I can't make her go. Not immediately. It would be so – obvious. Anyway, she's hardly important enough to make any real difference. You shouldn't have insisted on coming down here. Would you rather be back in London?'

Ulysses looked at him as if he had not heard. 'If you don't get rid of her soon,' he said, 'I'll fuck her.'

He did not discuss Melissa with Caroline. The following week, when Stephen was in London, Ulysses arranged to meet him in Harley Street and eat out afterwards. He caught a train up to town in the late morning and lunched with Caroline in a restaurant in Holborn. 'You eat too much,' she said, picking at a salad while he disposed of grilled trout. 'You'll get fat.'

'You don't eat enough,' he retorted. 'Like your father. The English are all too thin, especially the women. I like fat Greek women, with breasts.'

Caroline knew he was trying to annoy her. She found him childish but it did not trouble her; at least his thoughts and feelings were transparent, easily read, although she did not always understand the motives behind them. Presently she asked him: 'Is everything going all right?'

'I suppose so.' He paused, frowning speculatively. 'It is a beautiful house, but very cold.'

'There's central heating in all the rooms. Turn it up.'

'I meant, it is *unlived* in.' His sensitivity surprised her. 'It feels like a house where no one has ever been very happy, where no one ever dared to laugh or shout or spill things on the carpet. Your father told me, he bought it when somebody died. You can feel it in the atmosphere. She must have died slowly, without knowing about it, with lots of drugs and very little pain. It is easy to imagine people dying in that house.'

Caroline said, colourlessly: 'I was happy there, when I was a child.'

'You were an unnatural child. You never got your face dirty or ate too many sweets. I can tell.'

Caroline concentrated on her plate for a minute or two. She found herself separating the salad into its component parts, a habit she thought she had long outgrown. As an afterthought, she asked: 'How do you get on with my sister?'

Ulysses grimaced expressively. 'She's a nuisance,' he said. He didn't say any more.

When he and Stephen got home that night, Melissa's jacket was hanging in the hall and her bedroom door was closed. Ulysses, who was slightly drunk, laughed loudly and deliberately just outside. 'Sleep well, Melissa,' he murmured. 'Dream of *me*.' Stephen, who was trying to draw him away, flinched inwardly. In bed, Ulysses began to hurt him, pleasurably at first and then later, when he was weak and helpless with desire, more and more viciously, bruising his white flesh and biting until the blood came. Once, Stephen cried out. 'Make her go,' Ulysses whispered, filled with a horrible confusion of lust and fury, longing, in that moment, to thrust his thumbs into the sobbing windpipe, squeezing and choking until it was all over. Afterwards, lying in the darkness, he was frightened by his own loss of detachment. Often, with both men and women, he had made love with his body while keeping his mind apart, watching their pleasure and abandon with a sense of power untainted by any other sentiment. But increasingly, with Stephen, he found himself enjoying what was required of him, experiencing a perverse elation in hatred, in contempt, in the inflicting of pain. And even this time, he knew, his savagery had left Stephen somehow fulfilled. In the morning, perhaps, he would look at the bruises and be ashamed, but he would come back again the next night, and the next, for the luxury of further humiliation. In a moment of sudden panic Ulysses saw himself being drawn down by the other man's need, down and down into blackness. It was as though some rottenness in Stephen's soul had crept into Ulysses' vitals like a disease, and now he was corrupted with longings that were not his own. He tried to think of Caroline, of how it would feel to make love to her, the simplicity of her responses and the cool fragrance of her body. But the face he

114

pictured, rigid in coitus, the snarling mouth and drowned eyes, were Stephen's.

Outside, Melissa listened until the gasps and moans were over and silence supervened. She was shivering and under the arms her shirt was wet with perspiration. Even in sex, she feared her father might be aware of her presence, might hear the thread-like rasp of her breathing or see the heavy oak door quiver as she brushed against it. For a long time she stayed there, crouched down by the wall, listening to the silence with her ears stretched. When she thought they must have gone to sleep, she moved away. Halfway down the passage, glancing back nervously at the closed door, she caught her foot in a rug. The noise of her stumble, her indrawn breath, the slither of her foot, sounded horribly loud in the dead-of-night stillness. She picked herself up and ran down the passageway to her room, no longer looking back. Once inside she shut the door, too quickly, with a thud that seemed to echo through the house, crawled into bed, and buried herself under the covers like a child who is afraid of ghosts.

As Stephen expected, people did not realise the truth all at once. It happened by degrees: the social engagements rain-checked, the distant expressions on the faces of chance-met acquaintances, the false smiles of the female patients who encountered Ulysses on their way out. He seemed to hang around the hall deliberately, during surgery hours, looking rather as if he had only just got out of bed, his hair tousled, his chin unshaven, his shirt buttons left undone. The receptionist, always aloof and polite, became infinitesimally politer and more aloof, reporting without comment that Mrs Whatsit-Smythe could not make it this week, and Mrs So-and-So, whose back-ache had afflicted herself (and everyone else) for years, had been miraculously cured by acupuncture. She stayed on, though there was less and less for her to do, apparently indifferent to Ulysses' insolent stare and aggressive masculinity. Jobs were scarcer than ever and she was getting married in the summer. Mrs Bunce also stayed on. ('That poor girl,' she told her husband, referring, presumably, to Melissa. 'Her own father! Well, I know she's *difficult* but she wasn't a bad child, not really. Used to come into my kitchen and chatter away to me for hours, like no one else was interested. Who's she got to turn to, if I leave? When I think of all the things that happened, his poor wives and all, it makes you wonder, it really does. I always thought there was something funny about him. . .') It did not occur to Stephen to question either her motives or those of the receptionist, he merely felt vaguely relieved. And yet sometimes, paradoxically, he found himself wishing they would both go away, leave him alone, with the telephone off the hook and the unwashed crockery piled in the sink, waiting for some god to call it a day. One morning, Monica Anstey called, ostensibly to collect a book which she said she might have lent him. Stephen offered her a sherry and watched with humourless detachment as she sat on the edge of her chair, smiling too often and fondling her cultured pearls, her voice tinkling tinnily through an assortment of conventional phrases, her eyes fixed always on some point just to Ulysses' left. He pictured her, on her return, tottering into the drawing room, telling her family it was All True. . . Perhaps her daughter would hear the news, long distance, teeth agape as she listened to the gabbling receiver, inadvertently crunching up the mouthpiece as her jaws snapped in surprise. When Monica Anstey had gone, Stephen poured himself a small cognac and sipped, thoughtfully. Normally, he never drank cognac this early in the day, but lately he found the taste of sherry, even before lunch, faintly insipid. The level in the cognac bottle seemed to have fallen rather more than usual in the last week. Not that he ever allowed it to cloud his senses, but he liked the sting of the spirit in his throat. Like medicine, he thought: the sharper the taste, the more you feel it is doing you good. He rolled it round his mouth before swallowing, telling himself there was no hurry, he was not dependent; it was simply a pleasure he could easily dispense with. Ulysses watched him without comment.

11

'I suppose,' Caroline said slowly, 'I ought to come down for a weekend.'

She was talking more to herself than to Ulysses, but he heard. 'It is as you wish,' he said, with elaborate indifference. 'Don't you trust me?'

Caroline smiled faintly. 'Not very much,' she admitted. 'It isn't that. I just feel – it's my plan, my responsibility. I ought to be there. Would I cramp your style?'

'Of course not. You are just another tiresome daughter of Stephen's whom I do not want in the house. You will be very polite to me, and I will look sulky. You will say that you have visited Greece, isn't it beautiful, how could I bear to leave, and so on. You will be thoroughly banal and English and I will look even sulkier. Perhaps I will tell you, contemptuously, that it is not always sunny in Greece, and in the winter it rains a lot. I will speak of my starving peasant family, the leak in my bedroom roof, the dirt roads that turn to mud in bad weather, cutting us off from civilisation.' ('Don't get carried away,' Caroline murmured.) 'I will explain how we keep a single pot of soup on the stove and water it to make it last the whole season. Afterwards, I will tell Stephen that you are a proud, conceited sort of girl and very insular. It will be easy to deceive him. He *wants* to be deceived.' After a moment, he added, as though trying to convince himself: 'I would like you to come, I think. It might be amusing. Sometimes I get very bored.'

'I haven't been home for months,' Caroline said doubtfully (even now, it was the only place she referred to as 'home'). 'It would look rather strange. . .'

'No.' Ulysses sounded more definite, this time, as though he had come to some decision of his own. 'It's natural. You have come to see me. You are curious. It would look strange if you did not come.'

'Maybe.' She considered him, thoughtfully. 'You've changed your mind, haven't you? You really do want me there. Why?' She had always felt herself to be in control, a director on the set where Ulysses, and her father, were merely actors. Now, for an instant, it was as though their roles were reversed, Ulysses was directing her, drawing her into a situation she had not planned, did not want. But she knew she would have to go. She would have to *see* what she had done. It was not a question of curiosity, only necessity. She did not wish to gloat.

'I want you for your beautiful eyes, of course,' Ulysses was saying, mockingly. 'Your sister is very plain. It will be nice to see a beautiful woman again.'

'You see me now,' Caroline pointed out.

Suddenly she was conscious that he was standing very close to her.

'I know,' he said.

Even on the telephone, she could hear the reluctance in her father's voice. 'I want to see Melissa,' she said, seizing at random on some reason for her proposed visit.

'Melissa. . .' Her father did not sound enthusiastic but he seemed to accept this, as though it fitted in with some idea of his own. He did not appear to ask himself why Caroline should suddenly wish to see a step-sister with whom she had never had anything in common. 'Perhaps you can inspire her with some conception of maturity and independence. It is, after all, long overdue. She cannot expect to live under my roof for ever.'

He wants her out of the way, Caroline thought. Somehow, it was a possibility that had not occurred to her, though she knew it should have done. She had never thought very much about Melissa. The vehemence of her own reaction startled her.

'I saw Dick Willoughby Grant's mother the other day,' she said, abruptly. 'In Harrods.' In fact, they had not spoken: Mrs Willoughby Grant, absorbed in the purchase of Irish linen, had not noticed Caroline at all. But she did not mention that.

There was a short silence, disinterest or indecision. 'Really,' said Dr Horvath, in a strange, flat voice with no question mark in it. 'How delightful. I hope she is keeping well.'

'She seemed fine,' Caroline responded, carefully. 'Look – I'll be down on Friday, before dinner. If that's all right.' She gave him no time to demur. 'Till Friday, then. Goodbye. . .' She couldn't say: Goodbye, Dad. She supposed she must have called him Daddy when she was little but she couldn't remember it. For a long time now she did not think she had called him anything: not Father, Daddy, Dad, darling, dear. (She had once heard Glynis, on the telephone, call her father 'darling'.) There was just a gap between the words, a hesitation, the silence which was all that remained of their relationship. The receiver rattled on the cradle when she replaced it, as though her hand was unsteady. 'I don't care,' she told herself. 'I don't care any more.' But she knew it wasn't true.

She reached Cheyney, on the following Friday, rather later than she had intended. Her train had been delayed and it was raining, so she had to queue for a taxi. When she arrived at the house, dinner was on the table and Mrs Bunce was on her way out. She said, 'Hello, dear,' with an expression on her face that Caroline did not like at all, a sort of avid compunction that seemed both patronising and presumptuous. She murmured something in response and went inside, leaving her bag by the door. In the dining room her father, Ulysses and Melissa were seated round the table, waiting for her, with unnatural formality, hands poised over their soup-spoons. Even though she had been expecting it, had contrived it, the presence of Ulysses in that respectable interior was somehow shocking. The wall-brackets gave a thin, sallow light which made his dark face look even darker and dulled the glints in his hair. The whites of his eyes gleamed when he glanced up. He seemed far more out of place than Melissa, whose punk haircut and crude make-up merely served to emphasise her waif-life insignificance. Dr Horvath muttered an introduction which Caroline decided she could not catch and added: 'You're late.' She murmured something about trains but did not apologise. Her embarrassment, unfeigned, was all that he might have expected.

She sat down, not looking at Ulysses, and bent her gaze to her plate. The soup was vegetal in flavour and coloured a drab orange which spoke of carrots. Caroline stirred it, without appetite, for something to do with her spoon. She knew it was illogical to see Ulysses as an intruder, to feel this sudden impulse of panic at the realisation of her fantasies. She tried to think of Philip but the memory had receded, over the last few months, even the pain seemed to have grown faint and sweet, and she had no photographs, no sentimental keepsakes to bring it back. In desperation she looked at her father, searching for some resemblance, but although she had often seen the shadow of his parentage in Philip's face she could not find anything of his weakness and vulnerability in Stephen. Yet there was something in her father's expression which was almost like weakness, something which had not been there before. He had always had an air of tautness, of strain and the will to survive under strain. Now, the strain seemed to have lessened; his features had sagged, defeated, as though some elastic nerve behind his face was finally giving way. Here and there the elfin lines, formerly invisible, had broken through his skin, like the first hairline cracks in a surface long smooth and immaculate. She had always thought it would take only a hint of tragedy, no matter how fleeting, to bring out those lines, but tragedy had passed him by, leaving him unmarked, and it was the indulgence of desire, the fulfilment of the senses, which had begun the deterioration of his face. After dinner, she watched him pour himself a cognac; the bottle was new, nearly full, the price still stuck on the side. She wondered, remembering Ursula, if there was such a thing as justice after all, the unrelenting justice of some pitiless god who balanced all things in his immortal scales. But it was no god who had made this end (if it was the end). It was herself, Caroline Horvath, the perfect daughter. . . Briefly, she had a glimpse, gone in a moment, of a responsibility so appalling that her mind shrank. But she could not believe in it, not yet. Even now, seeing Ulysses at Cheyney and the lines on her father's face, she could not really believe what she had done.

* * *

On the Saturday, Stephen was supposed to be going to a sherry party, a long-standing invitation from a hostess too absent-minded, or too diffident, to cancel it. He had said he would not attend but eventually he went out, just before midday, in a dark suit which did not fit quite as exquisitely as it had once done and a tie that was inadvertently just a shade too deep a blue. Caroline almost thought he stooped a little, but perhaps it was an uncomfortable hunching of his shoulders. She wondered if it was her presence which had made him change his mind, in a final, ineffectual attempt to keep up appearances. Maybe Ulysses had said something. Melissa was out, probably all day, so they would be left alone. 'I shall go for a walk,' she said to her father, before he left. 'I need some country air.' She remembered him telling her once, years ago, about the view from the golf course. She had always meant to climb up there one day, very early, and watch the dawn come up behind the hills, but somehow she had never got around to it. The recollection gave her an odd stab of unhappiness which she could not quite explain. It was so very rare for her father to tell her things like that. When he had gone, she changed her shoes, as if she really intended to go for a walk. She did not want to be alone with Ulysses, not here, not at Cheyney. It occurred to her that she had never really been alone with him before. In London, they had always met in public places, in coffee houses and wine bars. In Greece, it was true, they had often been alone, but in the bar near the beach, with the door open, and people passing by outside who might decide at any moment to come in and buy a drink. She did not think she was afraid of him, but she felt that he might, in some unspecified way, try to upset things, just for the hell of it, to disrupt her plans, to disrupt *her*. When he did not come, she was definitely relieved. She picked up her jacket, opened her bedroom door, went quietly down the passage. She was not, she told herself, being deliberately quiet; she always wore crêpe-soled shoes for walking, it was practical. Her feet made little noise on the carpeted stairs.

He was waiting for her in the hall. In the poor light she could not see the expression on his face, but there was something vaguely threatening about his attitude, leaning against the front door with his back to it, his arms folded across his chest. It was as if he had read her mind, something she told herself was beyond his ability. All the same, she was not quite – not *quite* – surprised. On the bottom step, she paused. She did not want to hesitate but she felt if she tried to push past him it would bring her far too close. 'I'm going out,' she said calmly. 'I'll be back later.'

'You've been out,' said Ulysses. 'You had a lovely walk. It is very warm for March. I want to talk to you.'

Caroline said, rather more coldly. 'You know very well I haven't been out. I'm going now. I need some fresh air after being cooped up in London.'

'I want to talk to you.'

'What is there to talk about? You seem to be doing very well. Would you mind moving out of the way? If you want to make a melodramatic scene for some reason, do it in front of my father. It's wasted on me.'

Ulysses said shortly: 'Move me.'

Caroline was still standing at the foot of the stairs. She bit her lip. 'Don't be childish.'

'I told you, I want to talk to you. You know quite well we have certain things to discuss. When your father asks if you enjoyed your walk you can tell him a lie. It's time you told a few lies for a change. You're good at making plans but you don't much like the reality, do you? It's always me who has to get my hands dirty – not to mention my body. You seem to forget I am doing it for you.'

Caroline said: 'You didn't have to get involved. I thought this was what you wanted: a big house, plenty of money, the easy life. If you don't like it you can always leave. I can't stop you.'

'No.' The whites of Ulysses' eyes, fixed on her face, gleamed like two crescent moons. 'It's too late now. I've gone too far to be able to get out. So have you. You seem to forget, we are in this together: the three of us. You, me and *him*. We are inseparable.'

For a wild moment, Caroline visualised herself caught up in some ghastly modern play, trapped on a narrow stage with two or three other characters, none of whom she liked, being sucked down into the vortex of the author's psychoneurotic imaginings. She found herself saying, stupidly: 'I don't believe this.'

'Did you think that was all I wanted? The easy life? That

122

was not very clever of you.' He straightened up, moving away from the door. Towards her. 'No,' he said softly, searching her face, as though he was seeing something there which he had not seen before. 'You were cleverer than that, weren't you? You thought you could attract me, use me, eventually discard me, without ever having to commit yourself. You thought this was your game and you could make up the rules and it would never occur to me to break them. You were wrong. There are no rules. You are in this with me and you can't get out, any more than I could. I can do what I want with you.'

Caroline still stood at the foot of the stairs, unmoving. She was not afraid. Her insides felt horribly shaky, but it was not fear. She said as steadily as she could: 'That's rubbish. You can't blackmail me. We have done nothing illegal. Even if we had, you couldn't prove it.'

'I don't want to blackmail you.'

'What *do* you want?' (Fatal to ask. It sounded too much like the cue for a line she had no wish to hear.)

'Payment.'

He was touching her now, one hand on her shoulder, the other curving round the back of her neck. His own daring almost frightened him, so that he trembled inside, but he knew, even as she had known, that it would be disastrous to hesitate. She said, desperately: 'No. . .' but her voice died away. Never before had she been so conscious of him physically, of the muscle in his arms, the smell of his body, a strong, warm smell of rank masculinity. For her, the sense of smell was inexplicably connected with sexual arousal. She was horrified to feel herself melting inside like butter in a hot dish. She had always thought of him as a beautiful and dangerous animal, segregated from her by invisible bars, class, nationality, attitudes, customs, a deep-seated psychological taboo which had never been more than a chimera. He was very close to her now, so close she could not tell if it was he who was shivering or herself. His erection pressed into her, insistently, through his clothes. Her impulse to respond was so strong it shocked her. She tried to think of Philip, of being in love: she had never had sex without being in love, at least for a little while. But she could scarcely remember what love had felt like, she had been cold for so long, and

Philip was dead, ages dead, crumbling bones and rotted flesh, smoke on the wind, dinner for worms. As for his soul, if he had a soul, that was fled far away beyond thought or knowledge, in Paradise, in Purgatory, in the nethermost circles of Hell: what did it matter? It was out of her jurisdiction. She was alive and she wanted to live, to be *warm*. Her mind had retreated from the world into some far cold realm untouched by human affection, but her body betrayed her. Her hands crept around his neck, her knees gave, her mouth opened against his. She knew dimly that if she let this happen everything would be changed, but she could not stop, not now. She had denied herself too long. Somewhere at the back of her thought she had a glimpse of what those years of restraint must have done to her father, of how he must have felt, when his balked desires were released at last: a fleeting, terrible glimpse of helplessness, madness, despair. And she, his own daughter, she had taken advantage of that weakness, without understanding and without pity. No matter what he had done, how could she give herself the right to judge him? Her own lovelessness might, oh, so easily have drawn her down the same way. . .

'Your room,' Ulysses whispered. 'Come on.'

He took her by the hand and pulled her up the stairs after him, pausing on the landing to kiss her again, as though to reassure himself that she was there. He didn't ask her if this was really what she wanted, if she was excited or glad, if she loved him, if she liked him, if she was on the pill. In the bedroom, he didn't even trouble to shut the door properly. He was dizzy with lust, like a man who has missed breakfast three days running, and gone short at dinner. Close to, she saw his eyes were cloudy, his mouth so passionately serious she could scarcely believe he knew how to smile. His very seriousness aroused her. On the bed, his weight pressed her into the mattress, his thighs moved against hers. He began to talk to her, in Greek, soft hungry words whose meaning was unimportant: he only wanted her to respond to his voice. He was using it, like his hands and his mouth and his body, to excite her, to weaken her. She sensed the element of calculation, even in his lust, but it did not worry her, it made him more human, less animal; she feared to submit to something wholly animal. Perhaps, she thought, this was what she had

124

wanted all along. And afterwards, everything would be changed, they could start again from the beginning. . . His hands slid under her sweater, reaching for the buttons to unfasten her shirt. Foreigners, she reflected fleetingly, remembering a Frenchman she had fought off once on holiday, were so much more professional about zips and buttons. She was not wearing a bra and she could feel his fingers, teasing her left nipple until it grew hard. She moaned once, very softly, more to encourage him than because moaning came naturally to her. For some idiotic reason she was still wearing her jacket.

Somewhere in the house a door slammed. Faintly she heard it, on the edge of awareness, heard it and took note. A moment later, suddenly alert and unsure, she was thrusting her hands against his shoulders as though to push him away. But Ulysses was somewhere else. She did not hear the footsteps on the carpeted stairs. In the passage, a voice called out, disastrously close: 'Carla –' And then her sister was standing in the half-open door.

Caroline never remembered Ulysses releasing her, never remembered struggling to her feet. The room was quite still except for her fingers, fumbling stupidly at her shirt. When she spoke to him, her voice was cold, sharp with urgency and fear.

'Get out. I shan't tell my father; don't worry. Just get out.'

Tears, uncomfortably genuine, stung behind her eyes. Ulysses went out, unspeaking, leaving her alone with Melissa. As she tried to straighten her clothes she heard herself saying, listlessly, 'Thank God you came home.'

Downstairs, Caroline made herself some coffee, very black and strong, and sat at the kitchen table to drink it, vaguely conscious of Melissa's eyes fixed on her face. They were strange eyes, she thought, small and opaque, like round, shiny bits of some colourless stone. The heavy make-up made them look even smaller and there were dark lines underneath that would one day become pouches. 'Why is she looking at me like that?' Caroline wondered, without any real interest. She would have expected Melissa to exhibit her usual ghoulish triumph at the discovery of a disreputable secret, to gloat, to giggle, maybe to sneer. But there was an expression on her face which seemed both eager and, yes, wistful, almost envious. Caroline, filled with a strange new warmth, found her altogether pitiable and unhappy.

'What happened?' Melissa asked her, leaning across the table so that the rest of her face seemed to shrink back from her elongated nose like the face of a weasel. 'What did he do?'

'If you don't mind,' said Caroline, 'I'd rather not talk about it.' She didn't want to tell any lies, not even now. When she picked up her coffee cup she found her hand was shaking slightly, although she was not quite sure why. She hoped her sister wouldn't notice, not because it mattered, but because Melissa would misinterpret her distress and that, too, would be a kind of lie.

'Would you like a drink?' Melissa suggested presently. Her sympathy, whatever the cause, was so blatant Caroline felt she ought to respond to it.

'No. No, thank you. The coffee's fine.'

After a few minutes, Melissa said: 'Do you think he was really going to rape you?'

'Of course not.' Somehow, she must play down the incident, reduce it to a triviality, lightly disregarded, which Melissa would not think to brood over or discuss with anyone. With an effort which was less than she had anticipated, she managed a smile. 'That would be very melodramatic. I daresay he just thought . . . he hoped. . .' She could not go on. 'Some men are like that,' she said finally. 'They're good-looking, maybe, or simply conceited, and they think they can have anyone. He was just trying it on. That's all, really.'

'Ulysses is very good-looking,' Melissa averred.

Caroline glanced quickly at her. 'If you like that sort of thing,' she said.

At the sherry party, Stephen Horvath was standing on his own, nibbling a very small round biscuit decorated with a fragment of smoked salmon and parsley. He did not particularly like smoked salmon, he thought it overrated, nor did he usually eat any of the supposedly appetising titbits provided at parties of this kind. But his hostess, brandishing the plate,

126

had almost avoided him, and he had been unable to resist the temptation of annoying her by helping himself. The room was very crowded, but this somehow only emphasised his curious isolation. There was a small space all round him, the kind of space that opens up sometimes at social gatherings, by some undivulged manoeuvre, around the stammering girl whom nobody knows, the hearty man whom nobody wants to know. On either side of Stephen, there were people deep in conversations which did not quite include him, their shoulders half turned at just the right angle to appear discouraging without being overtly rude. Occasionally – and that was almost the worst – someone would come up and speak to him, duty-bound, determinedly natural: 'Hello, old chap. Not seen you for a while. How's business?. . . Yes, well, she's going to some coloured chap in East Grinstead, Indian or something. Straps her to a bed and sort of stretches her out – just like the rack if you ask me. Supposed to be frightfully good for the spine. All nonsense, of course, but you know what women are. Always keen on something new. . .' Stephen said yes and no and of course in his most bored voice and now and then allowed himself to smile, cynically, almost insolently, at his fellow-guest's defensive manner and uncomfortable condescension. Later, when the obtrusive enquirer had moved thankfully away, Stephen drained his sherry glass, rather too quickly, and wished in vain for cognac. The son of the house, a bespotted youth of university age, was circulating with a decanter. Perhaps he had heard the gossip from his parents; he certainly refilled Stephen's glass rather more assiduously than anyone else's, gazing at him with the mixture of awe and interest felt by the very young for those whom they see as rebels and social outlaws. Possibly he had learnt things in his first term at college that he had not learnt at school. But if there was any partisanship in his face Stephen had not noticed, and even if he had he would have considered the young man's sympathy as impertinent, as laughable as the condemnation of his elders. Stephen was not a rebel. He had courted these people, made use of them, insinuated himself into their lives, and now they had decided to reject him. It was as simple as that. He tried to be detached about it, to be wryly amused, like the loser looking back at the corner where he came to grief and seeing at last the grease

127

on the roadway. Soon (but not too soon) he could go home. He would have liked to leave now but that would look cowardly, an admission of deviance, of social crime, and he did not wish to give these people that kind of satisfaction. Not now he was here. He hadn't wanted to come, but Ulysses had taunted him, and the presence of Caroline, failing to meet his eyes across the dinner table, unsettled him more than he would admit. He had never been particularly conscious of it, but even as a child she had always been the sort of person who looked you in the eye. It was one of the things he most deprecated about her. Somehow, he felt it was an intrusion of privacy, that embarrassing, unwavering stare, demanding something which he could not give, trying, or so it seemed, to penetrate the very fabric of his mind. Margaret should have taught her that such overt candour was invalid in a contemporary society, if indeed any society had ever existed where candour had a place. But Margaret herself had been largely ignorant of the realities, brought up with the impossible ideals of Kipling and 'Invictus', unable to comprehend lack of normality, lack of principle, the complex dishonesties of the human psyche. He knew it was illogical that he should be in any way affected by Caroline's shrinking, her first contact, very probably, with an uncomfortable truth. It would have been easier, somehow, if she had over-reacted, perhaps become hysterical, instead of being polite and reticent. Melissa's furtive scrutiny, for example, did not trouble him at all; she was too shallow, too negligible, too easily understood. It occurred to him that Ulysses had not mentioned Melissa for some days now; maybe the arrival of Caroline had diverted him. Or maybe he had something else on his mind, more important, which Stephen admitted to himself, cravenly, he would rather know nothing about. He distrusted Ulysses, he reflected bitterly, more than anyone in this room.

He decided to leave eventually around one thirty. There were only a few people left by then and that meant that at least the entire community would not be holding an inquisition on his behaviour the moment he was gone. Fleetingly, he imagined them discussing him, his appearance, manners, drinking habits: 'Of course, he's *aged*. . . those bags under his eyes . . . he used to be such a handsome man. . . I even said hello to him, it seemed polite, after all these years, and do you know, he positively *ignored* me?. . . Not a good example for Nigel, I'm afraid. There's so much of this gay lib up at Cambridge. . . Did you see how much he drank?' Catching a glimpse of himself in the hall mirror on his way out, he thought: They're right. I look old. The flesh had sunk so deeply into his eye-sockets and the hollows of his cheeks his face resembled a death's head. Too many nights without sleep, too many demons and shadows, gathering just beyond the reach of his sight.

His host brought him his coat and mumbled something about 'glad you could come' and 'see you again some time'. His hostess fluttered safely out of reach. In the living room, he could hear Monica Anstey, last to leave, revving up for the first spate of gossip. She had not spoken to him at all. He thought of saying 'Thank you' and 'What a pleasant occasion', but he didn't. In the end, he didn't even say goodbye.

That night, Caroline slept badly. Usually, she slept well at Cheyney: as a child she had been reassured by the stillness of the countryside, the small night noises, the whisper of the wind in the leaves, the owl in the garden crying with its sad, human voice. Other sounds there were, beyond the edge of hearing, which she used to imagine, sometimes, as a kind of sigh running under the silence, like water running under ice: flowers closing, toadstools opening, spiders' feet in the long corridors. She was not afraid of spiders. Even when she felt wakeful these things soothed her, so that her thoughts could slip away, unhurriedly, until her mind filled up with sleep. She had slept badly in London, after Philip died, the grey sleeplessness of emotional exhaustion, of a dead spirit and a dull grief; but this was a different kind of insomnia. She lay rigid, unmoving, horribly alert. There was a soft creak, as of a floorboard settling, a distant noise that might have been merely someone shifting in the throes of a restless dream. Melissa's room was at the top of the stairs on the right: Ulysses' room, which had been Philip's, three doors along. Last night, it had troubled her, thinking of Ulysses in that bed where she and Philip, idiotically young (or so it now seemed to her), carefree, and rather drunk, had exchanged their first fumbling embraces; but it did not matter any more.

She reflected idly that Philip's lovemaking had always seemed rather amateurish, in spite of all his experience. She had liked it at the time. Presently, she heard the sound of a lavatory flushing, presumably the one between his room and Melissa's, and then footsteps in the passage. She stiffened, but they died away, and a door closed, at the other end of the house, with a soft decisive snick. She waited, hearing nothing, unable to relax. Her father slept at the back, between the bedroom which both Ursula and Celia had deserted and a sort of sitting room, still papered with preposterous giant sunflowers, which had once been used as a playroom, principally for Melissa's benefit. The windows were round the side of the house and let in very little sun: Caroline thought it had always had a bleak, unused, unhappy look. Her room was at the end of the corridor. Even if someone did go down to her father's room, she might not hear him, not if he were shoeless and very quiet. She lay deadly still, her whole being concentrated into the act of listening. She felt weighted down with a disproportionate responsibility, a helpless, childish apprehension founded on some age-old memory of disappointment. Her window was a little open and a draught of air stirred the curtain and blew coldly on her face. And suddenly she was a child again, lying tautly in the darkness, listening for the noises of footsteps and of doors, dimly aware of some terrible wrong in her secure young life which she would never understand or be able to put right. . .

Caroline did not know what time it was when she finally went to sleep. She heard the grandfather clock on the landing strike two, maybe three. She heard a hedgehog (she thought it was a hedgehog) calling in the garden. Sleep took her, unawares, and when she woke again it was already well into the morning.

12

Caroline left Cheyney on the Sunday afternoon. She wondered if she ought to say something more to her sister about the encounter with Ulysses, but Melissa did not mention it and in the end she decided there was no point. She wanted to speak to Ulysses, too, but she could not seem to find the opportunity. Mrs Bunce did not come in on Sundays so Caroline prepared the lunch, a proper Sunday lunch with a joint of beef she found in the freezer, roast potatoes, green beans. She opened a jar of horseradish sauce and put it on the table, in a china saucer, but nobody touched it. Once, she would have waited, probably in vain, for a complimentary word from her father; now, when he said, unexpectedly: 'You've turned into quite a good cook,' she hardly noticed. She registered that Ulysses ate with only moderate enthusiasm but whether that meant anything she didn't know. There was a moment when she felt him staring intently across the table at her, and her stomach tightened, although she did not look up, and she pushed her knife and fork together, unable to eat any more. It seemed impossible that she should leave without talking to him, but even if she stayed until the evening she felt the chance would never arise: Melissa would hang around, her father would be there, something or someone would always intervene. Afterwards, over the washing up, she waited for Ulysses to come into the kitchen with a sulky offer of help; surely he must wish for private conversation as urgently as she did. But perhaps he did not see the opportunity. She pictured herself running the tap, very fast and loud, to cover a soft-voiced discussion, pictured the dropped plate, caught just in time, when her father interrupted to call Ulysses away. 'How unusual,' he would say, sardonically, studying Ulysses with a faint suspicion. 'I never knew you were so domesticated.' It would be quite hopeless. Eventually, Caroline went straight after she had finished clearing the meal. On the train, she contemplated the long hours of uncertainty lying ahead of her with a vague incredulity. She had never felt this way, not in her whole life. Even after her first date with Clive, when she had not been quite sure that he would ask her out again, she had been able to concentrate on her work, to reply, coolly, to the enquiries of friends: 'He said he'd ring me up some time.' And with Philip, there had been no need for such tensions, unless she had created them herself, out of hesitation and temporary self-restraint. Philip had always been there, inevitable, a part of her world. Ulysses was a stranger. She realised that now, too late, seeing him suddenly as an individual and not merely a pawn on a chessboard. What, after all, did she know about him, his thoughts, his emotions, the motives which had persuaded him to come here? When he had kissed her, in the hallway at Cheyney, she had felt a sense of rightness, despite her reluctance, of something good born of all the pointless hatred that had wasted her spirit for so long. But that was her own private delusion. Supposing, in her lie to Melissa, there had been a core of truth. What had she said? 'He's only trying it on.' Perhaps, ironically, that was all it was, an extra in Ulysses' share of the takings, a moment of sound and fury, signifying nothing. And suddenly, looking back on her own actions, she saw herself as an ill-meaning fool who had summoned up an incubus she could not control, and now it preyed upon her family at will. Her father, herself, Melissa – yes, even Melissa, she thought, recognising at last the eager wistfulness in her sister's eyes. Maybe he had already taken her, one day when Stephen was in London, to while away the tedium of a dull afternoon. . .

Beyond the window, there was a sliding hillside, a procession of trees. Caroline stared unseeing at the sunlight slanting through a green mist of invisible leaves. This is useless, she told herself, savagely. I must stop. She wasn't a neurotic teenager, throwing herself into first love (or first lust) with an overdose of passion and despair; she never had been. Perhaps that was what was wrong with her. She had reached twenty-six without ever being sixteen, and for the first time in her life she felt out of control and painfully adolescent.

At the flat, she found Glynis, spending a rare evening in. Caroline forced herself to talk about *The White Hotel* and different ways of cooking duck and felt a little more normal. When the telephone rang, she started only slightly. She knew it would not be for her.

The following week was less agonising than Caroline had expected. She did not have the kind of job where she could sit idle, indulging in paranoid speculation: there were decisions to be made, letters to be answered, people coming in and out, constantly, asking her whether she had remembered to do this, and would she mind taking a look at that. In the evenings, she caught up on a backlog of reading. Glynis was there a good deal since her boyfriend, the extramarital Rodney, had gone away on business, and the two girls spent most of the time watching television and learning to play picquet. They had very little in common but Caroline did not dislike her flatmate, although she had always disapproved of her casual attitude to sex. If Glynis went to a party without Rod (she called him Rod) she would usually appear in the kitchen the next morning to make breakfast for some unknown young man, apparently quite unruffled by Caroline's obvious embarrassment. On one unforgettable occasion Rod had turned up without warning and tripped over the latest pick-up in the living room. The scene that followed, Caroline thought distastefully, was worthy of an American soap opera, with Rod storming and waving his arms and Glynis, in her dressing gown, standing there and saying nothing, watching him with her cool sibylline gaze, bored, amused, or possibly both; Caroline could not tell. 'It's no good,' Glynis said to her afterwards, 'I just can't say no.' At the time, Caroline had not understood. But now, remembering what had happened with Ulysses, she had a vague intimation of how it must feel to be subject to violent physical desire. She could not condone what Glynis did, but she realised, if reluctantly, what made her do it.

Around six thirty on Friday the telephone rang. 'It's for you,' said Glynis, looking, Caroline thought, with her newly awakened perception, almost pettish. Perhaps she was expecting a call from Rod. 'Some man. . .'

Caroline crossed the room, unhurriedly, and picked up the receiver, knowing already who it would be. Even so, the sound of his voice, altered by the telephone but still sharply familiar, gave her a curious shiver inside. (And when, she asked herself, had his voice become so familiar to her?)

'Caroline?'

'Speaking.' Glynis was looking at her, speculatively. She hated the feeling of covering up but she didn't want to say Ulysses' name in front of the other girl, not now. She knew she sounded cool and unencouraging, as if she were talking to any slight acquaintance who might happen to ring up on some pretext or other. It couldn't be helped.

'I have to see you.'

Glynis had moved away, perhaps conscious of discourtesy. Caroline hoped she would go into the kitchen. She could have asked, but she preferred not to.

'Yes,' she said. Just *yes*. It sounded inadequate to the point of idiocy.

'I'm in London – with Stephen. I thought I might be able to come and see you, but it's not possible. I can't talk long.' In the background, there was a constant eddy of noise, muttering voices, a door banging. A pub, maybe.

Caroline said carefully: 'I don't know when I'm free.'

To her relief, Ulysses seemed to understand. 'I thought you said your flatmate was out most of the time.'

'Not this week.'

'I can't come this week. Next week, maybe. I'll –'

'Call me.'

Pause. Perhaps Ulysses, distracted, had looked round for a moment. When he spoke again, his voice was lower and more urgent. 'I must go now. I will come next week. I can arrange it somehow. Be there.'

'Yes, but when –'

'Just *be there*.'

There was a click, and then the hum of the dialling tone. Caroline replaced the receiver, slowly, forgetful of Glynis, who was watching her from the other side of the room. Her casual question woke Caroline from a reverie that was not altogether pleasant. 'Who was it?'

'A friend of my brother's,' Caroline found herself saying,

134

without even pausing to think. Although it was a lie, it seemed somehow appropriate. 'Phil had some strange friends.'

'He has a sexy voice,' Glynis remarked contemplatively.

I suppose he has, thought Caroline. It was strange how much more aware of his voice she became, over the telephone, with no expressions, no features, no touch and smell to distract her. He had only telephoned her twice before, to arrange a meeting place: once at the office, when she was busy, once at the flat, when she was tired. It had not been very important how he sounded, not then. This has to stop, she decided, even as she had decided a hundred times in the past few days. It had gone on too long: the lying, the hatred, the whole fantastic rigmarole of revenge. Philip was dead because he had chosen to die and even if he came back, in a dream, in a nightmare, she would only say to him: 'Revenge is irrelevant. You opted out.' Too many people had been hurt, too many people, perhaps, were going to be hurt, because of Philip's cowardice. No, that was only an excuse: it was she who had been a coward, living on with a ghost, afraid to say goodbye. What harm might she have done, to herself, to her family – to Ulysses? She must take him away from Cheyney, somehow, away from the whole horrible mess that she had made. (Briefly, she thought how ironic it was, that only three months earlier she could think of nothing but how to get him there.) When she could see him, it would be easy. They would talk, and everything would become perfectly straightforward. Or so she told herself, resolutely, trying to crush the causeless doubt that was eating away at her residual certainties.

'He's foreign, isn't he?' Glynis' voice came to her as if from a long way off.

Caroline said with deliberate vagueness: 'I suppose so.'

He came, at last, on the following Wednesday, at a moment when she wasn't expecting him. She had just washed her hair and it hung down her back, still damp, looking very thin and lanky. Her kimono, which dated from her Cambridge days, was second-hand and had a slight tear under one arm. Glynis had gone out a little while earlier leaving the television on, and Caroline had found herself horribly fascinated by the latest American family saga, the incredible villainy of the villain, the sexual energy of the hero (who, as far as she could gather, was sleeping with every woman in the series except his mother), the trembling lip and moist eye of the juvenile heroine. She switched off, telling herself that if she watched it once she might become regrettably addicted, and wondered what to make herself for supper. She felt so tired lately, it hardly seemed worth the bother; she didn't really want anything. But if she did not eat she would only feel even more tired the next day.

When the buzzer went, she wasn't thinking about Ulysses at all. As she got up to answer it, she had almost begun to ask herself who it might be. But she knew really, even before she opened the door; she had been very nearly sure he would come that night. She had washed her hair and stopped thinking about him, to make him come. Catching sight of her face, bare of make-up, in a small mirror on the wall, she saw it was pale and shadowed. The shampoo had stung her eyes and they were reddened as though with real tears.

He didn't say anything when he saw her. He just stood there, in the corridor, looking, she thought, a little unsure of himself, like a boy scout come to collect some jumble from the house of a notorious miser. He seemed paler, too, as though the ingrained tan from years of Mediterranean sun was at last beginning to fade in the chill English climate. For the past week she had been trying to imagine this moment, if he would hold her, kiss her, maybe say he loved her, if she would experience the same sinking, whirling vertigo of passion she had felt that day at Cheyney. But now the moment was here, he did not touch her, and all she said was, 'Hello' and 'Come in'. His face assumed the half-mocking, half-threatening look which she was beginning to identify as a sort of bravado. In the doorway, he moved, ostentatiously, so as to keep the space between them, and although she found the manoeuvre both calculated and disingenuous it made her intensely aware of his body, his nearness, the inevitable fact that sooner or later they would make love. Suddenly, she wanted very much for him to touch her.

'Would you like some coffee?'

He followed her into the kitchen, filling it up; she had not realised he was so big. Or perhaps it was simply that the kitchen was very small. Wherever she turned, he seemed to be in her way.

'Are you hungry?'

'No.'

The murmur of the kettle grew into the silence, until it permeated the whole room. Caroline stood staring out of the window, trying desperately to think of something to say. She could remember feeling similarly blank, years ago, in that awful moment when you first turn over the question paper for a particularly important exam. She had rehearsed how she would speak to him over and over again, in bed, on the loo, in rare slack moments at the office, varying it from cold practicality to impassioned vehemence, according to her mood. But in her daydreams, she had always refused to allow the thought of his physical presence to distract her. She hardly ever fantasised about sex.

'You look tired.' When he spoke, she was startled; somehow she had imagined all the pressure was on her.

'I'm all right,' she said hurriedly. Suddenly, she didn't want him to know how much she had worried, how much she had thought about him. She poured out the coffee, stirred it, handed him the mug. 'Let's go next door.'

In the living room, they sat at opposite ends of the sofa. 'You have a nice place here,' Ulysses remarked, looking round appreciatively.

It isn't very nice, thought Caroline. He has no taste. The furniture was upholstered in too many different shades of green and the chocolate brown carpet showed every speck of fluff (neither of the girls had much time for the vacuum cleaner). She had never realised, before she came to live here, that carpet-fluff was always pale in colour.

Aloud, she merely said: 'It isn't mine. The flat belongs to Glynis. I believe her parents bought it for her.'

'Why doesn't your father buy you a flat? He could afford it.'

'It isn't his business to buy me things,' Caroline snapped, thrown off balance. 'Why should he? Anyway,' she added bitterly, 'you know him better than I do. You tell me.' For a minute, horrified, she thought she was going to cry. Her throat tightened: she stood up, abruptly, and went over to the window as if to draw the curtains. 'We must talk this out,' she went on, when she hoped she had control over her voice. 'There's no point in just sitting here exchanging compliments. That afternoon, when Melissa came in, I suppose I must have been very upset. I didn't know what to say to her. She isn't very stable and I think I was afraid – I don't know what I was afraid of. Anyway, I didn't want a scene, not just then. I knew it wouldn't be good for her.'

'She would have loved it,' said Ulysses. 'She is that type. A little excitement in her life.'

'It wouldn't have been *good* for her,' Caroline repeated vehemently. 'You might at least *try* to be a little more understanding. You just haven't time for anyone who is plain and unattractive, have you?'

'No,' Ulysses replied frankly. 'I haven't. What has that to do with the present circumstances?'

'We are all human,' Caroline said, with a strange little shiver.

'That is very profound. And now what? Why don't you talk to *me*, instead of to those curtains? What are you really afraid of?'

She turned round, her back to the window, facing him. 'I am not afraid,' she said levelly. 'Not now.' How could she tell him what she feared? She had drunk from the well once before and her thirst did not abate. She feared to drink and drink and be forever thirsty; she feared still more the well that might quench her thirst. That thirst, unsatisfied, was the one enduring pleasure, the one unendurable pain: anticipation, longing, lust, love. . . 'You were right,' she said at last. 'I should never have asked you to lie for me, to debase yourself. I think, after Philip died, I was a little mad. We must end it. Soon. It is very wrong for any human being to use himself, to *be* used, in this way. I don't know what you want to do now. Perhaps it was just as well that Melissa came in when she did. Lately, I have wondered –'

'Yes?'

'I won't let you take me for payment, or for revenge, no matter how I used you. It wouldn't rectify anything. We have to stop all this before it goes too far – before we can't stop. My father will suffer: I intended that and I can't prevent it, even though I would if I could. But I don't want anyone else to be hurt. I don't know if you have slept with Melissa yet –'

'Of course not!' He sounded indignant. Too indignant?

138

'I'm sorry. Perhaps I was imagining things. It is very difficult to look at everything dispassionately, when I feel suddenly so – involved.' Her gaze travelled from the table to the book-case, from the book-case to the wall. A sketch of Glynis was hanging there, chalk and charcoal, done by a friend. Worse than Philip, Caroline thought, irrelevantly. She did not want to find herself looking at Ulysses.

'You have always been involved.' He had put down the coffee-mug and now he was standing up, coming towards her. 'You were involved in Greece, when you made yourself so charming, because you had a use for me. Then, there was only you and I. Now, it is only you and I again. Do you regret it?'

'It happened,' Caroline said, tightly. 'When something happens, you have to live with it. Why regret?'

'That is no answer.'

He had imprisoned her against the window, his hands gripping the sill on either side of her. It was an attitude, she thought, of self-asserting virility, uniquely masculine, out of date. Suddenly, it was easy to meet his eyes.

'Yes,' she said. 'I would regret it, if I could. But there's no point. I have wasted too much time, wanting the wrong things. I don't want to waste any more regretting them. I wanted my father's love, but he couldn't love me, he wasn't capable of it. I wanted Philip's love, but it was too much for him. And now, I suppose, I want you. I'm not sure that it's love, but I want you. I may come to regret it – I don't know; but at the moment it feels right. I can't hurt you; you haven't that kind of sensitivity. You might betray me but you won't withdraw from me, or kill yourself, or leave me alone. And – you want me, don't you?'

He did not answer her at once. His fingers were running up and down her spine, filling her with a strange, glad shuddering; he was smiling slightly. 'I always wanted you,' he said eventually. 'Only you.' And he added, blinded by the moment: 'I knew, in the end, you would want me.'

His body was pressed against hers, invading her with a warm unfamiliar sensation of longing and yielding, of weakness and strength. And, like all women, every time, she found herself thinking: This is the first time. This time, it will be

139

special. This means something. This time . . . this time . . .
this time . . .

That afternoon, Stephen Horvath was sitting in his surgery
at Cheyney, looking out at the garden. There was no one
waiting to see him, although it was only four o'clock. There
had been no one waiting to see him for the past half hour.
He knew he ought to go next door, tell the receptionist she
could leave early (not for the first time), maybe retire to his
study with something to read. But he didn't want to move,
not quite yet. Outside, the sunlight looked deceptively warm,
the garden green and spring-like: the forsythia and the
Japanese cherry were covered in blossom and there were even
a few celandines scattered across the lawn. He had an idea
Old Joe had delayed using the mower in order to leave them
there. He would have to speak to him about it. Someday.
   Ulysses had gone to catch his train shortly after lunch. 'I
want to see my friends – the people I stayed with in London,'
he explained, sullenly, as though he resented having to
explain at all. 'I don't know when I'll be back.'
   'Who are they? Why must you see them?' Jealousy was
stupid, Stephen knew that, destructive and unnecessary. But
he was quite sure Ulysses was lying.
   'I thought you were my lover, not my gaoler. Why should
I tell you everything? I am going to London to see my friends:
that is enough. If I wanted to leave, I would leave. Mind
your own business.'
   'You'll be back for dinner?'
   'No.'
   Stephen felt a sudden spasm of panic. 'Why not?'
   'Why – why – why? Stop asking me *why* all the time. You
sound like a little boy, snivelling because you are going to be
left alone. I want to eat Greek food and talk Greek and listen
to Greek music. I want to relax and enjoy myself. We don't
enjoy ourselves, you and I: we just fuck. I want to have a
good time for once. I shall eat too much and I shall get drunk
and I shall be back *very* very late. Goodbye!'
   On his way out, he had slammed the door, as a parting
gesture. It was a very convincing performance, Stephen
reflected irritably, his fingers fidgeting with the papers on his

140

desk. He was almost sure it was only a performance. He wondered suddenly if he was really meant to be convinced, if he was meant to worry about it, to lose what little appetite he had, to go to bed early and lie awake, trying not to speculate on what Ulysses might be doing. He thought sometimes Ulysses experienced a malicious satisfaction in tantalising him in this way. But he did not really resent it; how could he? It was an aspect of the inherent cruelty which he needed so badly. He would fulfil his part of the relationship, he knew, later that night, waiting, sleepless, for Ulysses to return. He could not help himself. But it was not necessary to think too much about it now. Probably, Ulysses had told him a half-truth: he would visit his so-called friends, and then meet someone else afterwards ('some other man,' whispered a sweet inner voice). The thought of Ulysses with someone else, perhaps doing the same things he had done to Stephen, filled him with a complicated loathing, with frustration, finally with desire. He found he was crumpling the blotting paper, very slowly, in one hand; he smoothed it out again and tried to replace it in the blotter, but it was too creased, and in the end he threw it away. If he did not think about it too clearly he supposed it was bearable, knowing Ulysses was unfaithful. You can bear anything, if you have to. And he had never thought fidelity was one of Ulysses' qualities.

There was a light tap on the door and the receptionist came in, bringing him a cup of tea. He did not really want it but he said, 'Thank you' and put it on one side. She didn't ask him if she could go early. She just stood there, unsmiling, attentive, demure Lady Di fringe, demure grey skirt. He called her Miss Robinson (he rather thought her Christian name was Jonquil or something like that). When he told her she might go, she thanked him only briefly. He heard her high heels tapping down the hall in search of her jacket. When they asked her why she stayed on he could imagine her shrugging, carelessly: 'It's a job.' But he did not seriously try to decipher her thought processes: the ordinariness of her mind was beyond him, or so he felt. Doubtless she disliked him; quite possibly she always had; it didn't matter. He had never expected very much from people and now he expected nothing. On the facing wall, Philip's painting spoke to him of failure, of how this room would look, when he had vacated it for ever: the ball of blotting paper in the waste-basket, the prescriptions unwritten, the celandines strewing the sunlit lawn outside. And suddenly, he knew that he didn't have to go at all. He only had to sit there, and gradually his skin would flake off, his veins would shrivel, the stuff of his body would wither away, and only his fleshless hands would remain, still crumpling at the blotting paper, and his naked skull grinning across the empty desk.

He had heard the front door close some time ago. He got up, slowly, as though with an effort, went into the kitchen and tipped his untouched tea down the sink. Mrs Bunce would be there later, but not yet. No one was home yet. In the dining room, he fumbled with the key to the cocktail cabinet and took out the bottle of cognac.

Ulysses got home shortly after midnight. The door to Stephen's study, which he usually kept locked, stood a little ajar, and a thin glimmer of light leaked into the hall. Ulysses pushed open the door and went in, only half believing the light had been left on by mistake. Stephen was sitting at his desk. Beside him, the adjustable desk lamp had been pulled right down to his elbow so that the light spilled out in a horizontal line across the neat piles of correspondence, the blank pads of paper. The shadow of the ink bottle stretched long and black across the virgin blotter. Stephen was sitting so close to the lamp the light reached his face from underneath, a latent glow that cast inverted shadows around his eyes and in the hollows of his temples. When Ulysses came in, those eyes were already fixed on him with a baleful, vacant gaze, as though he had been sitting there, waiting, staring at the door, all evening. Suddenly, Ulysses felt afraid. He was not accustomed to feel fear. Once or twice before, with Stephen, he had known a curious prickling of the nerves, but he had always been able to dismiss it, telling himself, practically, that he was young and strong, while Stephen was old, not yet feeble but weakening, weakening in body even as his confidence and self-control gradually failed. But this time his fear was too strong for reason, the fear of something mis-shapen and incomprehensible which he had always sensed in the darkness of Stephen's mind, the primitive, human fear of that which is against nature. Centuries ago his peasant ancestors, slaves of similar fears, had driven the deformed from their gates, and shrunken from the voice of the god, crying out in the storm. Who knows where such memories live on, deep in the subconscious, stirring at a whisper? Not two hours before, he had been with Caroline. The thought of her had filled him to the exclusion of all else. He reached for that thought like a talisman, but even as his mind closed upon it, it had dwindled away. He felt oppressed by the room itself, as though in the ranks of books, smelling of old age and decay – even as Stephen would smell, very soon, under his clothes – there was concealed some unnameable secret, some ancient spell written in creased black letters on a yellowed page, whose consummation was rottenness. He tried to think of something to say, something sane and ordinary ('It's late. Why did you sit up for me?'); but for those first few seconds his mind was totally blank.

'You've come back.' Stephen's voice dragged.

'Of course I have.'

There was another silence. Ulysses wondered if he looked guilty but it did not seem to matter any more. Presently, Stephen got to his feet. He moved a pile of letters, automatically, from one side of the blotter to the other. It was a movement that did not seem to have any particular significance. 'Good,' he said at last. 'I was getting tired of waiting. Let's go to bed.'

He switched off the lamp and came towards Ulysses in the darkness. Perhaps inadvertently, his footfalls made very little noise. Ulysses took a step backwards, into the doorway. 'I'm very tired,' he said, too quickly. 'I need to sleep.' Normally, he would have said: 'I want to sleep.' But he was shaken by his fear, by the dreary look in Stephen's eyes. When the other man touched him, he was infected, as always, by the anticipation of loathing, by a sense of revulsion that was almost voluptuous. He felt his bowels weakening, the muscles shrinking in his loins. Already, his fear was beginning to drain away, to be replaced by other, less wholesome, sensations. He reached for it, even as he had reached for the memory of Caroline, but it was too late. Feeling Stephen's hand, moving across his breast, he knew a sudden urge to kick him, to hurt him, to drive his fists into that soft pale body, to squeeze the bloodless flesh until it split like over-ripe fruit and a thin red juice spurted out. . . In a few minutes, he knew, he would do everything Stephen required. In spite of Caroline, in spite of his own self-disgust, he would do it and enjoy doing it. Anger filled him, all the more violent for being useless. In Stephen, he saw all the things that most repulsed him: old age, corruption, perversion – and he could not resist them. He felt no pity for him; Ulysses was without pity. But he knew now that his whoredom with Stephen was merely the darker side of his obsession for Caroline, and he would never be free of it.

'Perhaps,' Stephen murmured, 'you have a headache?'

'No.'

'Then come to bed.'

Caroline had planned to go to Cheyney on the Friday, two days later. On Thursday, Harry called her from his office in Birmingham. He had a long, complicated saga about his car, which had apparently broken down last time he was in London. Would she mind very much collecting it from the garage for him? He would be down on Tuesday and in the meantime perhaps she would like to make use of it herself. Caroline said of course she would collect it and added, with less effort than she expected, that if he didn't mind she might use it to drive herself down to Cheyney at the weekend. She had passed her test in Birmingham but she would not allow Harry to buy her a car and now, although she could probably afford to pay for one herself, it did not seem very practical in London. Harry said of course, of course she could, with real enthusiasm in his voice (Caroline hated real enthusiasm), and she rang off hastily. Afterwards, she worried for an hour that she had not been adequately polite. In Birmingham, Harry sat silent at his desk, disregarding two incoming calls from the Middle East, thinking a little wistfully how much easier it would be if his step-daughter did not have quite such beautiful manners.

On Friday afternoon, Caroline left work early and drove out of London in the lull before the rush hour. Beyond Croydon, she chose an A road, avoiding the motorway, so she could enjoy the countryside. This was her favourite route home. If she ever ran a car in London, she decided, it would be just so she could drive down to Cheyney this way, once in a while. Sunlight blurred with tree-shadows patched the road in front of her; clumps of primroses grew on the verge. Beyond the forest, there were broad spaces of wind and gorse, short grass, tall firs. Caroline drove briskly and well. She knew it was illogical to be so happy, but she could not help it. From today, there would be no more lies, no more repressed desires or suppressed tensions. She would probably have to face an unpleasant scene with her father (not that it would really be a *scene*; she could not imagine him permitting himself to shout at her), but after that she would be with Ulysses and somehow, she felt sure, everything would be all right. She found herself making all sorts of good resolutions: to be nicer to Melissa, to talk Dostoyevsky with her father, even to have lunch with Harry (he always asked her) when he came down to collect his car. After today, if she could only be happy for a while, like other girls, like Angela and Glynis, she would try to be a better person, more understanding, less intolerant. You can't make bargains with God, she told herself severely, endeavouring to restrain her own optimism; but it was impossible. The road wound more as she drove south; familiar hills rose on either side. The sun sank towards the horizon, lingering between the trees. Ulysses had promised to tell her father the truth that afternoon, before she arrived. 'It is better that I speak to him alone,' he had said. 'If you were there, it would be too cruel. I will tell him only what is necessary: that I love you and it's over. The rest is unimportant.' She had agreed to that, surprised, as always, by one of his rare flashes of sensitivity. But she would not stay in London, out of the way. To avoid the inevitable meeting with her father would be an act of cowardice, a denial of responsibility. Caroline hoped she had never tried to shirk her responsibilities.

She reached Cheyney around half past six. Outside the house, she parked the car, locked it, carefully refrained from ascending the front steps at a run. Somewhere, she remembered having read something about the danger of walking into trouble with a light heart. Opening the door with her own key, she was reminded of her first visit to this house, and the boxer dog which had come out to meet her, barking. She didn't know why the recollection of that moment should

145

affect her so much. The dog was dead now, of course; it had died of cancer, years ago. . .

In the hall, the first thing that struck her was the quiet. She had not expected it to be quiet. Normally, it was a silent house, but this time, there should have been noises, voices raised or lowered, a hasty footstep, a slammed door. She hesitated for a moment, then called out, a little uncertainly.

'Hello?'

Ulysses appeared on the stairs so suddenly she wondered if he had been waiting on the landing.

'Have you spoken to my father? Where is he? I think I ought to – '

As he drew nearer, she saw that he was very pale. She had never seen him so pale. His face was almost grey.

He said, jerkily: 'You can't see him.'

'Why not?'

'You just can't. It's better not. You must listen to me. We must talk first. No, not in there – not there. Come upstairs, and we'll talk. Please, Caroline –'

The door to the living room was open a little way and Caroline moved instinctively towards it. She did not know what could have gone wrong, but she wanted to see her father *now*, to straighten things out, to say whatever had to be said. There was no point in putting it off.

'Not in there! You mustn't go in there. He's –'

Ulysses got between her and the door, but she thrust him aside easily, despite her bewilderment, as though it was she who was the stronger. The door rasped over the carpet as she went in.

At first, she thought her father wasn't there. Then she saw the huddle on the floor in front of the fireplace: an oddly small huddle for such a tall man. There was a moment when the whole universe shifted, just a fraction, and when it was still again the very sky was a different colour. He must have fallen, she thought stupidly. He must have fallen and knocked himself out. Why doesn't Ulysses call an ambulance?

She was on her knees beside him, feeling for his wrist. But she knew, even before she knelt down, even before she touched him, that he was dead.

146

PART 3

ULYSSES

13

She had never seen a dead body before. She found herself thinking stupidly, of a line she had once seen, carved on a gravestone. 'He is not dead, but sleeping.' REQUIESCAT IN PACE. The hand she held was still warm, but she knew this was not sleep; even in a room full of sleepers she would have known the difference. There was nothing there. No thoughts, no dreams, nothing. Suddenly, she felt she understood how they could bury people in mass graves, in war-time, like debris. This was only debris. She could hardly believe it had ever been a human being at all. He's gone, she thought: he doesn't live here any more. It seemed the height of absurdity to build pyramids and tombs, to cushion wooden coffins, to sing loud hymns and squander expensive flowers, all for a little mortal compost. Put it in a furnace and forget it. Garbage. There was blood on the back of his head, on his collar; a pool of blood soaking into the carpet. She did not want to look any closer, but she made herself do so. In his hair, there was a kind of pulpy mess where the base of his skull should have been: she thought she could see a white splinter of bone sticking out. . . Presently, she realised she was still holding his hand. She replaced it on the floor, very carefully, feeling somehow that it was important to show respect and consideration for this dead thing just because she felt none. Then she saw the poker.

It was lying on the floor a little way from the body, the heavy brass-handled poker that always hung beside the fireplace. For a few moments Caroline stared at it, blankly, unable to drag her eyes away. She could not seem to think at all. As far as she knew the poker had never been used, never moved before except for dusting. Her father had not liked open fires. He liked big marble fireplaces, the sigh of the wind in the chimney, bellows and firedogs, but he said actual fires were untidy, leaving smoke-stains and ash, rendered obsolete by the invention of central heating. The brass gleamed, pristine: Caroline found herself thinking how well it would retain fingerprints. Looking round, she saw Ulysses was still standing in the doorway, watching her, an expression on his face, both intent and uncertain, which she could not interpret, although she knew it was imperative that she should. He did not come into the room; she thought perhaps he was afraid to.

'*What have you done to him?*'

As soon as the words were out she knew she had made a fatal mistake. He did not seem to move but she sensed him flinch, inwardly, from the implicit accusation. No matter what had happened, no matter what might happen, he would never be able to forget – *she* would never be able to forget – that first instinctive assumption. She thought of trying to say she was sorry, that wasn't what she had meant, although she knew it would not do any good, but, meeting his eyes, the impulse died.

'It was an accident,' he said, too quickly. 'He tried to hit me with the poker. I pushed him, and he fell. I didn't mean to hurt him – he must have hit his head. When I turned him over it was all blood.'

As his words sank in, Caroline was conscious of an enormous sense of relief, out of all proportion to the circumstances. It was as though huge, unspoken fears had suddenly been allayed without ever having to be put into speech or thought. She should have noticed – surely, she *had* noticed – that there was no blood on the poker. The corner of the marble mantelpiece above the fireplace was smeared with something dark, but this time, she did not feel she had to look too closely. She could imagine the forensic specialist picking through it with a tiny pair of forceps: fragments of skin and hair, skull chips, cerebral matter. . . She had once seen sheep's brains frying in a pan, a pale, pinkish-grey pulp. She closed her lips very tightly for a moment and tried to think of something else.

'I told you not to come in,' Ulysses said presently. It seemed to her the stupidest remark she had ever heard.

'Of course I came in.' Her voice was curt. 'Someone had

150

to find him. Thank God it was only me.' She did not usually refer to God, even in the most casual way, but this time, she found she meant it. 'Why didn't you call an ambulance?'

'He was dead. It was no good. I told you, I saw his *head* –'

'Did you feel for his pulse?'

'N-no.'

Caroline got to her feet, her face closed. Ulysses, unsure of what she was thinking, found he could almost hear his own heartbeat. 'Tell me what happened,' she said at last. 'Tell me again. Slowly.'

'He tried to hit me with the poker. He –'

'Why?'

'We had an argument.'

She thought of her father's inflexible beauty, his chill dispassionate gaze. The archangel Gabriel in a smart black suit, officiating, unmoved, at the funeral of his son. She could not imagine him, red-eyed or loud-voiced with unaccustomed temper, reaching for the poker, raising it to strike – then she remembered the shadows round his eyes, the suggestion of snapped tension behind his face. Who knew what he might not do?

'What did you argue about?'

Ulysses almost shrugged. 'What do you think?'

'I see.' It came out in a whisper. Ulysses realised, only half understanding, that she felt herself in some way to blame; but he made no attempt to dispel this illusion. For a moment, she did not look at him; then she raised her eyes to his face. There was something in their expression that was both compelling and intensely painful. 'When they ask you,' she said, 'you mustn't say that. You mustn't mention me at all. If they knew about us, they might think –' She broke off.

Into the silence, Ulysses asked: '*They*?'

'The police.'

'I don't want the police!' His vehemence shocked her. She had been brought up to respect the police; they were honest, incorruptible, on the side of Right, slow maybe but invariably sure. It was a few seconds before she recollected that Ulysses had lived for a while under a military junta, had seen, possibly, both brutality and graft. 'The police are stupid,' he said. 'They will say I did this thing deliberately. Because I am a foreigner – a homosexual – I must be a murderer too. That is the British mind. They will put me in prison for many years – perhaps for life. I could not bear that. It is better that I go away. I have friends who will help me. You can talk to the police when I am gone.'

'No.' She must stop him, must make him see that to run would be fatal. She was standing in front of him now and she took his hands: in spite of his strength she was conscious of being stronger, far stronger, as though the force of her own will could mould him like clay. She began to explain what would happen if he tried to run: the ports and airports watched, his picture in every newspaper, on every station, the utter impossibility of a final escape. 'No one gets away like that,' she told him. 'Only with an organisation behind them – the IRA or something – and not often then. And when you were caught, it would be much harder to convince people what really happened. Running away is like an admission of guilt. If you stay, you may have to go to court – I don't know – but everything will be all right in the end. This is England. We don't put people in prison for something they haven't done.'

'I have heard of cases –'

Caroline shook her head, impatiently. 'Maybe once in ten years. Even in the best system people can make mistakes. But this is all perfectly straightforward. They'll find my father's fingerprints on the poker – they'll see the blood on the mantel-piece. All you have to do is tell the truth. There isn't any *reason* why you should have done it on purpose.'

'As long as they don't know about us?'

Yes. Her mouth shaped the word, but no sound came out. She said it again, louder: 'Yes.' Too loud.

Suddenly, Ulysses smiled, a glittering cruel smile that somehow caricatured the smile that had first drawn her to him, in the beachside bar nearly two years ago. Or perhaps the smile was unchanged, but now she knew what it meant. 'As usual,' he said, 'I am the one who gets my hands dirty.'

You did it, she wanted to say. You killed him. Not me. I didn't plan that. But she didn't say it. Perhaps she knew it would be unforgiveable; perhaps, even in her mind, the protest sounded hollow. Presently, she went on: 'They'll want

152

to know why you quarrelled. We ought to think of something. . .'

The smile lingered. 'It was an old quarrel,' Ulysses said. 'We had had it before many times. He was ashamed of me – he treated me like a prostitute. I said I would leave. I said he was an old man, an ugly old man, and I would find someone younger and sexier who would treat me properly. Perhaps my pride was hurt – we have pride, we Greeks, although it is not the same as your cold English pride which holds up its nose at the smell of shit.'

Sound and fury, thought Caroline, disregarding the bitterness in his voice. She said: 'So he tried to hit you, and you pushed him?'

'Yes.'

'You must have pushed very hard,' she said slowly, 'for him to hit his head like that.'

There was a short silence. 'Maybe,' Ulysses answered at last. 'I don't know. Perhaps he tripped over.' A little way from the body there was a low stool, barely calf-height, with wooden legs clasped in crocodile's feet. 'I remember,' he went on, evidently concentrating, 'when I knelt down to look at him, I picked up that stool. He must have fallen over it. He–'

'Why did you pick it up?'

'I suppose – it looked untidy. I don't know. At times like that, you *don't* know why you do things. I was very upset. . .'

'Of course you were.' He didn't, she thought, look quite so pale now, though the light was failing and it was difficult to tell. She saw him glance involuntarily towards the body; his eyes were empty and colourless like bits of glass. Somehow, she had almost forgotten the body. In a minute, she would have to call the police. Supposing someone had seen her arrive, fifteen, twenty minutes ago, half an hour, half an age. . . 'When you saw he was dead, what did you do next?'

'I didn't know what to do. I wanted to think. I went to my room and sat on the bed. Then you came. I don't know how long it was.'

'You must have been in shock,' she said, vaguely relieved. 'You need a doctor. I'm going to 'phone the police. We can't wait any longer.' Suddenly, she remembered something. 'Where's Melissa?' An afterthought, as always.

'Out. I'm not sure. She was here at lunch.'

At least she isn't here now, Caroline thought. She hoped fervently that just for once Melissa would not demonstrate her usual irritating flair for turning up whenever she was least expected or wanted. Not that they had anything to conceal, of course; it was merely that she did not feel she could cope with her step-sister just now. In the hall, she went to the telephone. It was a moment or two before she could think of what to dial. She had an idea Ulysses had gone into the room after her, drawn by she knew not what obscure fascination of death, but when she glanced round he was still standing in the doorway. He watched her playing with the flex, picking up the codebook and putting it down again. The 'phone rang only twice before someone answered. 'There's been an accident,' she heard herself saying, in the flat, cold voice of rigid self-command. 'My father. Horvath. Cheyney House, the Avenue, Cheyney. No, it's too late. I'm quite sure he's dead. . .'

There was very little time before the police arrived. Caroline and Ulysses stood in the hall, looking at each other, not saying anything. She took his hand and thought it felt almost as slack as the hand of the corpse, though far warmer. When they heard the sirens his fingers tightened abruptly round hers, so that she almost cried out: she had not realised how strong he was. After a few moments he released her. 'You'd better wait in the kitchen,' she said. She wanted to wish him luck but knew it would sound schoolgirlish and inadequate. There was another long moment when they faced each other and she thought he was going to say something, something vital and even terrible, but he turned away. She went to the front door and opened it, retaining the handle as though for support, so that the police would see her, standing there, waiting for them, as they came up the steps.

Caroline could never really remember what happened after that. They took Ulysses away quite soon and she was left sitting in the kitchen, wishing someone would tell her what was going on. She did not even known if Ulysses had been arrested or not. A policewoman made her some tea but it was too strong and very bitter: Caroline turned the cup round and round between her hands and let it grow cold. Once, looking into the hall, she saw they were bringing out the body. How small he looks, she thought again; why do the dead always look so small? It was impossible to believe that child-sized bulge under the sheet was really over six foot. Perhaps it was the living personality which accounted for size, size as others perceive it, and without that personality the body shrank in upon itself like an envelope when the letter has been removed. Philip's coffin, she remembered, had seemed ludicrously small to contain all that length of limb. She had had a nightmare, once, in which they cut off his feet, like Procrustes, to make him fit. But Philip's body had been shrivelled in the fire. . . Behind her, the policewoman said: 'You haven't drunk your tea.' Caroline murmured something noncommittal, swallowed a mouthful, stone-cold, and put the cup in the sink. She saw the policewoman was looking at her with dislike, saying to herself, perhaps: Snooty bitch, who does she think she is? What's wrong with my tea? But Caroline could not summon enough energy to mollify her, or to care about the incident at all. Later, the police surgeon looked in on her, and prescribed brandy. He fetched the bottle of cognac from the dining room; it was very nearly empty, Caroline saw: just enough for one glass. She wondered how you would breathalyse a corpse. The doctor poured the liquid into a convenient tumbler, and she found herself thinking how much it would have distressed her father, seeing her drinking his best cognac from the wrong type of glass.

'I don't really want anything,' she said, but nobody listened.

'You've had a shock,' the doctor explained, rather unnecessarily. He thought about patting her shoulder but the cool, distant expression on her face daunted him.

Caroline said: 'I am not shocked.'

The worst thing, she decided afterwards, was having to telephone her mother. Even now, she was not entirely sure that Margaret had ever realised the truth. She knew her mother was less fastidious than herself, but she could not help imagining the humiliation of that knowledge, feeling it as she would have felt, horribly degraded by the pity and interest of all her acquaintance. She pictured Harry, the proverbial

155

bull in a china shop, saying all the wrong things, treading heavily on feelings too delicate for expression. And the press. . . Of course, she thought stupidly, it'll be in all the papers. Folly to imagine she could protect the innocence of a middle-aged woman, in these days when the media bring every massacre into the home. Tomorrow, perhaps, her own family – she herself – would be there in blaring headlines, with the usual blurred photographs, thankfully unrecognisable, the gleeful reactions of Horror – Sensation – Outrage. She knew it ought to make her angry, but it was difficult, as yet, to believe in such a fantastic reality.

At the other end of the line, she heard her mother's voice: 'I'll come down right away. I'll take the next train. Just hold on, darling. Everything will be all right. . .'

The inanities of reassurance, thought Caroline. She said very carefully: 'You don't have to come. It really isn't necessary. I'd – I'd rather you didn't come.'

'But Carla –'

'Please, Mummy. I can manage.'

'Perhaps Harry –'

'*No!*'

She hadn't meant to shout. She sensed her mother's distress, even at long distance, and the startled, curious stares of the other people in the hall. She was over-reacting, she knew; but in a momentary blankness she could think of nothing to say that would nullify the effect of that instant's self-betrayal. 'It's not that I don't want him,' she lied, desperately. 'It's just – you must see how unsuitable it would be. Your present husband at the funeral of your ex-husband. It's – it's indecent. Anyway, I don't need anyone. Really I don't. I can cope with everything.' She hoped she could. 'It would only make it more difficult, if either of you were here.'

'Well, if you're quite sure.' Her mother had forgotten, Caroline noted, to ask about Melissa. Like everyone else. 'I do feel one of us ought to be with you, but. . .'

'No, Mummy. I'd much rather not. You'd only be upset.' She went on, picking her words: 'Father had changed a lot lately. He really wasn't himself. I suppose – he must have been under a lot of pressure.' She stopped, unable to continue without becoming painfully explicit, and in the pause that ensued she could imagine Margaret thinking.

'How did it happen?'

'An accident. I'm not sure.' She mustn't seem too well-informed. 'Ulysses – the au pair – was a bit incoherent. I think it must have been an accident.' Did her mother understand, beneath all the careful euphemisms, what had really been going on?

'You don't suppose he might have, well, tried to take something?' Margaret's voice held the very special brand of suspicion which she reserved for foreign young men.

'I shouldn't think so.' Impossible to leap to Ulysses' defence. 'I don't know. I must go now, Mummy. Try not to worry. I'll call you tomorrow.'

Afterwards, they took her to the police station. It was necessary to get a statement, they explained. No, they didn't know how long it would take. Caroline was anxious in case Melissa should come in while she was out, but the police-woman who had made the tea said she would be there to look after her. Caroline decided she must have imagined the woman's curt manner and air of indifference. She wanted to wait but the sergeant in charge (she thought he was a sergeant) insisted and she could only hope that Melissa, if she returned, would not be too drunk or stoned, or too ready to consider herself abandoned.

Outside, she was surprised to see so many people, unnecessary people who did not seem to be doing anything in particular, just standing about and staring. Neighbours, she supposed, or curious passers-by, who let their suppers grow cold while they gaped and wondered. She did not recognise any of them, but then, Dr Horvath had not been on very intimate terms with the other people in the Avenue. To be too friendly with your neighbours, he maintained, was at best a bore, at worst a disaster, since they were always popping round to borrow something you had not got, or lend you something you did not want, and once there they invariably stayed, drank your liquor or your tea, and showed you their holiday photographs. The best kind of friends were at least a short car journey away. Stephen was civil to his neighbours, but a little distant, and Caroline could not even remember their names. Looking round at the pale faces, the eyes that flickered away from hers, she found she was quite glad.

At the police station, they showed her to a small room with

157

very little furniture and brought her some more tea. This time, it was too weak, a thin, milkless liquid, yellowish in colour and not particularly warm. But the constable who brought it had acne and she did not have the heart to refuse. The light – the sort of strip-lighting common to all public buildings – was beginning to give her a headache. She would have liked some aspirin but she did not want to make a fuss or draw attention to herself. The constable stayed with her, standing just inside the door, his gazed fixed politely on the far wall, and she could not help thinking how little the harsh light flattered his acne, and wondering whether she should suggest that stuff Philip used, only she could not remember what it was called. She tried to picture his face, if she started talking about remedies for acne. Perhaps he would not be very surprised. Perhaps people often behaved like that, in moments of stress, fixing their minds on small, irrelevant details in order to keep themselves sane. Like Ulysses, picking up the stool because he thought it looked untidy. (Thank God he hadn't tidied up the poker as well.) 'I suppose, ' she reflected, 'I must be in a state of shock after all.'

About twenty minutes later the inspector came in. She knew he must be an inspector because the constable had mentioned it, when he brought the tea: 'The inspector says he will be with you shortly.' He was a tall, gaunt-looking man of indeterminate age, skull-faced, with thinnish, fairish hair scraped back from a high forehead, and steel-rimmed glasses. He wore no uniform and his coat hung loosely from his wide, fleshless shoulders like something on a coat-hanger. He shook hands with Caroline, but so briefly that she was scarcely aware of his grip before he had released her. 'Inspector Moyse,' he said. 'Sorry to keep you waiting.' He had an attractive, cadaverous voice, or so Caroline described it to herself, soft but with a hollow note in it, somewhere at the back: the kind of voice you might expect from a ghost with a sense of humour. When he took off his glasses she saw his eyes were hooded, the lids thin to transparency and creased with veins. The irises were a faded brown, the colour of parchment, holding little in the way of expression save a polite disinterest. For no specific reason, Caroline was conscious of relief.

The interview began easily enough. Caroline, uncomfortably aware of the one vital omission in her evidence, had half expected to be racked with guilt, to feel question after question probing her conscience until she was reduced to rigid monosyllables. But the inspector's manner was gentle, even sympathetic, and if there was a question she could not answer it did not appear to matter. Gradually, she began to feel that anything she had left out was not really relevant anyway. 'Contrary to popular belief,' the inspector remarked, 'we are more interested in getting at the truth than in making dramatic arrests for horrendous crimes which have probably never been committed. Fortunately, in this country we have very few horrendous crimes. . . By the way, I don't think you mentioned, was your father expecting you?'

For a fraction of a second, Caroline was unnerved. But Inspector Moyse was not looking at her: he was watching the constable, laboriously writing everything down in longhand. She took her time before answering. 'No, he wasn't,' she said at last. The temptation to tell a very minor lie, to make the circumstances look more natural, was almost irresistible; but she refrained. It would be too easy to lie. 'I only came on an impulse,' she explained. 'I had my stepfather's car for a few days, and – well – I thought it would be nice to get away. I don't much like London at weekends.'

'Did you often come down without calling your father?'

'Not usually.' She knew it was essential to stay calm, not to betray tension – not to *feel* tension. The inspector looked mildly intrigued, as though surprised at such casual behaviour. She made herself relax, very slowly, muscle by muscle, as she had learnt in yoga classes at college. 'You see,' she said, stumbling over her words, hoping the inspector would think her embarrassment perfectly natural, 'things weren't very comfortable at home these last few months. I've been frightfully worried about my sister – she's at a difficult age and she needs emotional security. I know my father wouldn't want me to come but I thought if I could get down here I – I might be able to talk to him.' She smiled, a little painfully. 'Silly, really. I've never been able to talk to him before. Only the sun was shining and suddenly everything looked easy. You know how it is when the sun shines.' (After all, she told herself, it's nearly the truth. As if nearly was any good.)

159

The inspector nodded. 'I only asked,' he explained, 'because your father seems to have given Mrs Bunce the evening off, and that would have been rather odd if he was expecting you. I understand Mrs Bunce comes in most days to cook the evening meal.'

Caroline had forgotten Mrs Bunce. She murmured, 'Yes' rather faintly and met the inspector's placid gaze as best she could. Thank God she had stayed so close to the facts. It occurred to her that she seemed to be thanking God rather a lot this evening, though she had rarely troubled to exchange a word with him in the past. Perhaps that was why so many religions were obsessed with sin: it was only the really sinful people who had any need of divine assistance. The good people, the people who didn't tell lies, who didn't attempt to salve their consciences with mere 'omissions', they could afford the luxury of atheism. At this point, she decided there was something badly wrong with her line of reasoning; but Inspector Moyse was talking again and there was no more time to think about it.

As the interview progressed, she was not sure if the questions got harder or if it was just that she found it more difficult to answer them. Perhaps she was growing tired; certainly her headache had worsened. She had to be constantly on the watch for sly, unobtrusive little queries which, if wrongly answered, would lead her into impossible mazes of reluctant deception. But Inspector Moyse did not look sly. He looked like a vaguely sympathetic person, friendly enough but not too friendly, the kind of person with whom she would have liked to feel she was being honest. When he smiled, she noticed, one side of his mouth lifted a little higher than the other, making a completely different set of wrinkles. She could see the lines all over his face, fine-drawn lines of amusement, of tolerance, of thought. She was reminded of her father, who never smiled, and whose lines were the stigmata of disintegration. Suddenly, she wished passionately that she had nothing to hide; that she could respond to every question without having to think at all; that she could go home, cry a little, after the manner of bereaved daughters, and sleep off her troubles. But of course, if she had nothing to hide she would not be there. None of it would have happened. For a moment, the enormous responsibility left her stunned: she could almost

160

have stood up and proclaimed, recklessly: I am a criminal; his blood is on my hands; arrest me. Melodrama. She told herself that if he had made up his mind to hit Ulysses with a poker, one reason would doubtless have done as well as another. And if not Ulysses, someone else. He was at the age when men go off the rails, or so she had heard. The male menopause. It was stupid to feel she was committing a crime, merely because she wished to avoid a lot of hideous publicity and unnecessary fuss.

'Was your father always a violent-tempered man, Miss Horvath?' Inspector Moyse echoed her thoughts.

Caroline considered for a minute, or seemed to. 'I'm not sure. I don't think I ever knew him very well. He had a lot of self-control but perhaps there were things going on underneath which I didn't see. I wasn't a very observant child. Once, I remember hearing him quarrel with Ursula – Melissa's mother – after we were all in bed. We – Phil, Melissa, and I, I mean. I heard crockery smashing, too.' (Suddenly, she wondered who *had* broken the Dartington glasses.) 'But he would never have let himself go when we were there. He was a very not-in-front-of-the-children sort of father.'

'Until just lately.'

It was not a question, but Caroline answered. 'I am not a child any more, inspector. And –' she voiced her thoughts '– my father was at a difficult age. I believe the psychiatrists say that's when people – break out.'

'So you never actually *saw* your father being violent?' the inspector murmured.

'No.'

'In fact –' a leisurely aside '– it could quite well have been Ulysses who initiated the assault?'

But here, Caroline felt on safe ground. 'I should have thought,' she said, very sweetly, 'the forensic experts could tell you who hit who with what.'

There was a short silence while Inspector Moyse studied a crack in the ceiling and the constable, who was now scribbling frantically, endeavoured to catch up. 'You are a very unusual young woman, Miss Horvath,' the inspector remarked, with a flicker of his lop-sided smile. 'Most people, in your place, would have been furiously vindictive, bristling with British prejudice, only too eager to cast the blame for anything and everything on the foreigner, the alien, the – er, dago in the woodpile. Yet you seem quite happy to exonerate him, even to apportion blame elsewhere. I find that very interesting.'

'I have always tried to be honest,' Caroline said, unhappily. 'With – with myself and others. You see –' she hesitated, just for a second, unsure of how to go on, but the words came to her as simply as truth '– at first, when I found out, I *did* feel all those things. I hope I wasn't vindictive, but I was shocked, and angry, and I suppose I blamed Ulysses much more than my father. I'd known he was a homosexual since I was sixteen, but I'd never actually *seen* it before. Not – not that he and Ulysses ever kissed or anything,' she added hastily, 'at least, not when Melissa and I were there. But I thought it was shameful and – well, as you say, it's easier to blame the stranger. Then I talked to Ulysses for a bit and although I didn't like him I couldn't really hate him either. There isn't anything there to hate. He's just greedy and indolent and rather shallow. He must be about my age, I imagine, but he seems very ignorant and I couldn't help feeling my father had taken advantage of that. After all, he – my father – was a highly intelligent, fastidious sort of person, and I thought he was behaving very irresponsibly. Particularly with Melissa still living at home. . . Anyhow, by the time I drove down – today – I was beginning to be angry with my father instead. And then I found him dead.' She gave a queer little shiver which was not entirely simulated. 'It's funny, but when something like that happens – death – you see everything quite differently. Suddenly, I didn't feel angry any more, just sorry. To go through life for so long without happiness or satisfaction. . . He looked so pitiful, too, lying there. Sort of shrunken. You can't be angry with the dead.'

'And Mr Stavrakis? Were you sorry for him too?'

'He looked *grey*,' Caroline said, after a pause (it took her a moment or two to work out who he meant). 'He must have been in shock. He couldn't really tell me what had happened. I think,' she added, rather diffidently, 'he's a little frightened of the police. I daresay the Greek police are a bit different.'

'I daresay,' said the inspector, so drily that Caroline wondered, in a moment of panic, whether Ulysses had a record, or whether the inspector merely thought he did.

'What will you do with him?' she asked presently, trying to keep the fear out of her voice.

'He'll be charged – remanded in custody – committed. The usual procedure. Violent death always makes a lot of work, I'm afraid, even if the circumstances are fairly straight-forward.' Caroline longed to know if these circumstances *were* straightforward, but she had decided it would be better not to ask too many questions. 'By the way,' the inspector was saying, 'I'd like to talk to your sister. I'll be round in the morning. I hope she's good at getting up early. And I shall probably want another word with you some time.'

Caroline said: 'Of course,' meaning to sound helpful and obliging, but it came out in a whisper.

Her statement was read back to her and she found herself wondering if she had really said all those stupid things, and thinking how unconvincing it sounded, in the policeman's flat monotone. She signed it, carefully, and was glad to find her hand did not shake. There was one question which she still had to ask, no matter what the inspector might think. She looked up from the paper and involuntarily met his eyes. 'What are you charging him with?' she said without preamble. There was no need to explain who she meant by 'him'. There was no need to explain anything. With a simplicity born of desperation, she added: 'I must know.'

The inspector arched an eyebrow in faint surprise.

'Murder,' he said.

14

It was dark when Caroline finally emerged from the police station. She had no idea of the time and was vaguely surprised to learn it was just gone half past ten: less than five hours since she reached Cheyney. It was as though she had slipped, unnoticing, into another dimension, an alternative existence, and even now the original Caroline was driving back to London with Ulysses, leaving her father sitting alone in his study, a book of contemplative verse unopened before him. 'Like a long-legged fly upon a stream, his mind moved upon silence. . .' Only his mind did not move, she realised, it merely planed, drifting in a void of air like a bird with still wings, like a leaf, falling, on a windless day. Whatever happened, she told herself, he would have died. He began killing himself long ago. Ulysses only held the sword; he fell upon it. As for her, she had won the struggle he lost, whether she wanted to or not, and now it was for her to bury him. The squad car pulled up outside her house even as she reached this point in her thoughts; the front door was open and she could see the same policewoman standing in the hall. 'Your sister is home,' she told Caroline. 'I made her some tea.' Her voice was definitely unenthusiastic. I haven't won anything, Caroline decided, feeling the eyes of the law following her into the kitchen. Nobody has won. We will all have lost in the end. . .

Melissa was sitting at the kitchen table, dribbling tea into an ashtray and pushing the floating cigarette-ends around with a careful finger. She wouldn't say anything until the police had gone. 'You're stoned out of your mind,' Caroline remarked, with a lassitude born of tiredness. She knew she disapproved but she couldn't *feel* disapproval any more.

Melissa nodded. 'I didn't tell them anything,' she said. 'The pigs, I mean. Duncan says you must never tell them anything. Then there's nothing they can get you for.'

'Nothing for which they can get you,' Caroline corrected absent-mindedly.

'They said,' Melissa went on, 'they said Father had had an accident. They said he was dead. I thought perhaps they were just pretending. To make me talk,' she added, by way of an explanation.

'No,' said Caroline.

There was a long silence while Melissa appeared to digest this. 'D'you mean,' she said at last, 'he really is – *dead*?' And then, seeing the answer in Caroline's face, she repeated, bewildered: 'Dead. Dead. Dead. . .'

She went on repeating it for some time.

'You ought to go to bed now,' Caroline said, as gently as

she could. 'There's no need to worry about anything. I'll look after you.'

Melissa's ugly little mouth, grown uglier from habitual expression, wrinkled up into a kind of defiant sneer. 'I'm glad he's dead,' she said. 'I hated him.'

Dramatising herself, thought Caroline. Like Philip. It seemed so strange that they weren't related. They both belonged to that section of humanity which always gave up, which was determined to give up, to wither in a slight frost, to drown in a wavelet. It was she who was the odd one out, the one with strength and stability, the survivor. Perhaps she had inherited something from her father, some element of his cold, abnormal force, while Philip and Melissa bore only a fatal germ of weakness from the distaff side. She did not like the thought of owing her father anything, but for some reason it never occurred to her that it might be her mother she resembled.

'You didn't really hate him,' she told Melissa. 'You only wanted to.' Like me.

'I *hated* him,' Melissa reiterated, as though reiteration would make it true. 'Are you going to tell me it's wrong to hate your father?'

'It's wrong to hate anybody.'

'He was a shitty father.'

'Yes,' Caroline admitted, impressed, perhaps because of exhaustion, by the simple truth of this statement. 'It doesn't make any difference, though. Hating someone – wanting revenge – is always mad, always futile. When you look back, you can see it wasn't real. The thought processes of insanity never are. You'll feel differently when you're sober. Would you like some Ovaltine before you go to bed?'

'There isn't any Ovaltine,' Melissa said smugly.

'Cocoa, then.'

An ungracious shrug. 'All right.'

When the cocoa was made Melissa let it stand and then complained about the skin. 'You really must try to get some sleep,' Caroline said, striving not to lose patience. 'There's an inspector coming to see you in the morning. He said he'd be round quite early. I assume he wants to take a statement.'

'Pig,' said Melissa, alluding, presumably to the policeman.

And then: 'Why does he want to talk to *me*? I wasn't even there.'

But Caroline was too tired for long explanations. 'I don't know,' she said.

In the small hours, Caroline started out of a restless dream to find Melissa standing beside her bed. She looked white-faced and very sober. It might have been mascara smeared under her eyes, it might have been natural shadows, but her small face looked haggard and horribly old.

'Sit down,' Caroline said, moving over. 'What is it?'

Melissa mumbled something and began to unpick the hem of her nightshirt. Caroline noticed quite a lot of it had been unpicked already.

'Would you like to get into bed with me?'

Her sister climbed in without a word. She was shivering and her thin legs felt clammy; Caroline wanted to draw away but she knew Melissa would be hurt. It was important not to hurt her, not to withdraw, to respond to her unhappy, resentful demands with at least the semblance of affection. She did not love Melissa and she knew Melissa did not love her, but she felt committed by her newfound responsibilities, by her own unlove; she even dwelt for a few moments on the idea of caring for her sister, selflessly, or as selflessly as possible, expecting (and receiving) nothing in return, as a kind of atonement for her past errors. Suddenly, uncomfortably, she wondered if she was beginning to enjoy the sweets of unappreciated martyrdom. She reminded herself that Melissa's mother was long dead and her late stepfather indifferent, that she had little charm or talent, few friends, no job. Caroline herself, on the other hand, was both talented and passably charming, with a good job, friends, a mother who loved her and a stepfather who was determined to exceed his stepfatherly obligations. What merit could there be in caring for Melissa, she told herself savagely, when she had so much, and her sister so pitiably little?

Beside her, Melissa lay motionless, acutely conscious of Caroline's proximity, her unspoken withdrawal. She wondered if she could be a lesbian, she wanted so badly for Caroline to touch her. Not an accidental touch but something deliberate and tender. She was afraid to move closer in case Caroline should somehow suspect, but she could not relax, and she shivered continuously despite the blankets. She began to hate Caroline for her stillness, for the inadequacy of her response, an old hatred based on old jealousies, imagined affronts, a miscellany of trivial incidents. Duncan, she knew, would say Caroline was regrettably bourgeoise, the conventional product of soft middle-class living. But Duncan wasn't there, and her very hatred only aggravated the bitterness and intensity of her need.

They lay for a while in silence, scarcely touching, each dwelling on her own private cause for pain. Presently, Melissa said: 'How did he die?'

The question was so abrupt, so unconnected with her previous train of thought, that Caroline was startled. She had not been considering the details of her father's death, only the consequences of it, her own culpability, her sister's dependence. She did not answer immediately, and Melissa went on: 'The policewoman said there'd been a fight. She said it was probably an accident. They've arrested Ulysses, haven't they?'

'I think it's just a formality,' Caroline said mendaciously, knowing she sounded inane.

'Was it you who found him?' Melissa asked. Her voice was oddly flat, toneless, masking, Caroline suspected, a morbid curiosity. Melissa was just the sort of person to feel morbid curiosity.

Caroline said: 'Father, or Ulysses?'

'Father.' She didn't think Melissa was still shivering but she stumbled on the word, though whether from fear or some other emotion Caroline did not know.

'Yes,' she said, 'I found him.'

'Was there – *blood*?'

Caroline felt the familiar surge of distaste. 'Does it matter?'

'If there wasn't any blood,' Melissa said, 'perhaps Ulysses broke his neck. It's quite easy to break someone's neck: you only have to twist it a bit. I've seen them do it in films. And I should think Ulysses must be very strong. Perhaps he did it deliberately. I would've, if I were him.'

'Father didn't break his neck,' Caroline said shortly. And

then: 'I hope you're not planning to talk to the inspector like this. It could cause a lot of trouble.'

Melissa turned away, hunching her shoulder. 'I don't want to see any inspector.'

'It'll be all right,' said Caroline, wishing she was sure of that.

'That policewoman was horrid to me,' Melissa went on. 'She made me drink her lousy tea and she pretended to be all sympathetic, just to find out where I'd been. But I wouldn't tell her. Stupid fucking cow.'

'I wish you wouldn't use words like that,' Caroline remarked. 'It always sounds so unconvincing. I expect it's because you weren't brought up to be foul-mouthed, so it doesn't come naturally.' Melissa, always conscious (particularly with Stephanie) that her bad language was forced and her left-wing opinions mere affectation, remained bitterly silent. 'I imagine,' Caroline added, 'the policewoman noticed you were a bit stoned.'

'So what?'

'You smoke too much,' Caroline said wearily, meaning dope. 'It's not good for you.'

'Piss off.'

Caroline did not say anything more. She knew – she had always known – that it would be useless. A little later she touched Melissa's shoulder, in a sort of tentative substitute for a caress, and murmured, not without difficulty: 'Sleep well.' She had never been any good at showing affection, particularly when she felt none. Melissa did not answer but she huddled herself more tightly in the blankets and after a while her heavy, regular breathing told her sister that she slept. Caroline lay wakeful for a long time. The bed was a double but Melissa fidgeted a good deal and had managed to appropriate most of the covers. Caroline held on firmly to the edge of the blanket and tried to control her own restlessness. As the night drew on she grew cold, and the possibility of sleep seemed to recede even further. She knew it must come in the end, if she could only stop thinking about it; she had known too many nights like this. But the darkness had already begun to lighten when she finally succumbed, and her dreams were haunted inexplicably by the memory of a fair-haired child, long dead, hiding amongst grasses grown wild and tall, and weeping in a thin bird-like voice for sorrows she did not understand.

She woke around nine, after perhaps two hours' sleep. There was a curious humming noise coming from somewhere below stairs which she identified presently as a vacuum cleaner; evidently Mrs Bunce had come in as usual. Caroline felt vaguely annoyed although she knew she ought to be grateful. She got up without disturbing Melissa and went into the bathroom. It was only while she was cleaning her teeth that she realised it was a Saturday: even under normal circumstances Mrs Bunce ought not to be there. She went downstairs in her kimono, preparing to say something chilly and even slightly cutting which would in some way relieve her pent-up emotions, but she did not get the chance. 'There, there, dear,' said Mrs Bunce, 'have a nice cup of tea, it's no wonder you look a bit peaky.' Caroline, who did not like being mothered, sat down at the table and allowed her good manners to get the better of her distaste. 'I thought I'd just pop in and tidy up a bit,' Mrs Bunce went on. 'Them police officers turned the place upside down yesterday. Come round to see me in the evening, they did; Mrs Wickstead from next door, she told them where to come. They asked me no end of questions. Wanted to know why I had the day off, when you was coming down. If I'd known, I said, I'd have come in. No trouble. But the doctor, he wouldn't think to mention it; he'd as soon open a tin of salmon as sit down to a proper roast. I wouldn't have kept on here if I hadn't been so long with the family,' she added – trying to impress me with her loyalty, Caroline thought. 'Particularly not with the goings on.' There was a hopeful pause, but Caroline, whatever her reflections, kept them to herself. 'Ah well,' Mrs Bunce concluded, rather reluctantly, 'the less said about that the better. It was a judgment, if you ask me, and as for that young man, I hope he gets what's coming to him. Bad, he is, bad all through. I knew it the moment I set eyes on him.'

'Neither bad nor good,' said Caroline. 'Just not very wise.'

'When I was a girl,' said Mrs Bunce, 'we didn't have none of this sort of thing. I blame the television. Puts ideas into people's heads.'

'I'm sure you're right,' Caroline assented politely.

Perhaps her quiet courtesy was beginning to take effect. Mrs Bunce continued a little doubtfully: 'You're bearing up wonderful, dear, but you ought to have some breakfast. I daresay you didn't get no supper last night, what with the police and all the upset. How about a nice boiled egg? Or a bit of toast?' Caroline started to refuse, but she was forestalled. 'Never mind; I'll make some anyway. There's nothing like the smell of toast to make you realise how hungry you are. Is your sister getting up soon?'

'I'd better go and wake her now,' Caroline said, rising. 'I'm expecting a police inspector to arrive shortly. As you're here, perhaps you wouldn't mind having some coffee ready.' Anything to stop the endless flow of tea.

'Of course, dear. A police inspector –! That reminds me, there was a young man on the telephone this morning, before you was up. Said he was from the *Daily Star*. He wanted to talk to you but I wouldn't wake you so he said he'd come round.'

Caroline said: 'Oh Lord,' and went to rouse Melissa.

Inspector Moyse arrived around a quarter to ten with attendant constable; the first reporter a little while later. Caroline admitted the police and instructed Mrs Bunce to deny the press. 'She might as well make herself useful,' she remarked. 'I didn't ask her to come in, after all.'

'I suppose this place belongs to you now?' the inspector said carelessly.

Caroline had not thought about it. 'I suppose it does.'

'Will you sell?'

She had not thought about that, either. 'I think so, yes. Oh yes, of course. There isn't any reason for me to hang on to it. Melissa would probably rather have a flat, or – or something.' Or move into the squat with Duncan. But she didn't mention that. She felt she ought to prevent it, if she could, though she was not quite sure how. Even if she could bring herself to invite Melissa to London, she did not think she would come.

'It should fetch quite a bit,' the inspector was saying, 'even in the present economic climate. Say, ninety thousand.

Without the contents. The practice must have brought in a fair amount, too. Rich people will have their aches and pains, no matter what the state of the nation, and when the FT index starts falling I daresay it only aggravates their ills. My wife always says I should have been a doctor. I gather business had been dropping off lately, but I trust young Stavrakis hadn't had time to ruin him yet. I assume you and your sister get half each?'

'I don't know.'

'She's adopted, isn't she? That probably makes a difference.'

Caroline thought of her father, who had loved none of his children. 'Not really.'

'Of course,' the inspector added, casually, 'the doctor might have left it all to our Greek friend.'

'No,' Caroline said flatly. 'He wouldn't do that.'

'In that case,' the inspector remarked, 'it looks like you're going to be a very wealthy young woman.'

Caroline could not repress a shudder.

Melissa was sitting in the kitchen, eating toast spread with marmalade and cottage cheese. She was given to making rather peculiar sandwiches (ham and blackcurrant jelly was another favourite) but she usually left them half finished and Caroline was surprised to see her chewing almost feverishly. When the inspector was introduced she looked sulky, but then, she very often did. Her spiky hair, unbrushed, was still flattened from sleep and her face had the pale, puffy look of someone who has only just got up and can't be bothered to wash, which was in fact the case. When the inspector asked her what she was eating she answered him with her mouth full.

'Would you like some coffee?' Caroline said, feeling a little like the hostess at an unsuccessful party.

'No, thank you. Perhaps if Miss Horvath has finished we could go somewhere more –?'

Caroline said 'Of course' and 'Would the study be all right?' Melissa went on eating toast. Bits of cottage cheese adhered to the corners of her mouth. When she stood up, she wiped her lips with her hand and then wiped her hand on her jeans. Caroline, knowing she was supposed to be provoked, carefully refrained from comment. In any case, she knew quite well it would not do any good.

The interview was brief and, as far as the inspector could manage, to the point. Melissa, with some hazy idea that it was expected of her, answered as much as possible in sullen monosyllables. She knew, or thought she knew, that among Duncan and his ilk the sullen monosyllable was considered the only suitable response to police interrogation. The inspector's gentle manner was largely thrown away on her; she was determined to feel threatened, and could only remind herself that his straightforward questions, apparently harmless, were merely a cloak for something far more sinister, an insidious attempt to lull her into a false sense of security. What Inspector Moyse thought would have been difficult to tell; his manner did not alter and his eyes, under their sleepy eyelids, were still pale and expressionless. Perhaps he was wryly amused; it would have been in keeping with the twist of his mouth and the flickering creases in his thin cheek. Anyway, he required very little information from this interview. Doubtless, if he had needed something more, he would have known how to obtain it. He must have dealt with a good many Melissas during the course of his career.

'So,' he summed up, while the constable, as usual, scribbled frantically, 'you were not there, you do not know anything, and you have no opinions. It makes a pleasant change to find a witness so succinct. Mostly, people tend to waffle.' Melissa opened her mouth, and then shut it again. 'I have had to listen to a hell of a lot of ramblings and conjecture in connection with murder cases.'

'Murder. . .?' Little more than a whisper.

'Under the circumstances, that is the charge, yes. Your sister didn't tell you?' For a moment, there was a gleam under the drooping eyelids, but Melissa did not see it.

'You mean – it wasn't an accident? Ulysses really *meant* to kill him?'

'That will be for his lawyer to disprove. What do you think?'

But Melissa, recollecting herself, had withdrawn again into sullenness. 'I don't know.'

'You lived in the same house with them,' the inspector pursued, allowing just a hint of flattery to colour his comment.

172

'I expect you saw more of their relationship than most. I'm afraid it must have been very uncomfortable for you.'

Melissa shook her head, unable to reply. She was remembering how she had fantasised about Ulysses, listening at doors for his voice, lingering in the passage, late at night, longing for a forbidden glimpse of his body. The inspector saw a dull red blush suffuse her face, which before had been as colourless as whey.

After a minute, he resumed: 'Would you have said your father was a violent man?'

'I don't know.' It was her standard answer.

'Have you ever seen him use violence, towards Stavrakis or – anyone else?'

'No.'

'Were you fond of him?'

This time, Melissa turned pale, even paler, if that were possible, than was usual of her. 'Of course. He – he was my father.'

'People are not always fond of their fathers,' the inspector remarked mildly. 'Particularly when they behave in such a very unfatherly way.' He let it hang.

'Leave me alone!' Melissa whispered, conscious at last of police brutality. 'I haven't done anything. . .'

'He wasn't your real father, was he? I understand you're adopted.'

'Leave me *alone!*' The whisper broke into a kind of shriek. Face and fists were screwed up with anger, with resentment, with the effort of forced hysteria. She no longer knew if she was being persecuted or if she merely wished to be persecuted, but it did not matter. It was so much easier to break down. A torrent of words burst from her in which abuse and melodrama and self-pity were jumbled together beyond all caution or coherence. 'Fucking pigs! Beastly fucking pigs! I won't say anything – I won't – I won't! I couldn't help it – it's not my fault. Anyway, he was cruel and horrid and a dirty queer. I hated him. I'm glad he's dead! I'm *glad*, do you hear? Glad – glad – glad. Sadistic fucking bastard. He didn't care about *me* – nobody ever cared about me. You don't know what an awful time I've had. My mother was an alkie and my b-brother killed himself. He hated Father too – we all hated him. Even my stuck up goody-goody sister hated him. If he was murdered it serves him right. I don't care if you arrest me – it's *true*. He was hateful – hateful –' When Caroline came in, she was sobbing drily, unable, perhaps, to produce any real tears. The constable, who was evidently rather inexperienced, had averted his face. Inspector Moyse looked thoughtful, but otherwise unaffected. When he spoke, it was in his usual detached tone.

'Your sister seems to be suffering from reaction.'

Delayed shock, thought Caroline. Like Ulysses. She had a premonition she was going to get very tired of delayed shock.

'Yes,' she said. 'She does.'

She put her arms round her, trying to repress distaste, conscious both of anger and a sort of uncomfortable pity. Melissa clung to her so tightly her fingers pinched. When the police had gone she quietened down a little, but her body still shook, uncontrollably, as though the furies to which she had abandoned herself had taken over, and would not let her go.

The funeral took place two days later. There were no other mourners and no flowers. Caroline's arm ached from slamming the door in the face of the press. She wore her winter coat, which happened to be grey, but that was her only concession to the occasion. Melissa inadvertently wore black; she often did, although it did not suit her. The doctor had put her on a course of anti-depressants and Caroline had a bottle of valium in her handbag, in case of emergencies, but she had not had to recourse to it yet. The rector hurried through the ceremony as though conscious of its hypocrisy. To her relief, he was a newcomer to Cheyney, a stranger; she thought she could not have borne the curiosity and sympathy of a familiar face. Just now, she only wanted to see strangers. When she and Melissa arrived, he had attempted a few words of conventional commiseration, but Caroline's polite disclaimer ended the pretence. Let it be done with, she said to herself, kneeling in the church, her hands clenched in prayer. Please God, let it be done with. There is no God, answered the silence, mocking her. God is dead. And she seemed to see his face, floating above the altar, as she had seen it when she was a child: the beautiful, pitiless face of an

174

immortal. She knew regret, and bitterness, and a sudden wild anger. She could hardly refrain from venting her contempt out loud, denouncing the cheats and the delusions and the whole pious insurance scheme, condemning the vicar and all his works to the Hell in which he professed to believe. Her eyes burned; tears of anger ran down her cheeks. Why do funerals always affect me like this? she wondered wretchedly, trying to rationalise. Why can I not be indifferent and accepting like everyone else? She fumbled in her bag for her handkerchief, but she had not brought one. 'You're crying,' Melissa whispered, staring at her in astonishment. 'Why?'

Caroline said harshly: 'I'm not crying.'

They buried Stephen Horvath beside his son, on the hillside above the church. The headstone would not be set in place for another year and without flowers there was little else to mark the grave. Let it be done with, Caroline repeated to herself, or to God, or to whoever might be listening. Let him be forgotten. Philip had a marble headstone with the statue of an angel whose wings covered his face. A blind angel, thought Caroline: how appropriate. A blind angel to watch over them both. She wondered what words she would put on her father's stone, when the time came, where other daughters put 'beloved' and 'deeply mourned'. No one had loved her father; none mourned for him. May he rest in peace, Caroline said to herself, bitterly. That was all she could wish for him now. Just that. Her anger was gone as swiftly as it had come. She brushed the earth from her fingers and, impelled perhaps by a sense of duty, took Melissa's hand. But her sister did not respond and she let it go, feeling both relieved and a little guilty.

At home, she found her father's lawyer, W. Pettigrew of Pettigrew & Farquharson, waiting to discuss the will. It had been drawn up shortly after Philip's death and, apart from an investment policy in Melissa's name which she could not touch until she was twenty-one, everything had been left to Caroline. A few cold words reminded her of her obligations to her adopted sister: that was all. Melissa was resentful, angry, and finally hysterical, although beforehand she had never given a thought to her possible inheritance. Caroline dosed her with valium and put her forcibly to bed. 'She's very easily upset just now,' she told Mr Pettigrew, by way of

excuse. And – a useful cliché – 'I'm afraid she feels rejected.'
The lawyer offered a suitable sample of legal wisdom and
took his leave, and Caroline sat at the kitchen table, nursing
a cup of black coffee between her cold hands, and trying not
to hear Mrs Bunce's persistent mothering, or the intermittent
shrill of the telephone, or the doorbell. Her mind touched
fleetingly on Ursula, under some foreign field, and Valerie,
lying, presumably, in unconsecrated ground. It was strange,
she thought, when so many had died, how difficult it was to
be alone.

15

For the next week or two Caroline was very busy – too busy
to be anxious, or so she thought, but her anxieties grew
underneath all her other preoccupations, manifesting themselves in moments of abstraction, turbulent dreams more
exhausting than sleeplessness, and fits of irritation, usually
with Melissa, where she had to struggle with clenched teeth
to keep her self-control. She had never found self-control
difficult in the past. Her employers had been very understanding and she was allowed as much compassionate leave
as she felt she would need, so she stayed at Cheyney, putting
the furniture up for auction, packing away the best of the
pictures, seeing solicitors and estate agents. Sometimes, she
thought it would have been better to go back to work, to the
welter of unread (and largely unreadable) manuscripts, the
irrelevant post and the unsympathetic telephone, rather than
remaining in the same environment surrounded by disquieting recollections. But the managing director was determined
to be understanding and Caroline gave in. Melissa had
decided to cultivate her depression, endowing it with a capital
D and a number of interesting symptoms, which, her sister
suspected, she had found in a recent magazine article.

Educational journalism, Caroline reflected, had a great deal to answer for. At the same time, she was uncomfortably conscious that Melissa had always been neglected and was long overdue for a little attention. Duncan came round once or twice, but his company, she felt, would do more harm than good. Like Melissa, he seemed to pride himself on his lack of tact, making a point of saying whatever he thought would cause the most embarrassment or outrage. It was not a trait which Caroline admired. 'So the old man really *was* a homo,' he commiserated (Melissa, curiously enough, had made little mention of Ulysses at the squat, and Duncan had only just read the story in the papers). 'Tough shit. Very tough shit. Yeah.' And then, profoundly: 'It just shows you what can go on, under the artificial façade of middle-class morality.' Caroline said, 'How very true,' and wondered when he had last had a bath. He started to roll a joint in Melissa's room but she dissuaded him firmly and left them alone together for as little time as possible. When he had gone, leaving behind a smell of unwashed hair and stale marijuana, Melissa talked at some length about his paintings and how 'vivid' and 'powerful' they were, but, Caroline thought, she did not really seem to regret his departure. For herself, although she knew it was quite possible for morons to paint well, she found it curiously difficult to believe in Duncan's artistic talent. Afterwards, Melissa was even moodier than usual. 'You're so conventional,' she told Caroline, petulantly. 'I suppose now you're going to sneer at Duncan because he doesn't have a snotty Oxford accent or – or a Y registration sports car or anything. He's really very clever only you're too stuck up to see it. You probably wouldn't understand his pictures anyway. They're symbolic.'

'I haven't seen them,' Caroline said, pacifically, 'so I can't judge.'

'You're like father,' Melissa went on. 'He pretended to know about art but he was only interested in what things cost and whether the artist was famous or not. He didn't really care. . .'

This was not entirely true, but Caroline did not say anything. She knew it would be a waste of time.

Fortunately, it had not been necessary for Melissa to attend the inquest. Caroline, who had expected witnesses, medical reports, and Coroner's platitudes of the kind delivered on Philip, was relieved to find it a mere formality, adjourned until after Ulysses' trial. As next of kin, she gave formal identification of the deceased, and Inspector Moyse detailed the circumstances and stated that a man was helping police with their enquiries. His face was curiously devoid of expression, inscrutable or simply noncommittal Caroline could not tell, and even his voice sounded level and dull, the voice of any policeman, anywhere. She found this faintly worrying, although she could not have explained why. She had never expected the police to be other than impersonal. Afterwards, walking down the steps from the Courts, she was not particularly surprised to hear him call her name.

'Perhaps Constable Ferris and I can give you a lift home, Miss Horvath.'

'I can catch a bus.'

But she knew really it had not been a request. 'I should like a few words, if you don't mind. The car's right here.'

They sat in the back, side by side. Caroline did not look at him. It was only a short drive from Sawsted to Cheyney but Constable Ferris, presumably under orders, took his time. In the rear view mirror Caroline saw he was the constable with acne who had brought her the tea, that evening at the police station. Or, if not the same one, it was another who looked very like him. Perhaps all constables under twenty-one had acne. Perhaps, like the height requirement, it went with the job. She wondered if the manufacturers of skin cleanser had discovered this yet.

The inspector's voice recalled her from her thoughts. It sounded soft and hollow again, the gentle disinterested voice of their first interview, and, thinking of his regulation court-room monotone, Caroline felt suddenly distrustful. 'After you found the body,' it pursued, very delicately, like someone prising the lid off a tin of sardines so carefully that neither the lid nor the sardines would notice, 'you are quite sure you didn't touch anything?'

'Quite sure,' said Caroline. And then, remembering: 'I held his hand. . .'

Possibly she hoped to divert him, to gain a moment's respite. But the voice went on. 'You didn't – for example –

touch the stain on the mantelpiece, before you realised what
it was?'

'Like in detective stories?' Caroline managed a faint smile.
' "When she drew her hand away it felt wet and sticky. She
thought at first it was red paint. . ." ' She glanced fleetingly
at him, but he did not look amused. 'No, inspector. No, I
didn't.'

'And the poker?'

Caroline said sharply: 'You must know I never touched the
poker. My fingerprints would be on it.'

'Fingerprints. . . yes. You seem to be very well up in these
things. Do you read many detective stories?'

'Some.' Caroline was bewildered. 'I read a lot of things.'

'Did you mention – fingerprints – to Stavrakis?'

'No – why should I? At least –' she checked herself, determined to stay as close to the truth as possible. She could only
hope Ulysses had done the same –'I *may* have done. When I
said I was going to call the police, he was very frightened. I
– I told you that. I think I explained about fingerprints and
things to reassure him – to show him how easy it would be
to prove what really happened. But I don't understand –'

'And then you telephoned the police?'

'Yes.'

'From the telephone in the hall?'

Again Caroline said yes. She decided she would give up
trying to penetrate the workings of the constabular mind.

'So Stavrakis was left alone in the living room?'

It was several seconds before Caroline turned to look at
him. But this time, her glance did not flinch away. She was
suddenly angry, angry at the inspector's petty suspicions, the
underhand way in which he had tried to lead her into a trap.
She felt betrayed as though by a friend. Probably he had
meant what he said about the 'dago in the woodpile', and to
him Ulysses was merely another dubious foreigner, too good-
looking to be honest, a sexual invert who had put himself
beyond the pale of human tolerance and understanding. She
said – and in her anger she was not completely accurate –
'Yes, inspector, he was. He stood in the doorway to watch
me telephone. I am afraid he was never out of my sight.'

The inspector said mildly that her evidence was very clear
and he was sorry she had been troubled. Caroline turned her

shoulder and stared out of the window, still agreeably conscious of her own anger and, for the first time in her dealings with the police, of being in command. Presently, she said coldly: 'Perhaps you could ask your driver to hurry up a little. I don't like leaving my sister alone for too long.'

Inspector Moyse murmured something to the constable and lay back in his seat, closing his eyes. He did not seem particularly disturbed by Caroline's attitude. If it had not been for the set line of his mouth, she could almost have believed he had fallen asleep.

That night, Melissa came into Caroline's room when she was getting ready for bed. For once, she had taken most of her mascara off and she looked, Caroline thought, little more than a child. It was impossible to believe she was nearly eighteen. Her eyelids were red-rimmed and swollen where the lotion had got in her eyes, her lips screwed into the sulky pout which usually meant she was upset about something. Caroline reflected that it might be important or it might not. So many things upset Melissa.

She watched Caroline in the mirror for a moment or two, over her shoulder. Then she said: 'What's that?'

'Night cream.' Caroline went on rubbing it into her face without turning round. 'Avocado.' And, on an impulse: 'Would you like some?'

'I hate avocados.'

There did not seem to be anything much to say to that. After a short silence, tense with the struggle of some invisible emotion, Melissa blurted out: 'Are – are you going back to London? I thought, now the inquest's over – I mean –'

'Not yet,' Caroline said gently.

'What about your job?'

'That's all right: I've fixed it. Don't worry, I shan't leave you.'

She half expected some indignant response, even a rebuff; she knew she had been too open with her kindness. But Melissa only said: 'Oh,' rather uncertainly, and then: 'When the house is sold – where shall I go?' There was a distant note of panic in her voice which did not escape Caroline.

'That's up to you,' she said. 'There'll be quite a lot of

money, remember. You could have your own flat, if you like. Or –' she hesitated fractionally '– you could come and stay with me. There's no need to make any definite plans just yet. When the time comes, we'll sort something out.'

'*I* shan't be rich,' Melissa said with a revival of resentment. 'Father left the money to you.'

Caroline shrugged slightly. She thought it would be best to be a little offhand. 'It all comes to the same thing,' she said. 'It belongs to both of us. You're my sister.'

'No I'm not,' Melissa whispered; but the whisper was scarcely audible.

After a little while, she picked up the subject again, very cautiously, as though it were an insect whose wings she feared to damage although its desperate fluttering filled her with loathing. 'That policeman knew I was adopted. He said so.'

'Did he?' Caroline squeezed a little hand lotion onto her palm and then offered it to Melissa. This time, she accepted. 'Well, there's nothing wrong with being adopted. Lots of people are. Anyway,' she added, 'you were his wife's child; it was perfectly logical for Father to adopt you. It's not as if you were found on a doorstep or anything.'

Melissa, she thought, would infinitely have preferred to be found on a doorstep. 'He was a stepfather,' she said sullenly. 'Stepfathers are always wicked. Like stepmothers.'

'Father wasn't wicked,' Caroline said. 'Just not very happy.'

'*You're* not wicked,' Melissa snapped. 'You're so good it makes me sick.' She rubbed her hands together and then sniffed them, wrinkling up her whole face. 'This stuff smells disgusting.'

Caroline said shortly: 'Lemon.'

'I hate lemons. I hate them worse than avocados.'

'What do you like?'

'I – I –' But Melisa could not tell her what she liked. Warm dark dreams, squirming sensual thoughts, little vengeances for little slights, a whole fantasy of being pretty and clever, of doing sweet obscene things with a dusky-faced lover who nibbled her like a rat. . . 'I like being high,' she said, 'being drunk. When I'm high I can get out of myself, be somebody else. I don't like being myself.' As an afterthought, or because she felt it would sound effective, she added: 'I expect I shall like being dead.'

'Don't talk nonsense,' Caroline said warmly. 'You could enjoy being yourself if only you thought less about it and more about other people. Unselfish people are always happy. You should try to be more –'

'Like you?' Melissa broke in, her voice rising. '*Goody-goody!*' She hesitated, groping for something even more cutting, but evidently without success. Perhaps because she had not been round to the squat for a while, she had forgotten to use any four-letter words.

'Of course I don't want you to be like me,' Caroline said listlessly. If only Melissa wouldn't make these scenes last thing at night, when she was always so tired. 'People are like themselves. Anyway – what makes you think I'm so very happy?'

She had not meant to make that last remark. She knew Melissa wouldn't understand. But fatigue, the apathy that comes from fatigue, betrayed her. To her surprise, it checked Melissa's impending hysteria. 'But – you're beautiful,' she said grudgingly. 'Everyone thinks so. Even Ulysses –' She stopped.

'Did he say so?' Caroline asked, her voice cold.

'No, but – *you* know what happened.' Something in Caroline's face closed, like a shutter over her thoughts. Absent-mindedly, Melissa picked up the hand lotion and squeezed a little more onto her fingers. 'I didn't tell the policeman,' she said airily. She glanced up, quickly, but her sister's face did not change. 'I thought you would prefer me not to.'

'I shouldn't think,' Caroline said at last, with an effort at indifference, 'that he would be very interested.'

Although she was so tired, Caroline slept badly again that night. She gave Melissa some valium and almost wondered whether to take one herself; but she knew it was not really necessary. She was not depressed or neurotic, only anxious and helpless – overstrained by her anxiety, frustrated by her helplessness. She told herself that there was nothing more she could do for Ulysses now; whatever happened, it was in the hands of God, or chance, or the police. She had played her part. Curious what a remote, unreal figure he had become, since his arrest, a phantom whose face changed with every new recollection, every half-forgotten detail dragged up from the depths of her memory and fitted into the past. Sometimes, she could hardly remember what he actually looked like. She had almost thought of him as 'young Stavrakis', the way Inspector Moyse said it. Young Stavrakis – fingerprints – the living room. Ulysses standing in the living room doorway, watching her dial nine nine nine. . . Only you can't *know* he was there, she told herself, cruelly, no longer warmed by a sudden anger but cold and clear-headed – too clear-headed – alone with the darkness. She couldn't know because she hadn't been looking at him. She had been staring at the numbers on the dial, wondering, stupidly, who to call, what to do. How long had she stood there, just staring? *How long?* 'What does it matter?' she said aloud, hoping to be reassured by the echo of her own voice. But the voice did not sound like hers at all, so thin and desperate, somewhere between a cry and a whisper. And afterwards the silence seemed more silent, the night darker, as though someone should have answered and had deliberately refrained. If only she could see Ulysses, speak to him, then she knew everything would be all right. She tried to remember their times together, but it did not comfort her. Policemen always think the worst, she decided. They saw so much of all that was violent and deformed in human nature it must be difficult for them to believe people could be any other way. Perhaps Inspector Moyse hoped to further his career, uncovering a supposed crime no one else had suspected. (What did that remind her of? Horrendous crimes which have probably never been committed. . . Who had said that?) Perhaps he was merely following a 'hunch'. In books, detectives were always having 'hunches'. She imagined him talking to his superior (the chief constable?): 'I know it's all perfectly straightforward, sir. It's just that I've got a *feeling*. . .'

'I've got faith in your "feelings", Moyse. Remember the Sheppard case – you were dead right then. I'm listening.'

'Well, sir, it's all been a little too slick.' (Wasn't that what they always said?) 'Stavrakis is a thoroughly bad lot: a homo, or more probably AC/DC, no morals, and Greek into the bargain. We all know what the Greeks are like.' *Timeo*

Danaos. . . 'As for the girl, I don't know if she's in it, or if it's just something she suspects, but I'm pretty sure she's lying to me.'

Yes, I'm lying, Caroline whispered. But it isn't an important lie. It isn't *relevant*. Not really. . .

The chief constable's voice, brisk and military, seemed to interrupt her unspoken pleading.

'Motive?'

There isn't any motive, she wanted to cry out: of course there isn't. It was all a horrible accident. Ulysses didn't have to kill him; he only had to come away with me. There isn't any motive at all.

You're going to be a very wealthy young woman. . .

With a start, Caroline jerked out of her dream. She was sitting bolt upright in bed and the sweat was cold on her forehead. For a few seconds her breathing came short and fast. I mustn't do that, she thought. I mustn't fall asleep brooding on things. I'll go mad. . . She knew really Ulysses was not capable of that kind of cold-blooded planning. He liked money, but he wouldn't kill for it – she was sure he wouldn't. Hadn't he always refused to be paid off, like a prostitute? She was allowing herself to give way under pressure, becoming as neurotic as Melissa, she who had always been so rational and unimpassioned. She lay down again and tried to remember her yoga, to relax, gradually, into sleep. Down the hall, the grandfather clock chimed once. Only once. It was a long way to morning, waking and trying not to think, sleeping and trying not to dream. She was learning to dread the nights.

A month went by. Auctioneers took away the furniture, slowly picking the house bare. Mrs Bunce roamed the huge empty rooms with her hoover and told her husband what a shame it was, though no one knew why. Melissa took her anti-depressants and continued obstinately depressed; Caroline allowed the doctor to prescribe her some mogadon though she hardly ever used them, lying, night after night, sleepless and enduring. In the garden, the celandines were replaced by daisies, and nobody cut the grass.

They saw few reporters, less police. Inspector Moyse stayed

away altogether, though Caroline still had the feeling he was watching her, from some concealed vantage point, like a naturalist, waiting, patiently, for the fox to emerge from his lair, for the chrysalis to hatch the dragonfly, for the mating rites of blackbeetles. One day, she drove Harry's car back up to London and, guiltily conscious that she had delayed returning it, agreed to have lunch with him. 'Keep it, love,' he said (if only he wouldn't call her 'love'). 'I can use your mother's Renault,' and 'Why don't you let me come down – sort things out for you? I'll get Jack Willis on the house. It'll sell in a week. No need for you to worry.' Caroline explained that she had already had an offer for Cheyney House which was being dealt with by her own agent and refused steadfastly to borrow the car any longer although her father's new Alfa was not insured for her. For a few moments, Harry seemed to be at a loss, but the arrival of the starters gave him the opportunity to notice her lack of appetite and complain to the waiter that the melons were unripe. Caroline, horribly embarrassed, abandoned any attempt to stop him. 'This place isn't what it used to be,' he commented, when the waiter had withdrawn in a cloud of apology. 'New management. You tell me straight off if your escalope isn't up to standard. I don't mind what I pay in a restaurant but I expect my money's worth. And I don't like to see you picking away at your food like one of Daisy's jerbils. You need some fuel in the boiler, young lady, with all you've been through. Tuck in.'

'I never eat much at lunchtime,' Caroline murmured excusingly.

It was no good, he decided; even as a child he did not think she had been the sort of girl who tucked in. If only she would let him *help*. . .

Afterwards, she thanked him with her usual politeness, sent her love to her mother, and resolutely declined his offer of a taxi-fare. Harry was left standing on the pavement, absent-mindedly flexing his Diners card, while Caroline escaped thankfully into the nearest Underground, making a private resolve never to borrow so much as a matchstick (let alone a car) from him again. With people like that, she reflected, if you let them do one small thing for you they immediately tried to interfere in every other aspect of your life. She had eaten far more of the escalope than she actually wanted in order to prevent further scenes with the waiter and she felt unusually solid and very warm inside. It was a long time since she had felt either solid or warm, and she was not sure that she liked it. She would have preferred to stay cool, empty, almost light-headed: the way she had felt for weeks past. On the train, rather to her surprise, she fell asleep.

The telephone call came about a week later.

Caroline took it in the hall (she never used the study 'phone if she could help it). When she lifted the receiver she said: 'Yes?' without giving the number. There had been too many anonymous telephone calls, particularly late at night.

A voice at the other end – a familiar unexpected voice, half pleading, half imperative – said: 'Caroline.'

Only one person spoke her name like that.

She sat down very slowly and deliberately in the chair – the only chair remaining in the hall. Quite suddenly, she was aware of several things: the hollowness of the empty rooms all around her, the shadows on the stairway, her own heartbeat. Melissa was in bed, hopefully asleep: Caroline glanced involuntarily towards the landing but nothing stirred. The grandfather clock had been taken away and the only sounds she could hear were the electric clock in the kitchen and the faint muted ticking of her own watch. Presently, she forced herself to speak.

'Hello, Ulysses. Where are you? I didn't think –'

'Don't worry.' He might have read her mind. 'It is all quite legal. I have not – what is the phrase? – done a bunk.' Ulysses' English was always fluent but occasionally he stumbled over colloquialisms. How *foreign* he sounds, she thought, with a sudden sense of alienation. She had not remembered he was so foreign. He went on: 'They let me out on bail. My lawyer managed it – he is very clever. They don't usually grant bail on murder charges but he explained at the committal that it was self-defence. They have taken my passport, of course.'

'Bail. . .' Once or twice, she had wondered about the possibility of bail. But she had not dared to make inquiries: it would have looked too suspicious. She said doubtfully: 'I thought it cost a great deal of money?'

'Only if I run away.'

'Yes, but – someone has to say they'll put up the money, don't they? Who –?'

'I have friends: remember? The Antoniades – at the restaurant. They have been very good to me. They found me the lawyer; I think he's a regular customer of theirs. And George Antoniades went over to Greece to stop my mother coming here. I didn't want my family mixed up in this.'

Caroline said unhappily: 'I know *I* ought to do something. But I'm tied down here – my sister needs me. The doctor's put her on anti-depressants. Anyway –'

'I know. You can't. It would be too dangerous.' She wasn't sure if he sneered or not. 'I want to see you.'

'*No.*' In her panic, her voice was too loud – too definite. 'We mustn't meet. You mustn't even call me any more. If someone found out it could jeopardise everything. Did you tell your lawyer about me – us?'

'Of course not.' She thought he sounded untroubled, almost leisurely. It did not reassure her. 'You are being ridiculous. Anyway, they are not allowed to tap telephones in England: I asked. Only if it's political. It's quite safe for us to talk like this. When can I see you?'

'I told you –'

Perhaps it was Ulysses' words; perhaps she heard something. She looked up at the stairs, and her hand moved automaticallly to cover the receiver, as though the gesture might somehow obliterate her own half of the conversation. She had no idea how long Melissa had been standing there. She was wearing her nightshirt and for a moment Caroline thought she must be shivering; she stood quite still but the material seemed to tremble slightly. Her eyes were like doll's eyes in a pale, smug, inexpressive doll's face. She said: 'It's Ulysses, isn't it? You're talking to Ulysses.'

Caroline murmured: 'Hold on a minute,' and put the 'phone down. For a second, her heart had jumped so violently that she felt a little sick, but now she was quite calm again. She went up the stairs until she was facing her sister. 'Yes, I am,' she said. (How much had Melissa overheard?) 'He's out on bail and there were one or two things he wanted to know. He thought perhaps I could help.' At all costs she must make it seem *natural.* 'Go back to bed now. I'll tell you about it in the morning.'

Rather to her surprise, Melissa allowed herself to be led back to her room. Caroline was not really convinced she would stay there but at least she had gained time. She returned to the telephone.

'Your sister?'

'Yes.' Her tone was guarded; she hoped he understood.

'I had forgotten about her.' Everyone always did, Caroline reflected. Even now. 'Do you know when she came in?'

'No.'

'I see. So – she may still be listening?'

'I don't know.'

There was a short silence. Evidently Ulysses was thinking: Caroline was still too unnerved for rational thought. At last, he said with a curious air of decision: 'I'm coming down. Tomorrow. I want to collect my things.'

'You can't.' There was no one on the stairs, but she felt watched. 'It won't be allowed. Anyway, I packed up your clothes and gave them to the police I expect they'll be sent on to your friends.'

'I'm missing two shirts and a watch-strap. I have to see you.'

'It's not possible.' She struggled to control herself, to keep her voice normal. 'You must see that it's best we don't meet. It could be very – awkward. If you really wish to come down I'll have to arrange to be out. . .'

'Don't be out. I'm coming tomorrow and I want to talk to you. The police aren't following me; no one will know. Incidentally –' he rolled the word off his tongue as though peculiarly proud of it '– I am impressed by your loyalty. As soon as I am in trouble you want to run out on me. That is very noble, very admirable. If it wasn't for you I wouldn't *be* in trouble. . .' Caroline, furious, could think of nothing to say which it would be suitable for Melissa to overhear. His accusations she dismissed as merely provocative, the product of childishness or pique, but his foolhardy behaviour might prove disastrous. 'I'll be there some time in the afternoon,' he concluded. 'Don't avoid me. It would be a mistake.'

'I won't –'Caroline stopped herself on the verge of an incautious retort. But he had already rung off.

In the morning, Caroline went to London. It was, or so she assured herself, the only safe, the only *reasonable* thing for her to do; but the compulsion that she followed was instinct, not reason. It would mean, too, evading a confrontation with Melissa, at least for a few more hours. She did not feel capable of confronting anyone just then. When she tried to analyse her reactions she could only think how strange it was, that she had wanted so badly to speak to Ulysses, to see him, and now, after one short conversation, she was so utterly averse to any meeting. That exchange over the telephone had done nothing to allay her fears; rather, those fears had changed, assuming new shapes, dim outlines, which she did not really want to bring into focus. It was not just the risk involved in an encounter with Ulysses – there was something more than that. She was – yes, she was *afraid* of him. Afraid to find him different from her recollection, stronger, more foreign, even more beautiful, with the brutal subhuman beauty of an ancient statue, gilded eyes in a mask of polished stone. Curious how blurred her memories had become, in such a brief absence, how little she could recall of his actual words, his looks, his smile. She tried to picture his face, in sex, softened and tender, but she could only remember a terrible solemnity, as though he took part in some fierce and sacred ritual of passion. 'I can't see him,' she reiterated, combing her hair with a hand that was not – quite – steady. 'Not *here*. Maybe elsewhere . . . later.' You *must* see him, whispered her conscience – the devil's advocate, she thought wretchedly. You must see him soon. You owe him that. After all, he is still your responsibility.

She put her head round the door of Melissa's room, but her sister was only half awake. 'I'm going to London,' she told her. 'I have to see my boss – get my leave extended. And I want a few things from the flat. You'll be all right, won't you? I'll be back this evening.'

Melissa mumbled something inaudible and pulled the blankets over her head.

'By the way,' Caroline continued, her voice a little high and unnatural, 'Ulysses will be down this afternoon – to collect some stuff. I thought it would be best if I wasn't here. Perhaps you ought to go out as well. You could go and see your friends –' she hesitated, disliking herself for a suggestion

189

that was purely expedient; but Melissa had so few friends '– at the squat. You haven't been there for a long time.' Her sister did not answer and Caroline repeated, rather awkwardly: 'I'll be back this evening.'

When she had gone Melissa drew back the bedclothes. Her small pebble eyes stared at the ceiling with a curious fixity, almost as though she had been staring upwards, through the blankets, for some time. She squeezed herself between the legs, conscious of a queer nervous excitement, but it did not develop into anything. A teaspoonful of sunlight sifted through the curtains and floated like an amoeba on the surface of the mirror. Melissa lay rigid, wide awake, watching, for nearly two hours, while it crawled diagonally across the glass and slid over the dressing table towards the floor.

Ulysses caught the two-fifty train and walked up from the station. He was pale after his weeks of confinement, the yellow-ivory pallor of a year-long tan fading away from sun and air. His hair looked darker, more brown than blond, and badly in need of cutting. He had lost weight. He thought it was unlikely that he would meet anyone who recognised him, since most of Stephen's acquaintances had met him only once or twice at the surgery, and no newspaper had carried his photograph; but anyway, the idea of a possible recognition did not trouble him very much. Cheyney had been his home, or so he argued, if only for three months; he had every right to return there if he wished. As long as he was back in time to report to the police station that evening. . . His shoulders twitched involuntarily at the thought of the law and all its associations, as though someone had laid a light, cold finger-tip on the nape of his neck. He did not want to remember those first slow hours in the narrow cell, the waiting and the suspense, the petty humiliation of his constant desire to piss. He had tried to think of Caroline, to give him something to hold on to, but in the midst of his thoughts he fell asleep and when he woke again he knew he had been dreaming of Stephen. As far as possible he wanted to avoid the memory of Stephen. As the hours of his imprisonment stretched into days, the days into weeks, he found the image of those last moments growing mercifully dim: the cold, impassive face disfigured with an anger more terrible than any lust, the eyes that stared at him, pale and empty, like the eyes of someone long dead, whose sleepless corpse is possessed by warring elementals. At last even his wildest fears seemed to wither in the implacable tedium of constant inaction and frustration. He spent a long time thinking about his home, the leisurely atmosphere of the bar and the white beach path and blue enamel sea framed in the doorway. They were getting into the season now and female tourists, tanned every shade of pink and yellow and brown, would lean across the counter, their breasts scooped together between their arms, making flirtatious eyes at his cousin Ari, or his friend Costas, or whoever was working there at the time. He had had plans for the bar, this summer: a proper coffee-maker, a new stereo, maybe even a portable television for the major football matches. The English were curiously obsessed with their football matches, even though they did not seem to win very often. He did not really regret what he had done – he knew, even better than Caroline, what a waste of energy it would be – but it helped to pass the time, thinking of home, reviewing plans which had never come to fruition. It was a distraction, and he badly needed distraction. He slept well, to the surprise of those who took care of him. A clean conscience, they said; or no conscience at all. He was always polite, although it cost him an effort. Good manners were something he used when he found them expedient. He did not complain about the food. His lawyer, who was unfortunately called Crump, spent a long time explaining to him all the conditions of bail, and the importance of complying with them. He was a small, tortoise-like man with an inoffensive tortoise face which always seemed just about to withdraw into his collar. His voice, too, was small: a thin, precise sort of voice. But in the courtroom, hunched up in his black robes, his very smallness became somehow malignant. His voice swelled until it filled the whole room. When he took off his spectacles, his blinking reptilian eyes darted to and fro as though seeking insects for him to devour. Bail was granted even as he had predicted and Ulysses was suitably impressed. Now, walking up the road to the Avenue, he considered yet again the possibilites of making a run for it. But he knew really it was unthinkable. Caroline was right: he would never get away.

And there was George Antoniades, who had put up twenty thousand pounds which he certainly could not afford to pay out. Ulysses was not given to considering other people very much, but he had his own kind of honour, and the Antoniades were old family friends. No: he would just have to hold on, keep his head and his nerve, and in the end, surely, everything would work out.

He did not seriously expect that Caroline would not be there. When they had talked over the telephone it had amused him in a bitter kind of way, hearing her sound less cool than usual, less sure of herself, catching the sharp note in her voice that betrayed the seeds of panic. The force of his own resentment had startled him a little. He had not known, until he heard her hesitations and evasions, how much he blamed her for what had happened. Not that she had actually *done* anything; it was impossible to imagine Caroline involved in an act of violence. But her will, her mind had spawned the deed, though other hands had performed it, and hearing her reject it – reject *him* – he felt used, the tool he had sworn he never would be. At heart, he knew she had to opt out, to be prudent: there was no other course of action for her to follow. But he could not help resenting it. Remembering (belatedly) that Melissa had overheard some, if not all, of their conversation, he told himself that the least she could do was to deal with her sister. Melissa, he reflected, was very tiresome. He had been right to want her out of the way.

Arriving at the house, he opened the door with his own key and let himself cautiously into the hall. He did not know what made him suddenly cautious, what gave him this curious shrinking inside. It was sunny out in the street, warm enough for England, but the hall, as always, was dark and cool. The kitchen door was slightly ajar and he pushed it open. He was painfully aware of how badly he needed to see Caroline, to speak to her again, confident that she would be there, waiting, watching him with this new element of nervousness, of reluctance, which both hurt and excited him. . . He went into the kitchen.

16

Caroline spent the night in London. It had not been her original intention but by the time she had seen her boss (who was still persistently understanding), endured the grating sympathy of her friends, and run through the backlog of work on her desk, she had managed to convince herself that she was far too tired to go home. She would still have to visit the flat, after all, though she had not formulated any specific reason for so doing. Perhaps she ought to see Glynis. Over lunch with Matt Hennessy, she listened to the catalogue of office disputes and production difficulties, the complaints about the new letterhead notepaper, the imminence of a strike among the warehousemen. All very ordinary, everyday worries. All blissfully trivial, even petty, in contrast with the darker troubles which she had pushed (temporarily) to the back of her mind. It was such a relief to worry about something ordinary.

At the flat she found Glynis, watching television and eating some rather peculiar camembert. 'Have some,' she offered. 'I brought it from France, the day before yesterday. But I don't think it liked the flight,' Her manner was just the same as usual, if anything a little more offhand. 'You must be fed up with everyone being kind,' she remarked later.

Caroline nodded.

'Of course,' Glynis added with wry candour, 'if you *do* want to talk about it, I'm devoured with curiosity.'

For once, Caroline found she was not offended. 'No thanks,' she said.

She watched television for a while without taking in what the programme was about and then realised she ought to ring Melissa. She rang twice but there was no answer. 'I suppose,' she reflected, 'she's at the squat in bed with Duncan.' She did not like the idea but it was better than leaving Melissa alone. If only she didn't have to worry about her sister. It was so tiring, so very tiring, trying to cope with her needs, her resentments, her irrational fits of anger or affection. They had no common ground, nothing to talk about, little on which to disagree. She knew she ought to be with her but it was so nice to be back at the flat, living something like a normal life, if only for one night, away from all those empty watchful rooms, the ghosts in the garden, the telephone. . . She tried to imagine Ulysses arriving at the house (did he have a key?) and finding her gone. But she felt warm and suddenly sleepy, and even that particular worry seemed vague and unreal. Anyway, she thought, I can't do anything *now*. She drifted into a hazy fantasy of a perfect existence, without excitement or pain, an unbroken routine of nine-to-five, nine-to-five, and endless evenings characterised by a restful sameness. . . On the television, a car rolled down a cliff-side and burst into flames, but Caroline did not notice.

They called her the following morning from the hospital. Normally, Caroline woke quickly in the mornings, but she had been sleeping heavily for once and she could not seem to take in what the ward sister was saying. Something about *Melissa*? 'I don't understand,' Caroline blurted out, knowing she sounded stupid. But she did understand. Suddenly, she understood horribly well. 'She took an overdose,' the sister explained. 'We are doing everything we can –' the standard reassurance '– but I think you should come down at once.' She sounded calm, gravely sympathetic, somehow unhopeful. Just so, Caroline felt, had she spoken to the daughters of ageing mothers, succumbing at last to cancer or double pneumonia, to lifelong wives who would soon be widows, to retired husbands who were losing their wives. All old people, dying predictably, by degrees. But Melissa was *young*. . . With an effort at concentration, Caroline said: 'What did she take?' Surely it wasn't usual to die of an overdose, not nowadays. There were stomach pumps and things. And afterwards you saw a psychiatrist, or perhaps several, and everyone said it was a 'cry for help'. Melissa had needed help, more help than her sister could give. She would enjoy the attention, the fuss, even the psychiatrists. So few people had ever taken an interest in her. But she wouldn't – really – want to *die*. (What had she said once? 'I shall like being dead. . .' But that was just self-dramatisation.) 'I'm afraid,' the sister was explaining, 'it was her anti-depressants. The doctor will give you the details when you get here.' Anti-depressants. . . Caroline didn't think you could kill yourself on anti-depressants. It didn't make sense. Perhaps Melissa was just high, stoned and ultra-stoned, superlatively anti-depressed. Perhaps. . . 'I'm coming,' she said, trying to pull herself together. 'Please –' But there wasn't really anything to plead for.

The hospital was at Sawsted. Caroline rang for a taxi and just made the fast train. On the way to the station, doing up her shoes, she found her hands were shaking. She couldn't think about anything except getting there – she had an idea it would be better not to. At the barrier, she muttered something about paying at the other end and ran through onto the platform. When she had eventually found a seat she pulled a hand mirror out of her bag and automatically applied a lipstick which had been left there the previous day. Idiotic really: she didn't have any other make-up. Her mascara wand was in the bathroom at the flat. Caroline hated going without mascara and even now she felt horribly conscious of her fair eyelashes. It made her feel so *unfinished*. . . The train slowed at a signal, lingered over points. Looking down, she saw her hands clench in her lap, and she made them relax, joint by joint, finger by finger, though no one was there to see and analyse her self-betrayal. Beyond the next station they began to accelerate, very gradually; the driver seemed to have all the time in the world. Caroline listened to the rhythm of the wheels, remembering herself as a child, going home, home to Cheyney, full of suppressed expectancy, knowing nothing of what life and time had in store for her. Thank God, she thought fleetingly, that she *hadn't* known. There had been moments in her life – a moment with Philip, a moment with Ulysses, the moment of finding her father and seeing he was dead – when she had said to herself: Nothing else can happen to me. This is the worst thing. . . And each time, there had been something else, something worse, yet to come. If Melissa died – but she wouldn't die. You might die of sleeping pills, of paracetamol (or so she had read); not anti-depressants.

She tried to stop thinking (if she couldn't think clearly, what was the point of thinking at all?) but even the beat of the wheels began to form itself into words in her mind. You should have gone home. . . you should have gone home. . . Mea culpa, Caroline reflected coldly, as always. As if that made it any better, knowing it was her fault.

At the hospital, she had to wait. She had always disliked hospitals: the smell of disinfectant, of closed windows and sick people, the pale impersonal corridors and cell-like rooms, the coarse, school-dorm atmosphere of the wards. She had only been in once, to have her wisdom teeth out, and she had never had to use a bedpan or otherwise humiliate herself. She did not think she *could*. She was not afraid of dying, or not especially, but she was afraid of helplessness, senility, incontinence, of lingering on in some cosy private bed under the gentle ministrations of an aloof nursing staff. She had seen an aunt of her mother's dying like that, while she was in Birmingham. A creeping, painless, sterilised death. . . She must stop thinking about death. Presently, a staff nurse appeared with a very young doctor and ushered her into an office. Afterwards the only thing she could remember about it was an enormous box of chocolates on the desk, doubtless the gift of some grateful patient, and a screwed-up piece of gold paper which had missed the rubbish bin. She wanted to ask again if Melissa would be all right but suddenly she was afraid of hearing him answer, like the sister on the telephone: 'We are doing everything we can.' 'The daily help found her,' he was saying, 'shortly after nine o'clock. She must have taken the pills at least twelve hours beforehand. After six hours there are complications –'

'Complications?'

'We're trying renal dialysis. But – there isn't much chance.'

There was a serious, I-won't-offer-you-false-hope expression on his face. She couldn't take it in. Even now, when the words had been spoken, she couldn't take it in. 'I understood,' she said blankly, 'she took her anti-depressants. I didn't know you could kill yourself like that.' Her voice sounded toneless and unreal, like a machine talking. She was not conscious of any emotion at all.

'It depends,' he explained, uncomfortably. 'The milder ones are all right. But your sister was on pills containing

196

something called amitriptylene which upsets the chemical balance of the body. I'm afraid her kidneys have been affected. . .'

'They shouldn't have given them to her,' Caroline said. 'The doctor should have *known* –'

'Has she ever tried to kill herself before?'

'N-no. She –' Caroline stopped. What did it matter if the attempt were genuine or merely a 'cry for help', since it had succeeded? It was only a question of irony. If she hadn't stayed in London, if she had been there to listen and sympathise – if she had returned late that night to find Melissa sleeping too deeply. . . If – if – if. But whatever guilt she might feel was no use to her sister now. She wondered what had happened to drive Melissa to the required nadir of despair or self-pity, whether it was merely loneliness or some other act of careless neglect which had proved the final straw. Perhaps someone at the squat (Duncan?) had upset her. Perhaps – perhaps she had seen Ulysses. . . Suddenly, Caroline knew it would be better to stop her speculations there. It was as though she had come to a wall in her mind, and beyond it was something she could not quite imagine and did not really want to. Ulysses, she felt, was the kind of person who might hurt, casually, without intent, and would not trouble to apologise or mollify. Malice afterthought. And Melissa had been attracted to him. . .

After a moment, she realised the nurse was offering her tea. It was strange, she reflected, how during all the most crucial events in her life people always wanted her to drink tea. She refused, but an elderly auxiliary had already appeared with a cup and an encouraging smile, rather like a genie who has been poised waiting for someone to brush against a lamp. Caroline said thank you and wished it wasn't so important to be polite.

Melissa died around midday. They said Caroline could go in and see her and although she did not really want to she felt impelled by the expectancy in their faces. Melissa lay flat, the way she had been arranged. Her eyes were closed and her mouth slightly open. She did not look unhappy, nor quiet, nor troubled, nor at peace. She looked as Stephen had looked,

197

an empty, useless husk, a doll. Caroline had to say to herself, consciously: This is my sister; because it was so hard to believe that limp lifeless thing had ever been anyone at all. Presumably it – she – had been cleaned up first, but there was still a faint smell of vomit, mingling with the usual hospital smell, and suddenly Caroline felt the tingling sensation in her jaw muscles which meant she was going to be sick. She went out quickly without saying anything.

The next few days were even worse than the time immediately after her father died. She had never realised how much of an anchor it had given her, having to look after Melissa, to make an effort. Now, there was nothing to keep her sane. She went from room to room in the huge empty house, sorting through the last debris of occupation: old photographs, paperbacks years out of date, unused tea sets and dinner sets, tins of screws and of buttons. One morning, she found a cracked china cup in which she remembered her mother collecting ha'pennies, in the days when the ha'penny was still currency. And in the attic she discovered a piece of marble, wrapped in cloth, which had once been called Humphrey, or Hector, or something like that. It reminded her a little of one of Philip's paintings. She sat for a long while absently stroking the smooth head. When she went downstairs again her jeans were grey with dust, and her face in the hall mirror looked grey too, except for the snail-track of a tear down her cheek. In the end, she put Humphrey (or whatever his name was) out with the rubbish. She had never been the kind of person who kept things merely for reasons of sentiment or remembrance. Your own memory, she felt, would hold on to what mattered, and the rest could be forgotten. In any case, there were too many things she did not want to remember at all.

She packed up the books in the study without looking at them and sold them to a dealer for a hundred pounds, although she knew really the collection was worth much more. There were a few books in the surgery too, modern medical books; she packed those up as well. Rather to her surprise, one of them was out on the desk. When she picked it up, it fell open at a page dealing with certain anti-depressants. Almost, Caroline thought, as though Melissa had checked

198

first, had known, in effect, that the pills she was taking would be lethal. But surely that contradicted everything Caroline had believed. . . Only if Melissa hadn't opened the book, who had? In the hall, she heard Mrs Bunce, moving around with her duster. She would have given almost anything to get rid of Mrs Bunce, to tell her that neither her dusting nor her mothering were required any longer, but somehow she could not do it. Perhaps it was Mrs Bunce who had consulted the book, inspired by some moribund impulse of curiosity. (But how had she *known* about the anti-depressants?) Perhaps – perhaps no one had looked at the book at all, and it was only a demon of coincidence which had make it fall open just there. When Inspector Moyse came to interview her again, she asked him tentatively: 'Is it – is it quite certain she took them herself?'

'Quite certain,' said the inspector. The expression in his eyes was hidden by the reflection on his glasses. 'Why do you ask? Did you imagine someone else might have given them to her?'

'Oh no,' Caroline said. 'No. I put it badly. What I meant was – could she have taken them by accident? Without realising. . .'

'So that's what you meant,' the inspector murmured. 'I beg your pardon. No, she couldn't have done that. She emptied the bottle, and from what her doctor says there must have been at least forty in there. I gather he'd just given her another prescription.'

Caroline did not say any more. She knew she had given herself away, but it did not seem to be very important. The inspector did not say any more either; he just stood there for a while, surveying her thoughtfully, before taking his leave. Possibly she imagined the shadow of pity and understanding in his gaze. She did not want pity and understanding. He must, she reflected bitterly, have dealt with so many like her, hesitant, fallible people, trying to live by certain standards and failing, failing all along the line. It made her feel commonplace and ineffectual. Hers was only a small part in a wearisome tale of experience, and in the end no amount of unofficial compassion would affect the attitude of the law, or of her own conscience. The thought of such compassion, such human charity, burned her like shame.

Ulysses had not called her again. Melissa's death had been in all the papers; he must have seen it. Every time the telephone rang she was afraid it would be him. But she would have to speak to him soon. Once, she would have hoped for reassurance from the mere sound of his voice; now, she could only trust he would avoid any confirmation of the suspicions she had left half-formed. She had not told the inspector (or anyone else) that he was supposed to have come down that day. After all, she reasoned, tritely, no one had asked her. When she was alone, she sorted through one of the boxes again, just for something to do. She dribbled the buttons onto the table and picked out all the red ones, then all the black ones, then all the pearl beads. But half way through she found her fingers had grown still, and in her mind the buttons had become capsules, rattling out of a marmite-brown bottle into a clammy palm.

It was almost a relief when her mother and Harry came down for the funeral. At least she had to assume a façade of normal behaviour, standard shock and distress, mechanical self-control. On her own, the mask slipped, but she knew as long as there was someone there she would not be able to let go. They stayed two nights. Her mother had never visited the house before but all she said was, 'Unfurnished rooms always feel rather bleak, don't they?' and 'I think you should get back to London as soon as possible, Carla – straight after the inquest. It can't be very amusing for you down here.'

Amusing. . . Caroline winced inside. Why was it that members of one's parents' generation – even the best of them – were so insensitive, so fatuous, so absurdly banal?

Harry, inevitably, was more forthright. 'Gloomy sort of house, if you ask me. Not surprising the poor kid got depressed. Shouldn't think there's much to do in a place this size, either – hardly more than a big village. Dull for a young girl.'

Caroline thought of the squat, the quiet country pubs, the old cinema which had been closed now for fifteen years. She said: 'I suppose you're right.'

'I was born in a village,' he continued unexpectedly. 'Smaller'n this. Kind of place where everybody knew your own business even better than you did. We moved to the city when I was eleven. I thought it was as exciting as a jungle. Couldn't live in the country again.' He added: 'I'm surprised your father didn't want to live in London – having the practice in Harley Street and all that.'

It occurred to Caroline that for all his tactlessness she had never heard Harry criticise her father, though there had been enough occasions when he might have done. Suddenly, uncomfortably, she found herself remembering their lunch together in London: Harry's clumsy, well-meant overtures of affection, her own prim, chilly response. What had Melissa called her? Stuck-up. And she had tried with Melissa, though not hard enough. She had never really tried with Harry. Poor dear bumbling Harry, leaping all over her – at least in spirit – like a great big dog who never got a welcome, but still kept on wagging its tail and hoping with the incurable optimism of the canine race. The kind of dog who knocked over your china ornaments and licked all your make-up off when you had just got it right. But did make-up and china ornaments really matter all that much?

She thought with a sort of horror: I am my father's daughter. And she had almost been proud of it. . .

'I suppose he wanted to get away from the traffic,' she said, trying to be forthcoming. 'He liked the quiet. Besides, Cheyney is very – up-market. Lots of stockbrokers and business people.' It was the nearest she too had ever come to criticising her father in front of Harry.

Margaret suggested she should stay for the inquest but did not really protest when Caroline said it wasn't necessary. 'I'm going back to London tomorrow, anyway. There's no point in my staying on here. I'll just come down for the morning.'

Their farewells were brief and far less awkward than usual. 'Take care of yourself, dear,' her mother said. 'You look so tired. It wouldn't hurt you to have a holiday. You know you can always come to us, but –'

'I know.'

When she said goodbye to Harry, she shook his hand. She thought he would have liked it best if she had kissed him, but Caroline rarely kissed anyone. Even her kiss for her mother was only an automatic touching of cheek against cheek.

After they had gone she went into the kitchen and sat down at the table with her face in her hands. She supposed it would be natural to make coffee (it was eleven o'clock) but she could not decide whether she wanted any or not. When she was alone she found it very difficult to make decisions, particularly the small, unimportant ones. After a while she felt the tears – meaningless tears of weakness and apathy – running down between her fingers. She did not know why she was crying, only that she seemed to cry a lot lately, though it brought her no relief.

It was easier in London – easier not to think, to occupy her mind with little things, easier to be alone, in the untidy flat, surrounded by fragments of someone else's life. Glynis' books in the living room, her scribbled notes by the telephone, the leftovers of her cooking in the kitchen sink. All utterly divorced from the events at Cheyney. Dinner with Rod, 8 p.m. – Richard, Blake's, 6.30 – 12th, drinks with Julia – party – theatre – drinks – C.: Matt called – C.: caller, no name – C.: caller. . . Caroline screwed up the notes, washed up in the kitchen, even vacuumed the carpet. Trifling, mindless tasks which required no effort, no thought. (She did not ask herself who might have called and left no name.) At work, it was a little more difficult: she had to concentrate, to catch up on what she had missed. Sometimes, in the middle of a telephone conversation, she would have trouble remembering what the conversation was about, or who she was talking to. But everyone was very understanding. Once or twice, she heard them talking, behind doors: 'Of course, she's been under a lot of strain. . .' She always passed the doors very quickly, without listening. The managing director, too, suggested she should take a holiday. 'Why not go to Greece?' he said. 'It's very beautiful, Greece. . .'

Caroline said that she had already been to Greece.

The inquest on Melissa brought in a verdict of suicide, with no surprises. It should have made Caroline feel more comfortable. The doctor talked glibly of teenage instability and depression following her father's death. An expert held forth on the subject of amitriptylene. It was suggested that the deceased had not known the possible effects of the pills and her attempt was actually intended to be unsuccessful. The coroner criticised the doctor. The doctor criticised the coroner (under his breath). Journalists composed headlines like: Suicide Pills Potentially Lethal – Doctor Denies Responsibility. Caroline thought of the book on her father's desk, and said nothing. If only the coroner had blamed her, too, it might have expurgated some of her guilt. She would have answered very quietly and calmly: 'Yes, it was my fault,' and the press would have written it down and the other people in the courtroom would have whispered and stared and she would have loathed the unwelcome attention and loathed herself and felt, in consequence, some kind of expiation. But no one even suggested she was to blame and Inspector Moyse, seated unobtrusively at the back of the room, went away without probing either her conscience or her fears. Caroline walked round to the station alone. She had a long wait for her train and to pass the time she bought a detective story. Perhaps it was a mistake: afterwards, she wished she had bought last month's *Vogue* (which was the only one they had) or *Harper's and Queen*. At the head of the first chapter the author had quoted two lines from the *Rubáiyát* of Omar Khayyam: 'There was a Door to which I found no Key; There was a Veil past which I could not see.' Like me, Caroline thought with sudden honesty, unable to read on. Only she did not *want* to find the key, nor lift the veil. . . It was very warm on the train and she drifted off into a kind of waking dream where she was going round a picture gallery with a guide who looked like the coroner, only somehow he hadn't noticed that all the pictures were covered up. They stopped in front of one huge canvas and Caroline caught hold of the cloth which was shrouding it and pulled, but it did not come away. Everyone was staring at her, stolid with disapproval, while she tugged and tugged in vain. And then suddenly there was a sound of breaking glass, and the cloth came away, and she was looking at a splintered mirror in which was her own reflection. Wet green stuff like slime was dripping down the rotten frame. And somewhere behind her left shoulder was her father's face. . .

* * *

She was not conscious of any moment when she thought, definitely: 'I must *do* something,' but by the time she got to London she had made up her mind. Or perhaps her mind had made itself up, independent of her will: she wasn't sure. She only knew she could not go on refusing to see, refusing to think, turning her face away from truth. If Ulysses had somehow driven Melissa to take those pills, deliberately or by accident, if he had seduced her, scorned her, encouraged her – Caroline wanted to *know*. In contrast, the details of her father's death appeared remote and insignificant; for a long time now she had hardly given it a thought. But Melissa's suicide had been too convenient, coming so soon after she overheard that fatal telephone call. When she knew the worst, Caroline told herself, then she would be able to face up to it. Fear is only incomplete knowledge. (Who had said that?) Perhaps, somewhere at the back of her mind, she still half dreamed of reassurance.

The Antoniades were in the telephone book (she had used the number once before, but had not written it down). It took her some time to get hold of a member of the family and longer still to make herself understood. In the background, she could hear a radio and the sound of people moving about. And then a familiar, all too familiar voice spoke into the 'phone, low-toned, carefully nonchalant: 'Hello? Yes?'

'It's Caroline.' She had already thought out what she was going to say. 'Come to my flat – tonight. Glynis is away. I think we should talk.'

She could tell, from the ensuing silence, that he was taken aback. 'I'm not sure –' This time, it was his turn to hesitate. But she knew it was only a matter of form.

'Let's not start playing games again.' Now she had come to a decision her voice sounded cool and self-assured, almost the voice of the old Caroline from before her father's death, though the assurance was mostly on the surface. 'We're wasting time. You wanted to see me: then see me. Tonight.'

She waited a few moments for an answer, but none came. Only partly satisfied, Caroline rang off.

He arrived after dark. Once before, she had washed her hair and neglected her make-up, to make him come. This time her hair was dry, silk-smooth and perfectly straight, her lipstick and blusher as immaculate as a mask. She looked (he thought) tearproof, kissproof, touchproof. He felt, as at the beginning of their relationship, like an instrument, a servant, who would never be able to reach her or have any lasting significance in her life. He tried to push the thought to one side, telling himself it was nonsense, but it persisted.

As before, he followed her into the kitchen. Then, his presence had seemed obtrusive, sexually disturbing; now, he was merely in the way. Caroline made coffee and took it into the living room.

'Sit down.'

He wanted to touch her, if only to prove that he still could; but he sat down.

Caroline sat opposite him, carefully arranging her body to appear at ease. She knew she was in control, for the moment, but she knew also how tenuous that control actually was, a fine thread which might snap at any second if she strained it too far. She was afraid, above all, to allow herself hope. Hope was a weakness, a chink in her armour. There could be no easy answers.

'Did you see Melissa?' The question came out harsh and cold.

Ulysses opened his mouth as though to answer, hesitated – then a faint smile curved his lips. 'Maybe.'

'I assume maybe means yes.'

'*You* weren't there,' Ulysses murmured; but she did not react.

'And maybe,' she went on, picking her words, 'maybe you talked to her. Maybe you upset her – deliberately. Maybe you thought you were being clever, capitalising on her neuroses, her instability, her – her physical plainness. You knew she was attracted to you.'

Ulysses shrugged. 'Your father told me once she was the suicidal type.'

'No,' Caroline said sharply. 'She was the type to take an overdose as a way of getting attention. She was not the type who would really wish to kill herself.'

'Then she made a mistake, didn't she?'

He sounded bored, uncaring. For a minute, Caroline felt as if it were all in her mind, a haphazard tragedy that just happened to fit in too well, a book that might have fallen open anywhere, suspicion, coincidence, her own private madness. She said: 'Did she?' But there was doubt in her voice.

Ulysses did not hear it. He got up and came towards her, resting his hands on the arms of her chair and leaning over her in one of those assertive would-be macho attitudes which she always found so contrived. 'Listen,' he said – perhaps it was unconscious, but his foreign accent was very apparent – 'what do you want me to tell you? That she made a pass at me, and I rejected her? That I told her she was ugly, her breasts were too small, her body that of a child? That I said no real man would ever want to make love to her – masturbating and peering through keyholes was the only sexual pleasure she would ever get? And so – because she was sorry for herself, because she wanted everyone else to be sorry for her – she went away and took too many pills, and that was that. What if I said those things to her? If it had not been me, it would have been someone else. I spoke only the truth. She was stupid, stupid and unattractive; there is no excuse for women to be stupid and unattractive. She was not happy in herself and she gave no happiness to other people. It is better – better for *her* – that she is dead.'

'You think of *no one* but yourself,' Caroline said, violently. She felt a little sick. 'It doesn't matter what she was like – can't you see that? She was a human being. She might have learnt to be happy. At any rate she should have had the chance.'

'That is nonsense,' said Ulysses. 'She was determined to be miserable. When someone has made up their mind, there is nothing you can do. You are a realist; you must know that.'

He was right, of course: Melissa would never have been happy. But that was only one aspect of the truth. Feeling suddenly constricted, Caroline got up and walked across the room. He moved aside without attempting to restrain her. On her feet, she found she was shaking, though whether with anger or horror she did not know. She said, obstinately: 'Melissa didn't want to die. That's all that matters. She didn't *want* to die.'

'Then she shouldn't have taken an overdose.'

'Do you know,' Caroline said abruptly, 'what she took?'

'It was her – what are they called? – anti-depressants. I read it in the paper. Why?'

'If she had taken aspirin,' Caroline said, watching him very steadily, 'she might have been all right.'

There was something in Ulysses' face that she did not understand, something compelling and intent. He said: 'Perhaps she could not find the aspirin.'

Did you hide it? thought Caroline. But she did not ask. 'In my father's surgery,' she continued, precisely, 'there was a book out on the desk. A medical book. It fell open at a page dealing with anti-depressants.'

'Possibly,' Ulysses said softly, 'Melissa looked them up, to see if they would work.'

'No.' Caroline kept her eyes fixed on his. 'If she had known how dangerous they were she would never have taken them. The risk was too great.'

'You forget,' said Ulysses, 'she was expecting you to come home, wasn't she? She was expecting you to come home and find her. . .'

Caroline's fingers curled into her palm until she could feel the nails pricking her flesh. I won't let him do it, she told herself. I won't let him use my own guilt against me. And then, the flicker of a thought: *He is getting to know me too well.*

'It is stupid to blame each other,' Ulysses went on. 'You meant well, I suppose; I meant – less well. But I at least am honest. You loved Melissa no more than I; your good intentions were just hypocrisy, a sop to your conscience. I don't offer my conscience sops. She was a nuisance; she is dead; I am relieved. So are you. Maybe it was our fault – both of us – but it is too late now to alter that and pointless to worry. Your good intentions – my bad ones – the result was the same. You cannot opt out as you are so fond of doing. I told you once before: we are in this together.' (The cliché – or its implications – made her wince.) 'Maybe you left Melissa to meet me on purpose, hoping I would deal with her for you, get rid of the nuisance. Whatever your reasons, we are accomplices. My deeds are your deeds. It is stupid to argue about it.'

He came towards her, pausing a little way off, studying her, she thought, almost gently. But there was calculation under the gentleness. 'I have not seen you for a long time, Caroline. We talk too much. It would be better to make love.'

She said: 'Would it?' just for something to say. His arms

207

slid round her; he pressed his mouth to hers – a hard, cold kiss which gradually softened into a deliberate tenderness. This is the moment, thought Caroline, when I am supposed to give in. She draped limp hands around his neck, turned her face into his shoulder. Inside her, there blossomed a sudden awareness of boredom – not reluctance, nor apprehension, nor any of the things she might have (or should have) felt, but the deadly familiar boredom of a wife ten years married going through an automatic performance with a husband to whom she has long been indifferent. It was illogical – she and Ulysses had made love on one occasion only – but the boredom was there; she knew it like a friend. Perhaps there had been a moment, a moment of passion and togetherness, when they might have made something lasting, if only in memory. But the moment had passed unregarded and in the intervening months they had grown too far apart ever to touch again. She could feel his erection – he never had any difficulty in becoming erect – the tightening of his muscles, but it was a passion without love, a cold, savage purpose. Almost as though the dullness of her response reminded him of some other lover, some other incident which he would rather have forgotten, and he took what revenge he could.

'We are accomplices,' he repeated, when they were in bed, trying to reach her, to make her angry, anything to break through that silent acquiescence. When at last she allowed him to arouse her it was almost an act of condescension, like a mother handing a sweet to her child to make him behave. She climaxed briefly and then lay, passive, waiting for him to finish. When it was over, she lit a cigarette. They talked about going away together, after the trial, but none of it was real.

17

The next few weeks passed very quietly. Afterwards, Caroline always looked back on that period as an attempt by Fate to lull her into the proverbial sense of false security, so that when her fragile peace of mind was destroyed – and it would take, she felt, such a little thing – the shock would be all the greater. By mutual agreement, she and Ulysses did not meet or telephone. Her mother rang at regular intervals and Harry came down once, presumably on business, and gave her a pub lunch in the City. The publicity surrounding the dual tragedy (as it was called) brought an assortment of letters from distant and usually mute relatives, including one from Celia full of conventional yet somehow awkward expressions of sympathy. Caroline was not quite sure why she had written since the associations were evidently so disagreeable. Inspector Moyse visited her once – he was in London on another case, or so he told her, and he 'thought he would look her up'. They talked mostly about Melissa's suicide.

'I heard someone saw Ulysses in Cheyney that day,' the Inspector remarked.

'Isn't he in prison?' Caroline said in faint surprise, hoping she did not sound disingenuous.

'He's out on bail,' the inspector explained. 'Of course, the witness may have been mistaken. There are several foreign students with rooms in Cheyney and to the average Englishman one young foreigner looks much like another.'

'Yes,' said Caroline carelessly, wondering if she was being lured down an escape route, only to show that she had something to escape. 'I didn't think you could get bail on a murder charge?'

The conversation drifted onto points of law and by the time the inspector left Caroline felt almost relaxed. She might have

been pleased with herself if she had not experienced so much distaste for her increasing skill at evading both lies and truth.

Angela rang her at work, the first week in September. Caroline had almost forgotten Angela. Since she had gone to Canada they had kept up a desultory correspondence consisting, on Caroline's side, of regular but conventional communications, and on Angela's of verbose rhapsodies on Michel and the Canadian scenery, not necessarily in that order, interspersed with long silences. Lately their correspondence had grown more desultory than ever. 'Are you in England?' Caroline heard herself saying, rather stupidly, she thought. Angela would never have telephoned her from Canada.

'I'm staying with Helen, darling. You know, *Helen*. I've heard all about it. You poor dear, it must have been simply frightful for you –'

Caroline interrupted ruthlessly. 'What are you doing here?'

'I've come to see the parents. Michel and I have decided to take the big plunge – wedding bells and orange blossom and all that. I'm not sure if it's awful or wonderful. I keep shaking whenever I think of it.'

Caroline said: 'I hope you'll be very happy.'

'Of course I shall – he's so lovely to me. He bought me a whole new set of luggage the other day, just because the handle came off my suitcase and there wasn't time to get it mended before this trip. I adore him. It's just so panic-making to think of me – *me!* – with babies and nappies and things. And having to say all that about 'from this day forward' and 'till death us do part'. It sounds so dreadfully permanent. Carla, do you think I'm doing the right thing?'

But Caroline knew Angela too well by now to be taken aback by the question. 'I should think so,' she said coolly. 'If it feels right to you.'

Angela, however, was obviously in one of those moods where she absorbed very little of what the other person was saying. 'How awful of me,' she went on, 'to be all bubbling over when you must be feeling simply shattered. Although perhaps it's good for you to be made to think about something *happy* for a change? Glynis said you looked dreadfully pale and wan.' So she's already interrogated Glynis, thought Caroline, annoyed. 'I tell you what, we'll go someplace where we can

get cream cakes – huge squashy ones with lots of calories – and you can tell me everything and I'll tell you everything and that will cheer you up. How about tomorrow?'

It was on the tip of Caroline's tongue to say she couldn't make it. She had forgotten all about the photographs until she found herself looking at an out-of-date Greek postcard stuck on the side of the filing cabinet. Photographs which had once been indiscreet and could now be disastrous. Angela had never sent them to her but she must have had them developed, might even produce them over coffee: 'Darling, guess what I've got? Do you remember that time in Greece. . .'

'Tomorrow will be fine.' Caroline's voice sounded flat, careful. 'Bring your photos of Canada – I want to see what it's like. And – I don't suppose you've got the pictures from when we went to Greece? I'd quite like to see those.'

'I don't know, darling. I'll have a look, I remember they were awfully good – that's a perfectly wicked camera. But I've got heaps of Canadian pics. You'll be bored out of your mind. Honestly, British Columbia is *so* beautiful. . .'

The next day, Caroline finished work at four and met Angela in a coffee shop in Covent Garden. It was the kind of place where all the furniture was made of pine and the crockery was cubist earthenware. The walls were covered with knotted string and instead of pictures there were two or three collages of the dead-leaf-and-leather variety. Besides the usual cream cakes and Sachertorte there was a carrot cake, leek tartlets, and small, wedge-shaped hunks of something that looked as if it was made from dried apricots and All-Bran. Caroline was not much surprised when Angela selected one of these.

'I love dried fruit,' she explained. 'Besides, I want to be *thin* for the wedding.' Somehow or other, she managed to pinch some loose flesh from her scanty hips. 'You have a cream cake. It'll do you good.'

Caroline dutifully had a cream cake. Afterwards, it occurred to her that she had probably done so to please Angela. The most unlikely things pleased Angela.

They sat down at a table in the corner and Angela held forth on her marriage plans, her (fortunately requited) passion for Canada, and what on earth was so-and-so doing

now, while Caroline picked at her cream cake and said little. Finally, Angela produced a sheaf of photo-folders, opened the top one and tipped a cascade of colour prints onto the table. With a curious sense of artificiality Caroline saw Ulysses' face, first next to a girl she did not recognise (of course – the courier), then beside herself, his lips pressed carelessly against her cheek. . . She picked up the photograph and studied it with vague incredulity. It seemed so impossible that she and Ulysses should ever have met like that, so casually, should ever have laughed together among a crowd of other people laughing or exchanged a playful meaningless kiss. Not quite a year ago, she thought, and it might have been another life, another time. But photographs lied – faces lied. Her own smile had hidden, even then, the lust for revenge, loneliness, bitterness, delusion. And in her mind the remembered laughter sounded frenzied and hollow, fools' laughter from some Jacobean tragedy. Mirth and madness.

Angela's voice broke into her thoughts, piercing and disastrous: 'It *is* him, isn't it? The one who killed your father? When I saw his name in the paper I knew it couldn't be a coincidence.'

Somehow, it wasn't unexpected. Perhaps she had feared it, deep inside, a small unexpressed fear which had lain at the back of fears far greater and more terrible since Angela's telephone call or even before. At least she wasn't entirely unprepared. The main thing with lying – she had learnt that by now – was not to answer too quickly. Take your time and use it. Think. Look at the cream cake, look up at Angela, pause to consider as though pausing to consider were the natural thing to do. Don't hurry. Don't panic.

'Yes,' she said slowly. 'Yes, that's him.'

'But darling, *how*? How on earth did they *meet*?'

Thank God, she didn't understand, didn't suspect. But why should she?

'It was my fault.' Caroline's voice was scarcely above a whisper. She hoped it might encourage Angela to lower her voice too, although she doubted if anyone was listening. 'I introduced them. I didn't know – didn't guess –'

'Darling, *no* –'

Angela's whisper, Caroline reflected, was almost more penetrating than her normal tones. 'I'd given him my

address,' she went on, picking out strands of the truth like different-coloured threads from a tangle. 'He said he was coming over here in the winter and I told him to get in touch. You know how one does that sort of thing on holiday. I never really thought he would.'

'Only he did?'

Caroline nodded. 'I told him to come to the flat. I'd forgotten my father was coming to tea the same day. He stayed later than I expected and they – met. I suppose Ulysses made up his mind to pursue him there and then.'

'But he seemed so *nice*.'

Caroline took refuge in a well-worn cliché. 'No matter how well one knows people,' she said, 'one doesn't ever *really* know what's going on in their minds. And after all,' she added, 'we *didn't* know him well, did we? Only the way you know someone on holiday. We got drunk together, and we flirted, but we didn't talk.' And she concluded, with an artistry which made her feel vaguely sick: 'I only wish I'd found time to talk to him. . .'

'What did you do,' Angela asked, after a suitable pause, 'when you found out he was living with your father?'

Involuntarily, Caroline looked round; but there was no one sitting nearby. 'What could I do?' she said. 'I didn't want to know. I didn't want anything to do with him – either of them. I was furious because of Melissa – she was still living at home – but I've never had any influence with my father.' She added, harshly: 'We weren't close.'

Perhaps the harshness was genuine. Even Angela seemed to sense the closing of a forbidden door. She said (not for the last time): 'It must have been awful for you.'

'Let's not talk about it.' Not for the last time, Caroline withdrew behind a natural *gêne*. 'I'd rather not. Most people don't realise that Ulysses and I – knew each other. I feel so responsible – so *ashamed*.'

'I won't tell anyone.' Angela had always enjoyed keeping other people's secrets, Caroline recalled. Anyhow, she would probably be too busy talking about her own affairs to talk very much about anyone else's – even if they did include violence and death. As long as she hadn't already discussed things with, for example, Glynis.

You know what Angela's like, Caroline imagined herself saying, carelessly. She always get things mixed up. . .

Aloud, she said: 'Anyway, haven't we had enough of my problems? I know I have. Show me your pictures of Canada.'

It wasn't difficult to divert Angela. Afterwards, Caroline picked up the folder of Greek photographs. 'You don't mind,' she said, 'if I borrow these? I'd quite like copies of those ones on the beach.' Angela, she reflected, probably wouldn't notice if she forgot to give them back altogether, and certainly wouldn't miss one or two prints. Or would she?

'Of course you can,' Angela said. 'I'm going down to my parents next week, but I'll be back in London the week after. If you could return them to me then –?'

'Of course,' Caroline affirmed. 'When are you going back to Canada?'

'The fifth of October.'

It was the date of the trial.

When Caroline returned to the flat Glynis was there, unpacking an overnight bag after a brief absence with Rodney. She seemed in an exceptionally laconic mood and, when Caroline mentioned Angela, only commented scathingly on the married state. Evidently they had not discussed Ulysses. With Angela, Caroline thought, you could never be sure. She would relate the most intimate personal information in public at the top of her voice and yet, under pressure, she might not say a word. As long as she had not shown anyone the photographs. Caroline could not remember if there had been one of Ulysses in any of the papers, but they were bound to come up with something for the trial.

Alone in her room, she pulled out the photo-folder and wondered how to destroy the evidence. She could tear the relevant prints and negatives (there were only three or four) into small pieces and flush them down the loo. She had an idea that was the standard procedure. But the loo didn't always work very well and a few pieces would almost certainly be left, floating round on the surface of the water, and she would have to wait for the cistern to fill up and then flush again, maybe several times, while Glynis outside would be wondering what the hell she was doing. Caroline's mind

214

shrank at the idea of such a grotesque charade. She had never found embarrassment – her own or other people's – particularly laughable. Briefly, she considered the more mundane possibilities of the dustbin. But although she couldn't seriously imagine the police picking through her rubbish she didn't quite like that idea, either. It didn't seem sufficiently *final*. The best way to dispose of the pictures, she decided, would be to burn them. . . There was a light tap on the door and Glynis came in without waiting for permission. She always came into rooms like that. Caroline slipped the folder hastily back into her bag and hoped she didn't look too conscious.

''Phone for you,' Glynis said. 'Some man.'

It would appear suspicious to shut the bag, worse to take it with her. With a sense of reluctance that was almost physical, Caroline left it lying open on the dressing table and went out. Not that she really believed Glynis would look in it, but. . . With indescribable relief, she felt rather than heard footsteps following her out of the bedroom, the swish of the door pulled not-quite-shut behind them. It was the endless ramifications of deceit that were so terrible, she thought. One small lie (to herself she called it 'small') bred a whole host of complications, spreading like ripples from a pebble dropped in a pool, disrupting the smooth clear mirror of her existence. And you couldn't go back. Untruth, once spoken, was fixed in your life: a footprint in concrete. Forever.

She hadn't stopped to wonder who it might be on the telephone.

'Hello, Caroline.'

The fool. She had *told* him not to ring her here.

'You're not alone, yes? Your flatmate is listening? Don't worry; I won't be long. Just tell me when I can come over. I want to see you again – before the trial.'

'Hold on.' Glynis might know his voice by now – not that it mattered, as long as she never realised whose voice it was she knew. 'I'll just check –' Caroline opened her diary, a peculiarly meaningless gesture, since she was already aware that it was empty. 'Would next weekend be all right? Sunday?' She made the words deliberately casual – ordinary words for an ordinary date. She couldn't show any anger at him now, not with Glynis there. She couldn't tell him about Angela, the necessity for more lies, more difficulties, the risk which (so it seemed) increased each day, each hour.

'Sunday,' Ulysses confirmed.

As she replaced the receiver, she looked blandly at Glynis. 'You will be away Sunday, won't you?' she said, with a half-smile that invited understanding.

Glynis grinned crookedly. 'Of course I shall. Lunch with the parents. You can have the place to yourself.'

She was thinking: Caroline is becoming almost human lately, in spite of all her problems. Or perhaps because of them? All the same, there must be a man in it somewhere.

Caroline was thinking: I'm getting far too good at this.

The next day, she had go to Cheyney to sort out one or two details on the sale of the house. It wasn't an essential trip, Pettigrew & Farquharson could have handled it for her, but suddenly she wanted to go. She didn't stop to analyse her reasons. Somehow, she hadn't had any opportunity to get rid of the photographs and she carried them with her, in her handbag, feeling curiously light-headed at the idea of danger. That was the trouble with taking risks: the fact that you could get used to it, after the first horrors had worn off, you could even grow to enjoy the feeling of recklessness, of freedom from certainty, like running blind, faster and faster, down a steep unknown road. And so, in the end, you deceived yourself into invulnerability, until a stone caught you, and you fell. Caroline knew she was not invulnerable. I should have burned them at the flat, she thought, placing an unconscious hand over her bag. I only had to wait until Glynis went out.

She entered the house cautiously, but there was no one about. She had half expected to see Mr Pettigrew, requiring her signature on some technicality, or even Mrs Bunce, still hoovering automatically at the uncarpeted floor. But there were no intruders, no ghosts. The rooms, bare of furnishings, seemed to have shrunken, as her father's body had seemed to shrink in death. If there had ever been any atmosphere, the bustle of life or the shadow of tragedy, there was none now. But there hadn't been, Caroline thought. That's what was wrong with this house. There was never any atmosphere at all.

She went into the living room. In one corner, a few frayed wires thrust through the wall, like the ends of torn arteries. Dust had gathered in the hollow fireplace. She had felt it would be appropriate to come here but now, in the bleak, unhaunted room, it seemed merely silly and dangerous. Still, she had to get rid of the photographs. She went down on one knee on the cold hearth and took out her cigarette lighter. The prints took a while to catch, burning with an uncertain flame that twisted them into half-blackened corkscrews and then lost interest and went out. Somewhere, Caroline thought she had read that pictures or writing on charred paper could be restored by chemical treatment. She blew on the ashes until they were cold and sifted them into powder between her fingers. It all took much longer than she had expected and the smell, like that of snuffed candles, seemed to pervade the whole room. She was so absorbed in what she was doing that she did not hear, or did not register, a faint sound from the hall.

'May I ask what you are doing, Miss Horvath?'

For a few seconds, Caroline did not attempt to stand up, did not even turn her head. She knew her face had gone deadly white. The voice was not loud, but it sounded loud, in the way a soft voice sometimes does in an empty room. She waited as long as she dared before speaking.

'Hello, inspector.' Her tone was peculiarly colourless. As she got to her feet a little warmth crept back into her cheeks. To gain time, she said: 'What are you doing here?' And then, with more confidence: 'How did you get in?'

'I have a key from the estate agents. You must have arrived when I was upstairs. I'm sorry if I frightened you.'

'This is a private house.' He must have heard her come in. The stairs creaked unless you were very careful. He must have come down quietly so as not to disturb her.

'You have moved out; the next tenant has yet to move in. I am not intruding on anyone's privacy. Is it really necessary for me to get a warrant?'

'What do you want here?'

'The – er – atmosphere of the crime.'

How could she ever have thought him mild, sympathetic, disinterested? His very gentleness, the softness of his voice, seemed suddenly sinister. His spectacles reflected the daylight, blankly.

'Your hands need washing, Miss Horvath. What were you doing?'

The tips of her fingers were smeared with ash. She looked down at them, thoughtfully, and then up at the inspector. Her gaze was very steady. It was all she could do not to appear defiant.

'I was burning some old photographs.'

(He knew there was something wrong from the steadiness of her gaze.)

'I see.' Burning photographs might have been the most natural thing in the world. 'Something you turned out from the back of a drawer, perhaps? Or in the attic?'

A trap. He was there before her; he must know she hadn't had time for searching through attics and drawers. Somehow, she must – she *must* – convince him that the photographs had nothing to do with the case. Whatever else he might have hinted, she did not think he suspected that she and Ulysses had known each other in the past, that Ulysses had seduced her father at *her* instigation. How should even a policeman imagine anything so monstrous? He did not know about Philip, about the whole wretched story of her life. But if he should begin to guess, it would be so easy, oh, so easy to start checking up. The Greek stamps on her passport (two trips). The bar that overlooked the sea. Angela. . .

The morals she had clung to so raggedly were long forgotten. To herself, she called it 'acting' not lying, though it made her feel no better: it came to the same thing. 'I brought them with me. I had to come down here and – it just happened that way. What has it to do with you?' She made the question surprised rather than resentful.

'It seems a slightly odd thing to do. When people behave oddly, it interests me.'

'Is it – odd?' She frowned. 'I suppose so. Does it matter?'

'That is what I should like to know.' He wasn't looking at her now. Instead, he had moved over to the window and the mirror-gaze of his glasses seemed to be fixed on the garden outside. No one had cut the grass all summer. Old Joe, Caroline recalled, had succumbed to rheumatism, or sciatica, or lumbago – one of those ills from which aged gardeners

218

invariably suffered – so the new tenants would have to find someone else. Wasn't it Old Joe who had told her about the ghost? The ghost in the garden – even as a child, she had never been able to imagine a ghost who would enter the house. But of course, there wasn't any ghost. Only in her own mind.

She murmured, almost apologetically: 'I don't really see that it's any of your business.'

'Isn't it?'

She had joined him at the window, leaning on the sill, taking a leaf out of his book. Her eyes wandered unseeingly over a weed-grown flowerbed. Presently, she gave a slight sigh. 'If you must know,' she said, 'they were photographs of my brother and me, when we were children. He died. I expect you know that. It was supposed to be an accident but – I always thought it was suicide. I felt very bitter about it. My father loved him the best, you see. He was going to help Philip in his career – get him an exhibition.'

'He was an artist, wasn't he?'

She nodded. 'I don't think he was much good though. And – he was weak. That's why he killed himself. It was a genetic thing – from his mother – no one's fault. Some people are born with that kind of cowardice. But I was afraid once or twice that my father felt responsible. They'd argued in the past. And in a family it's very easy to feel responsible for things that are not really your fault.' She added, with a twisted humour that the inspector, she hoped, would never see, never appreciate: 'I sometimes think, if Philip hadn't died, none of this would have happened.'

'You mean,' Inspector Moyse said, in a voice carefully devoid of irony, 'that Ulysses was a substitute for his son, not merely a lover.'

'Does that sound silly?'

'Not at all. Very Freudian. But – forgive me – I still don't quite understand the significance of the photographs.'

'I kept them, that's all. I don't usually keep things. I kept them to remind me, to keep the bitterness, I suppose. That *was* silly. Philip couldn't help himself – it was just heredity.'

'And now –' his tone was gentle '– you decided to bury your dead. All together, in the same grave. Is that it?'

He believes me, she thought, not with triumph, but dully,

with a dull relief. *He believes me.* 'Yes,' she said. 'Yes, that's it.' It was like concluding a prayer to a non-existent God. In her heart she denied Him, but her spoken word lent Him being. That's it. So be it. Amen.

Surely now the Inspector would go away. . .

'Even the dead deserve justice, Caroline –' (it was the first time he had called her by her christian name) '– if only for the sake of the living. A killer, for example, may kill again. It need not even be insanity; sometimes it is merely a lack of conscience, and the habit of ruthlessness. Vengeance is immoral but society must be protected. A cliché, I know, and like all clichés, immutably true. Bury your dead by all means. But do not forget what you owe to those of us who are left alive.'

Caroline stared blankly at him. She couldn't immediately think of any other way to react.

'You are a woman of imagination,' he continued. 'I want you to use your imagination. Imagine a young man – not perhaps a very well-educated young man, but one with a certain native intelligence uninhibited by affections or moral scruples. A young man who does not like work but who likes money – and the things you can buy with money. An extremely good-looking young man. He attracts the attention of an older man who, at a relatively small price, can give him everything he wants. At first he is perfectly content. But – er – custom stales. Gradually, he begins to grudge the price. He is – or so one of my WPCs assures me – attractive not only to older men but also to women. Possibly he prefers women; possibly it is a matter of indifference to him. Anyway, there are two daughters of the house. Perhaps he begins by intriguing with the younger daughter, but she is unstable and the affair becomes too risky. I don't know. Then he meets the elder, more beautiful daughter. And he thinks: if the old man were to die, I could have her, and the money as well. All this, and Heaven too. . .'

Caroline said clearly: 'You're mad.' She knew, too late, that that was what they always said.

'Imagine the scene.' His voice had dropped almost to a whisper; he was standing on the place where her father had died. 'An argument that sprang up in this very room. A snatched opportunity, with no time to think or to be afraid.

220

Or maybe there *was* no argument. It wasn't necessary, after all. Stavrakis is very strong. Maybe he just took the other man by the shoulders, or by the head, and forced him back, and back – until his skull stove in on the corner of the mantelpiece and his brains dripped onto the carpet. Only afterwards, when the body had fallen – here, wasn't it? – would Stavrakis begin to panic. He thought up a story – quite a clever story, in its way, because it was so near the truth, so simple, so difficult to disprove. He arranged the poker, though he probably forgot about the fingerprints until later. He was too frightened to think clearly. And then you came.' He had come quite close to her now, and he stood looking down into her face. Behind the glasses his pale-brown eyes expressed a sort of tolerant pity. 'What did you see, Caroline? All along I have known there was something you have not told, maybe something you have refused to acknowledge even to yourself. But you are a young woman of principle and it troubles you, doesn't it, even in your subconscious. Why don't you tell me? Is he so attractive that you can condone your father's murder for his sake? Or has he some other hold over you?' And then, when she did not answer: 'What did you see, that afternoon? Tell me, Caroline. What did you see?'

If he had shouted at her, threatened her, she might have felt brave and defiant. But he sounded only gentle and sorry. She could not think, could not reply. The picture he had drawn for her wasn't true, she knew it wasn't true, but it was horribly easy to visualise, in that room where it had not happened. Her father's body falling; the drip, drip, drip of blood onto the carpet. (*Had* there been blood on the carpet?)

She said at last: 'I saw nothing.' It was the truth, or the letter of the truth, but it did not sound convincing. Whatever she said would not sound convincing, not now. It didn't matter. She had run out of lies, and could only hold on to her denial. She knew the inspector wouldn't believe her.

'What about your sister? There was a moment when you thought Stavrakis had killed her too, didn't you? He says he wasn't there, but he can't prove it. Did you know he was here? Did you know why he wanted your sister out of the way? You must have guessed he had slept with her.'

'He – ' She checked herself. Another trap. Jealousy – the easiest road to betrayal. But she didn't care enough to feel jealous, or even interested. She said: 'Melissa committed suicide.' It wasn't necessary to say any more.

'There is such a thing as moral responsibility. The law does not recognise it, but you and I know it exists – don't we? Or can you close your eyes to that, too?'

How sad he sounded, she thought, how unutterably sad. He didn't see, didn't understand the bitter reality of what he had said. She knew all about moral responsibility. Because she, and she alone, was responsible. For everything.

'You don't understand,' she murmured, turning away. There was nothing he could say, nothing he could do, that would make her explain.

18

In the night, Caroline dreamed. It was a dream she had had two or three times in the days when she lived with Philip. She was at a party, or perhaps in the street, surrounded by a great crowd of people, and she could see him on the opposite pavement, looking at her, and he too was surrounded by people, laughing and talking indifferently, more and more people, so that gradually the two of them were being forced farther and farther apart. She struggled to reach him, but the street had grown wider, and the crowd had become a wild Dionysian mob, plucking at her with a hundred hands, and he was borne irresistibly away in a flood of merrymakers, still gazing after her helplessly, with a forsaken, wistful look on his face like an abandoned child. Waking from this dream, trembling and irrational, she had always tried to assure herself that it was merely the result of insecurity, symbolising, possibly, some of the difficulties of their situation. Such fancies of the subconscious were inevitable and not particularly significant. She had never been a believer in the importance of dreams.

After Philip died, the dream had not come again. Until now. But this time the face across the street – the face that had been her brother's – seemed to have changed, darkened: a dusky alien face with slanting eyes. In her dream, she knew it was familiar, but she could not think who it was. And its expression was no longer wistful and lost, but hungry, eager, searching. Gradually, she began to realise that the behaviour of the crowd, too, was different. It was the same laughing, indifferent crowd of revellers which had come between them in the earlier dreams. But instead of being forced apart they were propelled, inexorably, towards each other, while she struggled in a frenzy of helplessness to get away. . .

When she woke, it was a few minutes before she realised where she was. Somehow, she had been expecting to be at Cheyney, although there was no logical reason for this: she had never dreamed the dream at Cheyney before. But the window was in the wrong place and there was a faint rumour of early traffic which you always hear in London. She felt a strange sense of relief. For a moment she had imagined herself sitting up in bed, to find her room stripped of furnishings and the silent corridor waiting outside, and downstairs the living room with its cold fireplace and a slab of moonlight on the floor. She listened to a car revving somewhere and felt reassured. It was good just to sit there, her arms clasped about her knees, thinking of nothing, feeling nothing. Looking back briefly on her teens – useless, wasted years they seemed now – she wished she had concentrated more on *being*, less on longing and minding and all the finer graduations of self-inflicted anguish. Only now, when it was too late, could she appreciate how wonderful it was, just to breathe and be free. But that was the irony of life. You could only understand freedom – freedom from responsibility, from fear, from love and hate and pain – when you had lost it. And at last the inspector's words, which she had been trying to push aside all day, returned to her mind with all their implications, all their attendant possibilities, terrors, shadows, taking wing in the night like bats. Horror gripped her, the kind of horror that makes the flesh seem to hold too lightly too your bones and your heart grow cold and still. It's not true, she told herself, without conviction, without hope. She had known that such things could happen, that other people could be violent, brutal, avaricious, but not that the seed that spawned these things could be found in her own soul. If Ulysses had killed her father deliberately. . . But she *would not* think of it. Nothing is good or bad, but thinking makes it so. These were the phantoms of imagination and darkness, borne of suspicion, fantasy, fear. By day, surely, they would have no more substance than her dream.

She tried to get up, but her legs shook. In the end, she sat on the edge of the bed for some time, feeling her thighs grow cold, and waiting for the morning.

Ulysses came over, as arranged, on the Sunday. She had got past the stage of either wanting or not wanting to see him; she had no more positive feelings in the matter at all. He was her responsibility and therefore it was necessary: that was all that signified. After the trial, when he was acquitted, he would cease to be her responsibility and the chain of consequences which she had begun so long ago would be completed, not, as she had once envisaged, either rightly or wrongly, but inevitably. She did not try to think what might happen if he was not acquitted: the issues became too complicated. She had occasionally allowed herself to contemplate confession, not when Inspector Moyse had looked at her so sadly – in those moments, the instinct of self-preservation was too strong for her – but afterwards, when he was gone, and she remembered the regret in his face, and there was no self-seeking cowardice to restrain her. But confession would only implicate Ulysses further. And among all her webs of deceit and half-truth, she had not yet found a thread strong enough to hold, and subtle enough to clear him. Perhaps she was too inept for the spinning of such threads; perhaps, in the last resort, her respect for the truth would lead her to condemn him if not herself, eking out the appropriate measure of remorse to console her conscience. The little sincerity, the half-principles that most men live by uplift us all to different levels of hypocrisy, while only absolute evil remains absolutely honest with itself. Caroline, ruthlessly applying her own high standards of truth and justice to the rest of the world, was only just beginning to learn how easy it would be to achieve an even higher standard of false piety. But when it came to thinking about the future the lesson, like so many such lessons, only made a decision more difficult.

They went into the bedroom as a matter of course. Ulysses' love-making was more passionate than ever, but also harsher, more desperate, as though he knew he could no longer reach into her mind. 'I need you,' he whispered, with a frantic, loveless urgency, lapsing into his native language as an afterthought, because somehow it seemed more magical and seductive. 'Caroline moù. Glika moù.' It had touched her once. Only now, when he was with her, could he realise fully how afraid he was. The prison walls seemed to be drawing very near; he could see them in her eyes, doorless walls shutting him out, shutting him in, he did not know which. He imagined her, after he had been sentenced, looking at him with a calm unchanging face, turning her shoulder, walking away. 'I'm sorry: I can do nothing.' He knew it was true, but it only made him angrier. He tried to hurt her, as he had once hurt her father, but it was too easy, and therefore impossible. Orgasm, when it finally occurred, was more a pain than a pleasure, as though it had been wrung from him by necessity or exhaustion, and when it was finished his whole body shuddered with relief. Afterwards, he watched her expression glaze over as if he could actually see her mind slipping further away from him.

'Caroline –'

'Yes?'

'It doesn't matter.'

There was a silence, the kind of silence common to a love affair gone stale, while he waited for her to ask him what was wrong, and she didn't. She was thinking about Angela, wondering whether to tell him, knowing at the back of her thought that she had never really intended to do so. The urge to confide in him, once so strong, had become merely an automatic pang, a part of that desire to talk to someone, anyone, which existed continually behind her compulsory reserve, like an ache to which she had grown so accustomed she did not notice it any more. She would sooner have talked to the inspector. She did not analyse her reaction: there was too much fear in it. Melissa had been a nuisance, in the way – and Melissa was dead. Her father, too. . . Of course, Ulysses had always liked Angela. He had not liked Melissa at all. She supposed he had not liked her father, although she did not really know. But with Angela, it was different. Nothing could possibly happen to Angela.

'Caroline – why don't you talk to me? Why don't you say something? What are you thinking of?'

'Nothing.'

She shifted her body, turning towards him, hoping vaguely that the movement would do as a substitute for reassurance. Her hair fell over her face and he pushed it back with a hand that was not quite steady.

'You don't care any more, do you?' he whispered. 'You just don't care. You have already abandoned me, in your heart. Everything I have done was because of you –' for a moment, she thought, he faltered on the edge of a confession, and her very pulse hesitated '– yet you have turned against me. What you started you were afraid to finish, so you looked away while I finished it for you, and now you want to see me in prison. I am not a tool that you can use and throw away because there is blood on it! You are like your father; did you know? You want to do – to *feel* – whatever you think it is –' he reached for a word '– *proper* to do and feel. You want to be a "nice girl". Your father wanted to be a "nice man" but he was not a nice man and now everybody knows it. Do you really believe you can ever be a nice girl again?'

I suppose that is what I want, she reflected, faintly amused. How ridiculous that I should still mind so much *what* I am, after everything that has happened.

'You have deserted me,' Ulysses went on, 'for a conscience you do not possess. Even when I make love to you, you are not there. Don't you understand –' he might have been about to accuse or threaten, but some instinct made him change his tactics '– don't you understand how that hurts?'

He looked very foreign and excitable, his dun-yellow eyes dark with unexpected pain. She found herself thinking, as she had thought in the early stages of their relationship, how utterly alien he was, how irreconcilably different from everything that belonged in her life. Once, his words would have left her silently furious: she had always felt deeply the indignity of such scenes, particularly in the bedroom. But now she could not even rouse herself to resentment. In her eyes, he saw an abstraction as distant as the moon. Don't you

226

understand, he had pleaded, but she had lost track of whatever she was supposed to have understood.

'Not really,' she said.

She met Angela the following week to return the photographs. As predicted, Angela did not even look at them. 'I wish you could come to the wedding,' she remarked. 'My family are flying over specially, of course; so's Helen, and Sue. Sue Parsons, darling: she's my very oldest friend. You must have met her. *Why* don't you come too? You could make it a holiday. I'm sure Helen would take you on with her to Vancouver. She's got these cousins there, simply rolling, *two* swimming pools. You can afford the fare, can't you? I thought your father left you lots of lovely money.'

'I have to stay for the trial,' Caroline reminded her.

'Oh Lord, I'd forgotten; how perfectly awful.' Angela's face melted into an expression of easy sympathy; she reached across the table to press Caroline's hand. 'Darling, don't look so *anxious*; I can't bear to see you looking anxious. Everything's going to be *all right*.'

Caroline, summoning up a vague smile to repudiate the charge of anxiety, wished that she could be so sure of the outcome, or even that such an outcome were possible.

After the long period of suspense, the trial itself brought a curious sense of anti-climax. Like a party, Caroline thought, which you have been looking forward to for ages, and which passes in a few swift hours of shallow chit-chat, a blare of music, a drunken whirling of lights. She had not expected the same laws of anticipation to apply to an unpleasant event as well as a pleasant one. Most of the first day was spent waiting to give her evidence, in a barren little room with pale walls and a lot of sunlight coming through a window at her back. Although she had kept her coat on Caroline got rather cold and sat as close as she could to the radiator, reading a novel by Paul Scott which she had brought with her to pass the time. Afterwards, though she could recall very little of what she said in the witness box, she remembered the novel in peculiar detail. But when she came to re-read it, some years later, she found herself imagining, not the yellow Indian sky and fleshless earth, but a pale memory of walls, uncertain as mist, and the light of a chill sun touching the nape of her neck. The novel itself had lost all conviction.

The clerk of the court called for her in the mid-afternoon. It was the wrong time of day, Caroline felt, for doing anything disagreeable or difficult (she always arranged dental appointments in the morning). She stood in the witness box, reciting the words of the oath – words which might have been in a forgotten language for all they meant to her – wondering if she would have to perjure herself, and how often. Somehow, it seemed much easier, less dishonest, to tell lies in a courtroom, to an unknown counsel for the prosecution, than in the intimacy of private conversation. She had a vague feeling everyone told lies in court, big lies, small lies, according to their need. The lawyers trained them in their lies and the judge made an elaborate pretence of not knowing they were so trained, because it was expected of him and a part of the sacred mechanics of Justice. The whole proceedings reminded Caroline of one of those plays where the characters have no names, only capital letters – First Juror, Second Juror, the Witness, the Accused – and even the costumes are symbolic rather than convincing: wigs that show the hair underneath, flowing robes worn over suits and ties. As for the God to whom she swore so solemnly, He was no more real to her than any other deity. Her childhood God was dead and she had never found a credible replacement.

The questions were far less alarming than she had expected, if only because she had answered most of them before. She could not remember whether she had to tell any actual lies. Sometimes, she looked at the counsel asking the questions; sometimes at the public, who had flocked there sensation-hunting like ancient Romans to the circus. She did not look at Ulysses at all. Gradually, she began to see the crowd, not as separate individuals, but as a vast many-headed entity, a thousand pair of eyes flickering to and fro with her every movement, all exactly together, or so it appeared in her growing vertigo, a single murmur in a thousand different throats. She could not focus on anything, and her voice sounded small and brittle in that huge room, a tiny quaver of clear sound in a place that was all silence and whispers. When she sat down, she realised she must have imagined the room far bigger than it actually was, and the crowd, although there were no empty seats, could not have exceeded a hundred. But in the witness box, she felt as if half the world were watching, both avid and indifferent, while she went through the ritual compromise of her integrity. Yet in the end the whole performance was curiously painless, like an operation under local anaesthetic: she knew it had happened because she had been there, but she had not felt anything at all.

The afternoon dragged on. Caroline crossed and re-crossed her legs to prevent pins and needles and tried not to fidget with the strap of her handbag. She was longing to smoke. Sometimes, she caught herself half wishing for a familiar face, her mother's or even Harry's; but she knew she did not really want them: they might look at her too keenly, glimpse the tension of her spirit behind the pale mouth and watchful eyes. She had been glad, at the time, that Margaret had not been called as a character witness. She could not have borne, on her mother's behalf, the ruthless exposure of private humiliations which she herself had never seen and could only conjecture. Perhaps, in the event, Margaret would have proved less sensitive than her daughter, but Caroline did not think of that. It was better, far better, that she should endure this alone. Enduring things alone had always been one of her obsessions.

Once or twice she looked at Ulysses, now she was not on the stand, but that only increased her sense of isolation. He was the stranger who had intruded into every facet of her existence, every fibre of her being, and yet remained a stranger, a maverick whom she knew at the last she could neither understand nor control. There were moments when she almost wished that he might be found guilty and locked away from her for a long, long time, so that she need never see or speak to him again. His eyes were fixed on the floor, whether in sullenness or resignation she could not guess, and did not meet hers. His hair stood out around his head, dark fraying into gold where the light caught it, like a sombre halo. On one occasion when the judge interceded he glanced up, and the sudden white gleam under his lowered brows made her shiver, though she did not know why.

* * *

229

The second day. The prosecution called Hilda Bunce. Defence cross-examined. The doctor, she said, always seemed such a nice, quiet man, not at all violent. But you never knew, did you?

'What did you never know, Mrs Bunce?'

Well, really, that he wasn't quite – *normal*. You know. That he was one of *them*.

'You mean, you never realised until the arrival of the accused that Dr Horvath was a homosexual?'   ¿

Well, yes. No. No, she didn't.

'Would you expect your employer to explain his sexual preferences to you during the course of your work?'. . . And so on.

Caroline had taken an extra sleeping pill the previous night and despite her inner tensions she could not stop yawning. Her inevitable craving for a cigarette started about mid-morning and became acute towards the lunchtime recess, but she could not smoke in the court precincts and she dared not go outside for fear of being waylaid by reporters. Dimly, she realised from the trend of the questioning that the prosecution had no real hope of the murder charge and was aiming for manslaughter: a spur-of-the-moment killing, possibly in the course of a fight, with no specific motive. She wondered what the inspector had said when he gave his evidence. He could not, she thought, give voice to suspicions which were based solely on speculation; not in court, anyway. But he had taken the stand towards the start of the trial, before she came in, and she had not seen him.

No one said very much about Melissa.

By the last day, Caroline was almost sure what the verdict would be. Counsel for the defence had proved, at least to his own satisfaction, that her father's personality had changed dramatically during the last few months of his life. Gerald Anstey, posing as former intimate of the deceased, said his behaviour had become 'unfriendly and bitter'. Jonquil Robinson, ex-receptionist, called him 'moody, sometimes curt, easily irritated'. One Vincent Gable, manager of the Charioteer, described the doctor's five years of voyeurism and his 'dangerous' over-reaction to even a tentative attempt at a pick-up. A psychiatrist and fellow Harley Street practitioner spoke of 'opening the floodgates', and 'the disastrous release of banked up passions, sweeping away the barriers of self-control'. Defence, questioning Ulysses, painted the picture of a childish mentality, stupid but not wicked, flattered by the attentions of someone as rich and successful as Dr Horvath and easily led astray. The jury, reminded of ancient customs, were invited, not too blatantly, to find his sexual ambiguity more understandable in a Greek. Ulysses himself managed to appear helpless and slightly inarticulate, the bewildered victim of circumstances which had little to do with him. Caroline, watching him gain time over one of the prosecution's more awkward questions by hesitating as though he had not immediately understood, listening to him stumble on English words which she had once heard him enunciate without difficulty, was unable to feel much amused. Yet there was something about his air of would-be innocence which remained oddly convincing, even to her. He doesn't *regret* anything, she thought, with a sort of hostile wonder. What was guilt, after all, but a surfeit of regrets? And innocence – innocence was only the inability to distinguish between right and wrong, the state of the savage. There was nothing admirable about it.

The judge summed up, dismissing the murder charge as the evidence was too thin, stating the case for manslaughter or self-defence so impartially that Caroline began to be afraid all over again. She wondered what she would do, if Ulysses was sentenced, if she would faint, or cry, or try to protest, crawling to her feet and mouthing like a fish, voiceless with terror; or if she would just sit there, saying nothing, until the people faded away, and bars grew over the windows, and the sky outside sombred into a perpetual night. The court rose and the jury filed out. There were five women and seven men. I counted them out, Caroline quoted or misquoted to herself, and I counted them in.

They were out for some time.

It was late and growing dark when Caroline got back to the flat. She had promised to ring her mother immediately, although she was not sure why it was so important, except to forestall the newspapers. Margaret answered the 'phone herself, so promptly that Caroline could almost have believed she had been sitting beside it. She was glad not to have to speak to Harry.

'He got off.'

'I'm glad,' her mother responded surprisingly. 'That was what you wanted, wasn't it?'

Her intuitions were always so finely tempered, Caroline thought. She would fail completely to see the core of an unpleasant truth while somehow perceiving certain external details with uncanny sensitivity.

'Yes,' she said. 'Yes, I did. I don't know what really happened, but I shouldn't have wanted him to go to gaol. I don't think it was entirely his fault.'

There was a pause – almost a restful pause.

'Stephen was a strange man,' said Stephen's ex-wife. 'I always meant to tell you about him, when you were old enough, but somehow I never got around to it. It doesn't seem to matter so much now. I expect it's better that I don't say anything after all.'

Caroline said: 'No, don't.' For the first time in her life she thought how much she loved her mother, and how little she had ever noticed it.

The next day's papers carried the story in full. Several had photographs of Caroline leaving the court, a grey trilby hat bought specially for the occasion tilted well down over her eyes. There were pictures of Ulysses too, fortunately rather blurred, masked by stolid official shoulders and a huge pair of dark glasses. (Caroline had felt dark glasses would be a little too dramatic.) She bought *The Times*, *Telegraph* and *Guardian* from a newsvendor who evidently did not recognise her without the hat and retreated to a corner table in the nearest coffee house to look through them. Nothing would have induced her to buy the *Sun* although they had made the story a front-page item. (Tragedy of Secret Homosexual: Harley Street Doctor Destroyed by Illicit Passion.) The reports in her three papers were more restrained, but she found she could not be bothered to read them in any detail. Buying the papers, she supposed, had been a purely automatic gesture, like an actress buying the reviews of a play which she knows has already folded. She lit a cigarette and wondered about giving up; she had given up so many things, taking a bizarre pleasure in the pangs of abstention, it was odd that she had never been able to give up smoking. I shall give up giving things up, she resolved, though she had no real idea how to set about it. The waitress brought her a cup of coffee and although it was rather early in the day Caroline ordered a plate of prawn sandwiches. Food was one of the things she had given up too often lately. Involuntarily, she wondered how Angela was doing, on her pre-marital diet which, like most of Angela's totally superfluous fits of dieting, would probably disintegrate in the face of a well-endowed menu. Presumably she was immersed in wedding preparations. Caroline visualised her falling rapturously on a set of Wedgwood finger-bowls from some long-lost cousin, or swathed in oyster silk and pins, surrounded by dressmaker's minions, worrying that the train was just too short, or just too long, and would her orange blossom be the wrong shade of white? There was something very reassuring about picturing Angela like that: distant, happy, *safe*. Don't be ridiculous, Caroline told herself, sharply; Angela was never *un*safe. It was only a brainstorm, a temporary madness of the imagination born of over-anxiety and giving too many things up. It was over now, to be forgotten like a nightmare on waking, or a daydream that never came true. The court's decision had absolved her as well as Ulysses, and her most secret fears could no longer rise up in public to threaten her. For all the play-acting and the lies, Caroline had always had great faith in the British judicial system.

Ulysses arrived shortly after the prawn sandwiches. The waitress stared, but not, Caroline thought, because she recognised him. He was wearing a bomber jacket and faded denims and he looked almost obscenely handsome, radiating assurance to a degree which Caroline found, under the circumstances, both vulgar and disquieting. The acquittal seemed to have restored his self-esteem, or perhaps merely bolstered his ego; she was not sure any more. He took his time about sitting down, towering over her in the hope that she would look up at him. But when she did, the fading smile on her face seemed to mock him, and he sat down quickly, chilled.

'Have a sandwich,' she said. She was glad to see he could still feel chilled. She had so few advantages left.

He took the sandwich and began to eat with familiar voracity. He had been going to say something about how pleased he was to see her, but her smile killed the impulse. Even while he ate, licking the mayonnaise from his fingers, his eyes never left her face. Yellow cat's eyes seeking to mesmerise her into doing or saying something she had never really intended. When he had finished, he asked, reluctantly: 'What now?'

She had known, of course, that she would have to answer that question some time. She had known it when the verdict was announced, and she realised Ulysses would be able to keep their last appointment. Even if he had gone to gaol, in a year, or two years, or three, they would have been sitting in a cafe somewhere and he would have asked her the same question, made more significant and more compulsive by the pallor of long confinement, the shadows behind his eyes. What now, Caroline? What indeed? Her fingers played with her empty cup, stroking the rim, turning and turning it in the saucer. When the waitress came she ordered more coffee for both of them.

'What had you planned?' she retaliated presently. They had made so many plans together, but none of them seemed relevant now. Even at the time they had been little more than after-sex daydreams.

'To be free,' Ulysses replied. 'To be with you.'

Caroline said abruptly: 'Why?'

She thought he would say: 'Because I love you,' but he did not.

'We are in this together.' His favourite theme. 'I have been arrested, imprisoned, tried – and all for your benefit. I might have had to go to prison for a long time. But I kept silent, I said nothing to implicate you.' ('Nor I you,' Caroline murmured.) 'You were free to go where you pleased while I had to report to a police station every day. Even at the beginning, when I was in the cell, I thought always of you. When this is over, I said to myself, she will be there waiting for me, and she can refuse me nothing. Not her body, nor her mind, nor even her heart. Her most intimate feelings will be mine to share.'

'And?' Caroline's expression was deliberately opaque.

234

He shrugged. 'It is over. This is the pay-off.'

'What about —' she hesitated, wondering if she dared to name them '— the dead? Have you forgotten them already?' She did not know why, but she was thinking of them all, even Philip, as though Ulysses had to answer for his death, too. She visualised the three graves, huddled together on the hillside, their grey stones growing quietly out of the sleeping turf. The standing angel hid his face from the sun.

'What about them?' Ulysses was undisturbed. 'They are dead. They will not come back from Hell to trouble us. Anyway, I do not believe in Hell.'

'That is sufficiently obvious,' Caroline remarked pointedly.

'I intend to concentrate on the living,' Ulysses went on. 'Like us. When you are standing in the dock waiting for the verdict, knowing that maybe you will go out of the courtroom between two big policemen, into a van with bars at the windows, then into a prison with more bars, and high walls, and no sun — then you start thinking how wonderful it would be, just to walk out into the street by yourself, and be alive. I have not got enough life to waste any more of it behind barred windows and locked doors, feeling guilty about nothing. In any case, what good would my guilt do Stephen, or your sister? They are not going to rise up and forgive me. You can feel guilty if you must but I want to enjoy myself. I have earnt it, haven't I?'

There was a brief, unquiet silence. The coffee arrived and was deposited on the table with a clatter of saucers, a rattle of spoons. 'You are very brutal,' Caroline said, when the waitress had moved away.

'I am just practical,' Ulysses retorted. Then he added, as though struck by a sudden thought: 'I suppose your father *did* leave his money to you?'

Caroline considered him coldly and steadily. 'No,' she said. 'He left it to a home for decayed homosexual doctors.'

For a moment, Ulysses looked uncertain. Then: 'You are joking?' he suggested doubtfully.

Caroline smiled. 'The money is very important to you, isn't it?'

'It's nice to have money.' Ulysses was guarded.

'Well, then,' Caroline spoke carefully, summoning all the

blandness she could command, 'let us talk business. After all, that is what this is all about. What is your price?'

He did not answer immediately; perhaps he did not understand. 'You said this was the "pay-off",' she continued. 'So what is the price? You don't have to take my body or my mind or any other portion of my anatomy. I can pay in pounds and pence. Shall we run through the bill?' She had thought she was quite calm but to her horror she felt angry tears stinging behind her eyes. When she could speak again, her voice sounded brittle and treacherous. 'Item: your imprisonment and trial, including the risk of a further period in prison. There will be a service charge to cover bail and the resulting inconvenience and mental strain. Item –' she swallowed painfully '– the suicide of my sister, which you were considerate enough to arrange for me. Item: my father's death, including the seduction and general deterioration which preceded same. Item: your noble reticence with the police concerning my involvement in the aforementioned seduction, suicide, et cetera. It's an impressive account, isn't it? Perhaps you would like to give me an estimate?'

Now, he understood. She watched with a sort of detached fascination as the different expressions flicked across his face in rapid succession: bewilderment, comprehension, incredulity, rage. He was so transparent, she thought; perhaps too transparent. Always, beneath the violent obvious moods, she sensed a kind of calculation. She wondered if he was going to bring his fist crashing down on the table and discreetly moved his cup out of the way. 'Do you really think that what you owe me can be paid only with *money*?' Strangely, his scorn washed over her, like wind over stone. 'At the beginning, this was all your idea: remember? Did you really imagine that if you paid me enough I would take responsibility for what you did? You cannot make me the scapegoat for your own conscience.'

It used to be a prostitute, Caroline thought. Now, it is a scapegoat. But the principle was the same. All she said was: 'My conscience is my own affair. Keep your voice down.'

The tirade went on but Caroline barely listened. She was glad she had chosen a coffee house where the background music was reasonably loud. 'All this is unnecessary,' she said

236

at length, when he had temporarily run out of indignation or breath. 'I'm not going to haggle. Just tell me your price.'

'There – is – no – price.' He spoke slowly, spacing the words for emphasis. 'I have told you. You cannot *buy* peace of mind.'

She hardly seemed to hear him. 'The price,' she repeated, very deliberately, 'of my freedom.'

She was staring down at her hands, lying motionless on the table. Slender, childish hands with unvarnished nails and no rings. She wondered if a gypsy would be able to read her future in the spider-thin creases on her palm. There could not be much future in those few, shallow lines.

She did not look at Ulysses. Whether she feared to expose her own humiliation, or, still worse, to realise his, she did not know.

'Freedom?' he echoed, stupidly. 'From the law? Bah! I was acquitted. They cannot charge me again – my lawyer said so. I could tell them everything and they would still be helpless. We have nothing to fear.'

'There are laws against perjury,' Caroline said. She wasn't sure if she could be charged as an accessory even if the police knew the truth. But that wasn't what mattered. She and Ulysses were bound together by their mutual complicity, a form of two-way emotional blackmail where each of them was blackmailer, each victim. Neither of them could ever betray the other now. 'I didn't mean that kind of freedom.'

'What kind of freedom?' Ulysses asked, without thinking. And then, after a long, long pause: 'Do you mean – freedom from me?'

She didn't say anything. She didn't have to. He knew her now in all her weakness and desolation. He knew that for all the stillness of her face she was pleading with him, she who had never pleaded with anyone. This was the moment he had worked for and dreamed of, the moment when he felt himself at last in control, in possession, as though he had finally penetrated the smooth cold shell of her outward personality and deflowered her forever. He wanted to revel in her subjection, to smile a slow cruel smile and deny her everything, driving her to further self-abasement, further self-revelation, but he could not. Reality, as so often, was bitterly different from the dream. Instead of the sweet sensual feel of mastery there was only the dull realisation that whatever he demanded of her, whatever he forced on her, she did not need him any more. He had been so sure that she could never release him, even as he could never release her. She might hate him, fight him, curse him, but in the end she would respond to him, reluctantly, bound like her father by his sexual power, by their shared responsibility for past deception and death. Only of course Caroline would neither fight nor curse him. It was not in her nature. Even her hatred was a dark silent wellspring which their passing relationship had never touched. This was the moment of his triumph, and in the end, all he saw was how little he had ever meant to her. For no logical reason, he found himself remembering a night when Stephen had looked at him with dreary eyes.

'If we were alone,' he said, almost dispassionately, 'I think I would kill you.'

He means it, she thought numbly, without surprise or fear. She could see the desire reflected in his face. This time, neither accident nor suicide, but killing for its own sake, an almost orgasmic pleasure in the act of death.

'The price,' she said. It seemed to her that the main thing was to keep to the point.

It was a moment or two before he remembered what they were talking about.

'Always money.' He managed a sort of sneer. The superfluous anger which he had used earlier seemed to have drained away, leaving him without any particular façade. He continued, bleakly: 'Oh yes, I like money. Everyone likes money. Even you like money, though you pretend to be so high-minded about it. If you had ever been poor you would know how nice money is.' She wondered fleetingly if he *had* ever been poor. She knew so little about him. 'But if I have you the money will be there too. It will be *our* money. We can spend it – together.'

She said, too quickly: 'I would rather give it away.'

Her reaction was like a chink in her self-containment, a taste of his power. 'Who to?' he said. 'Some charity for starving children or abandoned cats? Or that asylum for homosexual doctors that you have invented? You cannot do without the money, Caroline. You do not know how. You are stuck with it, just as you are stuck with me. You will never be free.'

238

For a moment, his lust for mastery was so strong, so intensely physical, that he felt himself growing erect with anticipation. She looked at him without speaking. She could refuse to see him, move away, change her name and her telephone number. But in the end, he would find her. He would hang on to her like a starving dog with its teeth clenched on a steel bone, in the blind belief that one day he will find meat on it. Only death would loosen his hold. Lately she had grown very familiar with Death, even dependent on him. Perhaps he would not fail her this last time. Perhaps Ulysses would drown in the blue Hellene sea or crash on some precarious mountain road or get bitten by one of the greeny-brown island snakes that found its way somehow into his bed. She was shocked how easily, how naturally the idea occurred to her. As though it had been germinating in her subconscious for some time, and now the moment had come for it to crawl out into the daylight. Where had she been, these last two years, what had happened to her, that her brain could hatch out horrors? Once, in the darkness, she had had another fantasy – but that was a world ago. She had come a long way since then. Or had she?

What have you gained? whispered a voice that came from nowhere in her mind. She had reached out for love, passion, revenge – and her hands were empty. She was a cold thirsty spirit trapped in an enchanted well: she bent her head to drink, but her thirst remained unsated and her mouth as dry and arid as a desert of stones. She had drunk the stones, eaten dust. She was dry and the well was dry and the water for which she thirsted had never been more than a hallucination, born of fever and parching, which shrank from the touch of her lip and seeped away into dirt. She wondered if she would ever have the courage to try and drink from the well again.

'When can I move in with you?' Ulysses' voice intruded on her thoughts. She seemed to see him through a veil of loneliness, as though already he was little more than a ghost.

'That's not possible,' she said at last. 'You must go back to Greece. We cannot be seen together, not yet. It would be too dangerous. I'll send you some money. Later, I can come after you.' Courage, she discovered, is a part of life, as instinct as breathing. You go on because you must.

'When will you come?' Ulysses asked, distrustfully.

'When I can.' Always the same question, though the words differed. Always the same useless evasion given in answer. The dispute might drag on, Caroline thought, all through midday and into the afternoon, and evening and night and morning again, stating and re-stating the same irreconcilable viewpoints, going nowhere. Unable to agree, unable to agree to disagree, incapable of hanging on or letting go. It was the same trap, the undrinkable well, and they were both in it, eternally apart, imprisoned in the impossible human dilemma of longing and futility. Freedom, like love, like passion, like everything Caroline had ever wanted, was always just out of her reach. And Ulysses, in his turn, reached for a Caroline who did not – quite – exist, a phantasm of the senses which would forever elude him. There was no way out. There would never be any way out.

When will you come? When? When?

When.

In the street outside, people passed carrying the headlines of her father's death. The next day, they would carry different headlines. But not for Caroline. Whatever she did, whatever she did not do, she had made of this hour, this moment of her life, a moment that would endure for all time.

For both of them.